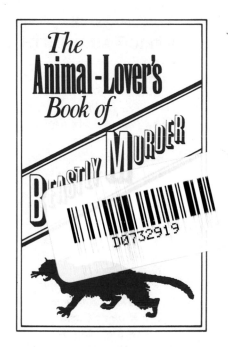

The
Animal-Lover's
Book of

BEASTLY MURDER

D0732919

BOOKS BY

PATRICIA HIGHSMITH

NOVELS
Strangers on a Train
The Blunderer
The Talented Mr Ripley
Deep Water
A Game for the Living
This Sweet Sickness
The Cry of the Owl
The Two Faces of January
The Glass Cell
A Suspension of Mercy
Those Who Walk Away
The Tremor of Forgery
Ripley Under Ground
A Dog's Ransom
Ripley's Game
Edith's Diary
The Boy Who Followed Ripley
People Who Knock on the Door

SHORT STORIES
Eleven
Slowly, Slowly in the Wind
The Black House
Little Tales of Misogyny
The Animal-Lover's Book of Beastly Murder

The Animal-Lover's Book of BEASTLY MURDER

PATRICIA HIGHSMITH

MYSTERIOUS PRESS

THE MYSTERIOUS PRESS
New York • London • Tokyo

The Animal-Lover's Book of Beastly Murder
was originally published by William Heinemann, Ltd.,
London, England

Copyright © 1975 by Patricia Highsmith

All rights reserved.

 Mysterious Press books are published in association with
Warner Books, Inc.

The Mysterious Press, 129 West 56th Street, New York, N.Y. 10019

Printed in the United States of America
First Mysterious Press trade paperback Printing: May 1988
10 9 8 7 6 5 4 3 2 1

Library of Congress Cataloging in Publication Data

Highsmith, Patricia, 1921—
    The animal lover's book of beastly murder.

    1. Amimals—Fiction.   I. Title.
[PS3558.1366A5   1986]   813'.54   86-91481
ISBN 0-89296-942-3

ATTENTION: SCHOOLS AND CORPORATIONS

MYSTERIOUS PRESS books, distributed by Warner Books, are available
at quantity discounts with bulk purchase for educational, business,
or sales promotional use. For information, please write to: SPECIAL
SALES DEPARTMENT, MYSTERIOUS PRESS, 666 FIFTH AVENUE,
NEW YORK, N.Y. 10103.

**ARE THERE MYSTERIOUS PRESS BOOKS
YOU WANT BUT CANNOT FIND IN YOUR LOCAL STORES?**

You can get any MYSTERIOUS PRESS title in print. Simply send title and
retail price, plus $2.00 for the first book on any order and 50¢ for each
additional book on that order, to cover mailing and handling costs.
New York State and California residents add applicable sales tax. Enclose
check or money order to: MYSTERIOUS PRESS, 129 WEST 56th St.,
NEW YORK, N.Y. 10019.

For my cousin
Dan Coates
of Box Canyon Ranch,
Weatherford, Texas

CONTENTS

Chorus Girl's Absolutely Final Performance

THEY call me Chorus Girl – shouts of 'Chorus Girl' go up when I stand and swing my left leg, then my right, and so on. Before that, however, maybe ten, twenty years ago, I was 'Jumbo Junior', mostly 'Jumbo'. Now it's Chorus Girl entirely. My name must be written on the wooden board at the front of my cage, along with 'Africa'. People stare at the board, sometimes say 'Africa', then start calling me 'Chorus Girl! – Hey, Chorus Girl!' If I swing my legs, a small cheer goes up.

I live alone. I never saw another creature like myself, in this place at any rate. I remember when I was small, though, following my mother everywhere, and I remember many creatures like myself, much bigger, a few even smaller. I remember following my mother up a sloping wooden board on to a boat, the boat a bit unsteady. My mother was led and prodded away, back the same board, and I was on the boat. My mother, wanting me to join her, lifted her trunk and bellowed. I saw ropes flung about her, ten or twenty men tugging to hold her back. Someone fired a gun at her. Was it a deadly gun or a dope gun? I will never know that. The smell is different, but the wind was not blowing towards me that day. I only know my mother collapsed after a little while. I was on the deck, screaming shrilly like a baby. Then I was shot with a dope gun. The boat finally moved, and after a very long time during which I mainly slept and ate in semi-darkness in a box, we arrived in another land where there were no forests, no grass. Into another box I went, more move-ment, another place with cement underfoot, hard stone

3

everywhere, bars, and foul-smelling people. Worst of all, I was alone. No little creatures my own age. No mother, no friendly grandfather, no father. No play. No baths in a muddy river. Alone with bars and cement.

But the food was all right, and there was plenty of it. Also a nice man took care of me, a man named Steve. He carried a pipe in his mouth, but almost never did he light it, just held it between his teeth. Even so he could talk and I could soon understand what he said, or at least what he meant.

'Kneel, Jumbo!' and a tap on my knees meant to get down on my knees. If I held my trunk up, Steve would clap his hands once in appreciation, and toss some peanuts or a small apple into my mouth.

I liked it when he got astride my back, and I would get up, and we would walk around the cage. People seeing this would clap their hands, especially little children would clap.

Steve kept the flies off my eyes in summer by means of a string fringe which he fixed around my head. He would hose the cement floor, the shady part, so I could lie down and keep cool. He would hose me. When I became bigger, Steve would sit on my trunk and I would lift him into the air, being careful not to tip him, because he had nothing to hold on to except the end of my trunk. Steve took special care of me in winter also, making sure I had enough straw, even sometimes blankets if it was very cold. One particularly bad winter, Steve brought me a little box with a cord attached which blew warm air on to me. Steve nursed me through an illness caused by the cold.

The people here wear large hats. Some of the men carry short guns on their belts. Once in a while one pulls a gun and fires it into the air to try to scare me or the gazelles who live next door to me and whom I can see through the bars. The gazelles react violently, leap into the air, then huddle together in a far corner of their cage.

A pitiable sight. By the time Steve or one of the caretakers arrives, the man who fired the shot has put his gun back in his belt, and looks like all the other men – who are laughing and won't point out the man who did it.

This reminds me of one of my pleasanter moments. There was a red-faced fat fellow about five years ago who on two or three Sundays fired his loud gun into the air. It annoyed me, though I would never have dreamt of showing my annoyance. But the third or fourth Sunday when this particular fellow fired his gun, I quietly took a snoutful of water from my trough and let him have it full force through the bars. I hit him in the chest and he went over backwards with his boots in the air. Most of the crowd laughed. A few of the people were surprised or angry. Some threw a few stones at me – which didn't hurt, or missed entirely, or hit the bars and bounced in another direction. Then Steve came trotting up, and I could see that Steve (having heard the shot) knew exactly what had happened. Steve laughed, but he patted the shoulder of the wet man, trying to calm him down. The man was probably denying having fired the shot. But I saw Steve give me a nod which I took for approval. The gazelles came forth timidly, staring through the bars at the crowd and also at me. I fancied they were pleased with my action, and I felt proud of myself that day. I dreamt even of seizing the wet man, or a man like him, of squeezing his soft body until he died, then of trampling him under my feet.

During Steve's time with me, which must have been thirty years, we would occasionally take a walk in the park and children, sometimes three at a time, would ride on my back. This was at least amusing, a nice change. But the park is anything but a forest. It is just a few trees growing from rather hard, dry soil. It is almost never wet. The grass is close cut, and I was not allowed to pull any grass up, not that I much wanted to. Steve managed everything, managed me, and carried a stick made of

5

woven leather with which he prodded me to make me turn in a certain direction, kneel, stand up, and at the end of the outing stand on my hind legs. (More cheering.) Steve did not need the stick, but it was part of the show, like my turning in a couple of stupid circles before standing on my hind legs at the end. I could also stand on my front legs, if Steve asked me to. I remember my temper was better in those days, and I would avoid without Steve's telling me the low branches of some of the trees so the children on my back would not be knocked off. Given a chance, I am not sure I would be that careful any more. What have people, except Steve, ever given me? Not even grass under my feet. Not even companionship of another creature like myself.

Now that I am older, my legs heavier, my temper shorter, there are no more rides for children, though the band still plays on summer Sunday afternoons – 'Take Me out to the Ball Game' and lately 'Hello, Dolly!' Sometimes I wish I could take a walk again, with Steve again, wish I could be young again. And yet, what for? For more years in this place? Now I spend more time lying down than standing up. I lie in the sun, which doesn't seem as hot as it used to. The people's clothing has changed a little, not so many guns and boots, but still the same broad-brimmed hats on the men and some of the women. Still the same tossed peanuts, not always shelled, that I used to stick my trunk through the bars for so eagerly when I was younger and had better appetite. Still the same popcorn and sweet Cracker-Jack. I don't always bother getting on my feet Saturday and Sunday. This infuriates Cliff, the new young keeper. He wants me to do my stuff, as in the old days. It is not that I am so old and tired, but I don't like Cliff.

Cliff is tall and young, with red hair. He likes to show off, cracking a long whip at me. He thinks he can make me do things according to certain jabs and commands. There is a sharp point of metal on his stick, which is annoying, although it doesn't break my skin by any means. Steve approached me as one creature to another, making acquaintance with me and not assuming I was going to be what he expected. That is why we got along. Cliff doesn't really care about me, and does nothing to help me against the flies in summer, for instance.

Of course when Steve retired, I continued to go through the Saturday and Sunday rounds with the children, once in a while with adults on my back. One man (another trying to show off) dug his spurs into me one Sunday, whereupon I put on a very little speed of my own accord and did not duck under a low branch but deliberately trotted under it. It was too low for the man to duck, and he was swept neatly off my back, landed on his knees and howled with pain. This caused a lot of disturbance, the man groaned for a while, and what was worse Cliff took the man's side, or tried to placate the man, by yelling and prodding at me with the pointed stick. I snorted with rage myself – and was gratified to see the crowd fall back in terror of me. I was nowhere near charging them, which I'd have liked to do, but responded to Cliff's prods and headed back to my cage. Cliff was muttering at me. I took a snoutful of water, and Cliff saw it. Cliff retreated. But he came back after nightfall when the park gates were closed, and gave me a whipping and a lecture. The whipping did not hurt at all, but must have exhausted Cliff who was staggering when he finished.

The following day Steve turned up in a wheelchair. His hair had become white. I had not seen him in four or five years, perhaps, but he was really the same, with his pipe in his mouth, the same kind voice, the same smile. I swung my legs with joy in my cage, and Steve laughed and said something pleasant to me. He had brought some small red apples to give me. He came in his wheelchair into the cage. This was pretty early one morning, so there was hardly any of the public in the park as yet. Steve said something to Cliff and gestured towards Cliff's pointed stick, so that I knew Steve meant that Cliff should get rid of it.

Then Steve made a sign to me. 'Up! Lift me up, Chorus Girl!'

I knew what he meant. I knelt, and stuck my trunk under the seat of Steve's wheelchair, sideways, so he could grab the end of my trunk with his right hand and with his other hand press against my head for balance. I did not get to my feet for fear of toppling Steve's chair, but I lifted him off the cement by quite a distance. Steve laughed. I set the chair down gently.

But that was years ago, Steve's visit. It was not his last visit. He came two or three times in his wheelchair, but never on the two days of the week when there were the most people. Now I have not seen Steve in about three years. Is he dead? This possibility makes me sad whenever I think of it. But then it is equally sad to expect, to hope for Steve to appear some morning of the quiet days, when just a few people straggle in, and Steve is not among them. Sometimes I raise my trunk and bellow my chagrin and disappointment because Steve doesn't come. It seems to amuse people, my bellowing – just as my mother bellowed on the dock when she couldn't reach me. Cliff pays no attention, only sometimes puts his hands over his ears, if he happens to be near.

This brings me close to the present time. Just yesterday, Sunday, there was the usual crowd, even more than usual. There was a man in a red suit with a white beard ringing a bell in his hand, walking about talking to everyone, especially to children. This man appears every now and then. People had peanuts and popcorn to give me through the bars. As usual, I held my snout through the bars, and my mouth was open also, in case someone aimed a peanut correctly. Someone threw a round object into my mouth, and I thought it was a red apple until I crunched on it, whereupon it started stinging my mouth horribly. I immediately took some water into my trunk, rinsed my mouth and spat. I had not swallowed any of the stuff, but the whole inside of my mouth was burning. I took more water, but it did little good. The pain made me shift from foot to foot, and at last I trotted around my cage in agony. The people laughed and pointed. I became angry, furious. I took as big a snoutful of water as I could manage and walked rather casually to the front of my cage. Standing a little way back from the bars so I could hit them all, I forced the water through my snout with all my power.

No one quite fell, but more than twenty people staggered, fell back against each other, choking and blinded for a few seconds. I went to my trough and took on more water, and not a moment too soon, because the crowd had armed itself also. Rocks and sticks came flying at me, empty Cracker-Jack boxes, anything. I aimed at the biggest man, knocked him down, and used the rest of the water to spray the whole assembly again. A woman was screaming for help. Others retreated. A man pulled his gun, shot at me and missed. Another gun was being drawn, although the first man who had shot was at once jumped on by another man. A bullet hit me in the shoulder, not going through but rather skimming the surface. A second bullet knocked off the end of my right tusk. With the last of my trough water in my snout, I attacked one of the gunmen squarely in the chest. It should have been enough to break his bones. At any rate he flew backward and knocked a woman down as he fell. Feeling I had won that set-to, in spite of my burning mouth, I withdrew prudently to my sleeping quarters (also of cement) where no bullets could hit me. Three more shots rang out, echoing in empty space. I don't know what they hit, but they did not hit me.

I could smell blood from my shoulder. I was still so angry, I was snorting instead of breathing, and almost to my own surprise, I found myself barricading the entrance to my sleeping quarters with the bales of hay which lined the place. I pulled the bales down from their stacks against the walls, shoved and kicked them, and with my trunk managed to boost one up on to the top of the heap of eight or nine, thereby closing the doorway except at the very top. This was bulletproof, anyway. But the bullets had ceased. Now I could hear Cliff outside, shouting to the crowd.

'Take it easy there, Chorus Girl!' Cliff's voice said.

I was familiar with the phrase. But I had never heard the fear, like a shaking, in Cliff's voice before. The crowd was watching him, of course. Cliff had to show himself powerful, able to control me. This thought plus my dislike of Cliff set me off again, and I butted my head against the barricade I'd made. Cliff had been pulling at the top bale, but now the whole heap fell on him.

The crowd gave a cry, a scream of shock.

I saw Cliff's legs, his black boots kicking underneath the bales.

A shot sounded, and this time I was hit in the left side. Cliff had a gun in his hand, but it was not his gun that had gone off. Cliff was not moving now. Neither was I. I expected another shot from the crowd, from someone in the crowd.

The crowd only stared back at me. I glared at them, with my mouth slightly open: the inside of my mouth was still burning.

Two uniformed men of the place arrived via the side door of my cage. They carried long guns. I stood still and did nothing, barely looked at them. Crazy and excited as they were, they might have shot me at once out of fear, if I had shown any sign of anger. My self-possession was returning. And I thought Cliff might be dead, which gave me pleasure.

But no, he wasn't. One man bent over him, pulled a bale of hay off him, and I saw Cliff's red-haired head move. The other man prodded me rudely with the point of his gun towards my sleeping quarters. He was yelling something at me. I turned and strolled, not hurrying, into my cement room which was now bestrewn with hay and bales in disorder. Suddenly I was not feeling well, and my mouth still hurt. A man stood in the doorway with his gun pointed at me. I regarded him calmly. I could see Cliff getting up. The other man was talking with Cliff in an angry tone. Cliff was talking and waving his hands, though he didn't look like himself at all. He looked unsteady on his feet, and he kept feeling his head.

Then a man with greyish hair, not as grey as Steve's, came to the gate with another man who carried a bag. They were let into the cage. Both of them came quite close to me and looked at me. Blood was dripping from my left side on to the cement. Then the grey-haired man spoke to Cliff angrily, kept on talking when Cliff interrupted – a string of words from both of them. The grey-haired man pointed to the cage door, a sign for Cliff to leave. The next moments are vague to me, because the man with the bag put a cloth over my snout and tied it firmly. He also gave me a prod with a needle. By now, during the loud talk, I had lain down. The cloth smelt cool but awful, and I went into a frightening sleep in which I saw animals like huge cats leaping about, attacking me, my mother, my family. I saw green trees again, high grass. But I felt that I was dying.

When I awakened, it was dark, and there was some kind of grease in my mouth. My mouth no longer hurt, and my side hurt only a little. Was this death? But I could smell the hay in my room. I got to my legs and felt sick. I threw up a little.

Then I heard the side gate clang as someone closed it. I recognized the step of Cliff, though he was walking softly in his boots. I considered going out of the small sleeping-room, which was like a trap with no other exit but the door, but I was too sleepy still to move. I could barely see Cliff kneeling with a bag like the one the man had carried. Then I smelt the same sweet, thin smell that the man had put over my nose. Even Cliff snorted, and turned his head away, then he came at me with a rush, tossing the cloth around my nose and pulling it tight at once with a rope. I flicked my snout and knocked Cliff down with a blow against his hip. I beat my trunk against his fallen form, trying more to get the cloth off than to hurt Cliff, who was writhing and groaning. The rope loosened, and with a toss I managed to shake off the cloth. It fell on Cliff's chest and part of his legs – stinking, evil, dangerous. I went out into the purer air of my cage.

Cliff was getting to his feet, gasping. He too came out for air, then rushed back, muttering, seized the cloth and came at me again. I rose a little on my hind legs and pivoted away from him. Cliff nearly fell. I gave Cliff the merest bump with my trunk and it lifted him off his feet. He fell his whole length on to the cement. Now I was angry. It was a fight between the two of us, Cliff with the evil-smelling cloth still in his hand. Cliff was getting to his knees.

I gave Cliff a kick, hardly more than a prod, with my left foot. I caught him in the side, and I heard a cracking sound like the breaking of tree branches. After that Cliff did not move again. Now there was the awful smell of blood mixed with the sweet and deadly smell. I went to the front corner of my cage, as far from the cloth as possible and lay down, trying to recover in the fresher air. I was cold, but that was of little importance. Slowly I began to feel calmer. I could breathe again. I had one brief desire to go and stomp a foot on Cliff, but I hadn't the energy. What I felt was rage. And little by little even the rage went away. But I was still too upset to sleep. I waited in my cement corner for the dawn.

And this is where I am now, lying in a corner of the cement and steel cage where I have spent so many years. The light comes slowly. First there is the familiar figure of the old man who feeds the two musk oxen. He pushes a cart, opens another cage where there are more horned animals. At last he passes my cage, glances twice at me, and says something with 'Chorus Girl' in it, surprised to see me lying where I am. Then he sees Cliff's form.

'Cliff? – Hey, Cliff! What's the matter?'

The cage isn't locked, it seems, and the old man comes right in, bends over Cliff, says something, holds his nose and drags the big white cloth out of the cage. Then he runs off, yelling. I get to my feet. The cage door is slightly open. I walk past Cliff's body, nudge the gate wider and walk out.

There is no one in the park. It is pleasant to walk on the ground again, as I haven't done since they stopped the week-end rides so long ago. The dry ground even feels soft. I pause to raise my trunk, pull some green leaves off a branch, and eat them. The leaves are tough and prickly. but at least they are fresh. Here is the round fountain, that I was never allowed to pause at, or drink from, on the week-end outings. Now I take a long cool draught.

Behind me there are excited voices. The voices are no doubt back at my cage, but I don't even bother looking. I enjoy my freedom. Above me is the great blue sky, a whole world of emptiness overhead. I go into a thicket of trees growing so close that they scrape both my sides. But there are so few trees, I am immediately out again, and on a cement path where apes and monkeys in cages stare goggle-eyed and chatter in amazement as I stroll by. A couple of them huddle at the back of their cage, little hairy fellows. Grey monkeys yell shrilly at me, then turn their blue behinds at me and scamper to the far corner of their cage. But perhaps some of them would like to ride on my back? From somewhere I remember that. I pull some flowers and eat them, just for amusement. The black monkeys with long arms are grinning and laughing, holding on to their bars, jerking the bars up and down and making a clatter.

I stroll over, and they are only a little afraid, much more curious than afraid, as I stick my trunk around two of the bars and pull the bars towards me. Then a third bar, and there is room for the black monkeys to scramble out.

They scream and titter, leaping along the ground, using their hands to boost them. One grabs my tail mischievously. Two of them take to a tree with delight.

But now there are footsteps from somewhere, sounds of running feet, shouts.

'There she is! By the monkeys!'

I turn to face them. A monkey scrambles on to my back, using my tail to get up. He slaps my shoulders, wanting a ride. He seems to weigh nothing at all. Two men, the same as yesterday, with the long guns, come running towards me, then halt, skidding, and raise their guns. Before I can lift my trunk in a gesture that might indicate friendliness, before I can kneel even, three shots go off.

'Don't hit the monkey!'

But they hit me.

Bang!

Now the sun is coming up and the tops of the trees are greenish, not all the trees being bare. My eyes go up and up. My body sinks. I am aware of the monkey leaping nimbly from my back to the ground, loping off, terrified by the gunshots. I feel very heavy suddenly, as if falling asleep. I mean to kneel and lie down, but my body sways sideways and I strike the cement. Another shot jolts my head. That was between the eyes, but my eyes are still open.

Men scamper round me as the monkeys did, kicking me, shouting to one another. Again I see the huge cats leaping in the forest, leaping on me now. Then through the blur of the men's figures I see Steve very clearly, but Steve as he was when he was young – smiling, talking to me, with his pipe in his teeth. Steve moves slowly and gracefully. So I know I am dying, because I know Steve is dead. He is more real than the others. There is a forest around him. Steve is my friend, as always. There are no cats, only Steve, my friend.

14

Djemal's Revenge

DEEP in the Arab desert lived Djemal, with his master Mahmet. They slept in the desert, because it was cheaper. By day, they trudged (Mahmet riding) to the nearest town, Elu-Bana, where Djemal gave rides to tourists, squealing women in summer dresses and nervous men in shorts. It was about the only time that Mahmet walked.

Djemal was aware that the other Arabs didn't care for Mahmet. A faint groan came from other camel drivers when he and Mahmet approached. There was much haggling over prices, dinars, between Mahmet and the other drivers who would at once pounce upon him. Hands would fly and voices rise madly. But no one exchanged dinars, only talked about them. Finally Mahmet would lead Djemal to the group of staring tourists, tap Djemal and yell a command for him to kneel.

The hair on Djemal's knees, front legs and back, was quite worn off, so his skin looked like old leather there. As for the rest of him, he was shaggy brown with some clotted patches, other patches nearly bare, as if moths had been at him. But his big brown eyes were clear, and his generous, intelligent lips had a pleasant look as if he were constantly smiling, though this was far from the truth. At any rate, he was only seventeen, in the prime of life, and unusually large and strong. He was shedding now because it was summer.

'Ooooooh! – Eeeeeek!' a plump lady screamed, jolted from side to side as Djemal stood up to his impressive full height. 'The ground looks miles away!'

'Don't fall! Hang on! That sand's not as soft as it looks!' warned an Englishman's voice.

Little filthy Mahmet, in dusty robes, tugged at Djemal's bridle, and off they went at walking pace, Djemal slapping his broad feet down on the sand and gazing about wherever he wished, at the white domes of the town against the blue sky, at an automobile purring along the road, at a yellow mountain of lemons by the roadside, at other camels walking or loading or unloading their human cargo. This woman, any human being, felt like no weight at all, nothing like the huge sacks of lemons or oranges he often had to carry, or the sacks of plaster, or even the bundles of young trees that he transported far into the desert sometimes.

Once in a while, even the tourists would argue in their hesitant, puzzled-sounding voices with Mahmet. Some argument about price. Everything was price. Everything came down to dinars. Dinars, paper and coin, could make men whip out daggers, or raise fists and hit each other in the face.

Turbaned Mahmet in his pointed, turned-up-toed shoes and billowing old djellaba, looked more like an Arab than the Arabs. He meant himself to be a tourist attraction, photogenic (he charged a small fee to be photographed) with a gold ring in one ear and a pinched, sun-tanned visage which was almost hidden under bushy eyebrows and a totally untended beard. One could hardly see his mouth in all the hair. His eyes were tiny and black. The reason the other camel drivers hated him was because he did not abide by the set-price for a camel ride that the others had established. Mahmet would promise to stick to it, then if a tourist happened to approach him with a pitiable attempt to bargain (as Mahmet knew they had been advised to do), Mahmet would lower the price slightly, thus getting himself some business, and putting the tourist in such a good mood for having succeeded in bargaining, that the tourist often tipped more than the difference at the end of the ride. On the other hand, if business was good, Mahmet would up his price, knowing it would be accepted – and this sometimes in the hearing of the other drivers. Not that the other drivers were paragons of honesty, but they had informal agreements, and mostly stuck to them. For Mahmet's dishonesty, Djemal sometimes suffered a stone thrown against his rump, a stone meant for Mahmet.

After a good tourist day, which often went on till nearly dark, Mahmet would tie Djemal up to a palm tree in town and treat himself to a meal of couscous in a shack of a restaurant which had a terrace and a squawking parrot. Meanwhile Djemal might not have had any water even, because Mahmet took care of his own needs first, and Djemal would nibble the tree leaves that he could reach. Mahmet ate alone at a table, eschewed by the other camel drivers who sat at another table together, making a lot of merry noise. One of them played a stringed instrument between courses. Mahmet chewed his lamb bones in silence and wiped his fingers on his robes. He left no tip.

Maybe he took Djemal to the public fountain, maybe he didn't, but he rode while Djemal walked into the desert to the clump of trees where Mahmet made his camp every night. Djemal could not always see in the darkness, but his sense of smell guided him to the bundle of clothing of Mahmet, the rolled up tent, the leather water-bags, all of which were permeated with Mahmet's own sweaty, sharp scent.

In the early mornings, it was usually lemon-hauling in the hot summer months. Thank Allah, Mahmet thought, the Government had established 'camel ride' hours for the tourists, 10–12 in the mornings, 6–9 evenings, so it left the drivers free to earn money in the day-time, and to do all the tourist business in concentrated hours.

Now as the big orange sun sank on the horizon of sand, Mahmet and Djemal were out of hearing of the muezzin in Elu-Bana. Besides, Mahmet had his transistor on, a little gadget not much bigger than his fist, which he could prop on his shoulder amid folds of djellaba. Now it was a wailing and endless song, with a man singing in falsetto. Mahmet hummed, as he spread a tattered rug on the sand and threw down some more rags upon this. This was his bed.

'Djemal! – Put yourself there!' said Mahmet, pointing to a side he had discovered was windward of the place where he intended to sleep. Djemal gave out considerable heat, as well as blocking the gritty breeze.

Djemal went on eating dry brush several yards away. Mahmet came over and whacked him with a braided leather whip. It did not hurt Djemal. It was a ritual, which he let continue for a few minutes before he tore himself away from the dark green shrubs. Fortunately he wasn't thirsty that night.

'Oy-yah-yah-yah . . .' said the transistor.

Djemal knelt down, turning himself slightly against the wishes of Mahmet, so that the light wind very nearly stuck him straight in the tail. Djemal didn't want sand up his nose. He stretched his long neck out, put his head down, almost closed his nostrils, and closed his eyes completely. After a while, he felt Mahmet settling against his left side, tugging at the old red blanket in which he wrapped himself, settling his sandaled heels in the sand. Mahmet slept as he rested, almost sitting up.

Sometimes Mahmet read a bit in the Koran, mumbling. He could read hardly at all, but he knew a lot of it by heart, since childhood. His school had consisted, as the schools consisted even now, of a roomful of children sitting on the floor repeating phrases uttered by a tall man in a djellaba who prowled among them, taking long strides over their heads, reading phrases from the Koran. This wisdom, these words were like poetry to Mahmet – pretty enough when one read it, but of no use in everyday life. This evening, Mahmet's Koran – a chunky little book with curled corners and nearly obliterated print – remained in his woven knapsack along with sticky dates and a stale hunk of bread. Mahmet was thinking of the forthcoming National Camel Race. He scratched a flea somewhere under his left arm. The camel race started tomorrow evening, and lasted for a week. It went from Elu-Bana to Khassa, a big port and a major city of the country, where there were even more tourists. The drivers camped out at night, of course, and were supposed to carry their food and water supplies, and make a stop at Souk Mandela, where the camels were to drink, then push on. Mahmet went over his plans. No stop at Souk Mandela, for one thing. That was why he was making Djemal go dry now. When Djemal tanked up tomorrow, and just before the race started in the evening, he could go seven days, Mahmet thought, without water, and Mahmet hoped to make it in six, anyway.

Traditionally, the Elu-Bana to Khassa race was very close, drivers flogging their camels at the finish. The prize was three hundred dinars, quite enough to be interesting.

Mahmet pulled the red blanket over his head, and felt secure and self-sufficient. He hadn't a wife, he hadn't even a family – rather he had one in a faraway town, but they disliked him, and he them, so Mahmet never thought about them. He'd stolen as a boy, and the police had come a few times too often to his family's house, warning him and his parents, so Mahmet had left aged thirteen. From then on, he'd led a nomadic existence, shining shoes in the capital, working for a while as waiter until he was caught stealing out of the till, then picking pockets in museums and mosques, then as assistant pimp for a chain of bordellos in Khassa, then as runner for a fence during which time he'd been winged in the calf by a policeman's bullet, giving him a limp. Mahmet was thirty-seven or thirty-eight, maybe even forty, he wasn't quite sure. When he won the National Camel Race money, he intended to make a down payment on a little house in Elu-Bana. He'd seen the two-room white house with running cold water and a tiny fireplace. It was up for sale cheap, because the owner had been murdered in his bed, and nobody wanted to live there.

The next day, Djemal was surprised by the relative lightness of his work. He and Mahmet cruised along the lemon mountains on the outskirts of Elu-Bana, and Djemal's two huge sacks were loaded and unloaded four times before the sun went down, but that was nothing. Ordinarily, Djemal would have been prodded much faster along the roads.

'Ho-ya! Djemal!' someone shouted.

'. . . Mahmet! . . . F-wisssssss!'

There was excitement. Djemal didn't know why. Men clapped their hands. Praise or disapproval? Djemal was aware that no one liked his master, and Djemal took some of this ill-feeling, therefore apprehension, upon himself. Djemal was ever wary against a sneaky blow, something thrown at him, meant for Mahmet. The huge trucks pulled out, loaded with lemons brought by scores of camels. Drivers sat resting, leaning against their camels' bellies or squatting on their heels. As Djemal walked out of the compound, one camel for no reason stretched his head forward and nipped Djemal's rump.

Djemal turned quickly and lifted a protruding upper lip, baring powerful long front teeth, and snapped back, not quite catching the camel's nose. The driver on the other camel was nearly thrown by his camel's recoil, and cursed Mahmet roundly.

'. . . !' Mahmet gave back as good as he got.

Though Djemal was already full of water, Mahmet led him again to the town trough. Djemal drank a little, slowly, pausing to lift his head and sniff the breeze: he smelt the perfume of tourists from afar. And he also heard loud music, not unusual as transistors blared all day from every direction, but this music was bigger and more solid. Djemal felt a wallop on his left hind leg. Mahmet was walking, in front of him now, pulling his rein.

There were flags, a grandstand, tourists, and a couple of

loudspeakers whence the music came. All this at the edge of the desert. Camels were lined up. A man was speaking, his voice unnaturally loud. The camels looked good. Was it a race? Djemal had once been in a race with Mahmet riding him, and Djemal remembered that he had run faster than the others. That was last year, when Mahmet had acquired Djemal. Djemal had a fleeting recollection of his first master, who had trained him. This man had been tall, kind, and rather old. He had argued with Mahmet, doubtless over dinars, and Mahmet had won. That was how Djemal saw it. Mahmet had taken Djemal away with him.

Djemal was suddenly in a line with the other camels. A whistle blew. Mahmet whacked him, and Djemal loped ahead, taking a minute or two to get into stride. Then he was galloping straight into the setting sun. He was ahead. It was easy. Djemal began to breathe regularly, settling down to keep the pace for a long time, if necessary. Where were they going? Djemal could not smell leaves or water, and he was unfamiliar with the terrain.

Ka-pa-la-pop, ka-pa-la-pop ... The hoof beats of the camels behind Djemal faded out of hearing. Djemal went a trifle slower. Mahmet did not whack him. Djemal heard Mahmet chuckle a little. The moon rose, and they kept on, Djemal walking now. He was a little tired. They stopped, Mahmet drank from his watersack, ate something, and bundled himself up against Djemal's side as usual. But there was no tree, no shelter where they lay that night. The land was flat and wide.

The next morning, they set off at dawn, Mahmet having had a mug of sweet coffee brewed on his spirit lamp. He switched on his transistor, and held it in the crook of his leg, which was cocked over Djemal's shoulder. Not a camel was in sight behind him. Nevertheless, Mahmet urged Djemal on at a fair pace. Judging from Djemal's firm hump behind him, he was good for four or five days more without showing any sign of flagging. Still Mahmet looked to right

23

and left for any lines of trees, any kind of foliage that could give shelter from the sun, however brief. When noon came, they had to stop. The heat of the sun had begun to penetrate even Mahmet's turban, and sweat ran into his eyebrows. For the first time, Mahmet threw a cloth over Djema's head to shelter it from the sun, and they rested till nearly four in the afternoon. Mahmet had no watch, but he could tell time quite well by the sun.

The next day was the same, except that Mahmet and Djemal found some trees – but no water. Mahmet knew the territory vaguely. Either he had been over it years before, or someone had told him about it, he couldn't quite remember. There was no water except at Souk Mandela, where the contestants were supposed to stop. That was a detour off the straight course, and Mahmet had no intention of stopping there. On the other hand, he thought it best to give Djemal an extra long rest at midday and to make up for this by travelling far into the night. This they did. Mahmet navigated a bit by the stars.

Djemal could have done all right for five days without water, with moderate pace and load, but Djemal was often loping. By the noonday rest of the sixth day, Djemal was feeling the strain. Mahmet mumbled the Koran. There was a wind, which blew Mahmet's coffee brewer flame out a couple of times. Djemal rested with his tail directly towards the wind, his nostrils open just enough to breathe.

It was the edge of a windstorm, not the storm itself, Mahmet saw. He patted Djemal's head briefly. Mahmet was thinking that the other camels and their drivers were in the worst of the storm, since the gloom lay in the direction of Souk Mandela to the north. Mahmet was hoping they'd all be seriously delayed.

Mahmet was wrong, as he discovered on the seventh day. This was the day they'd been supposed to finish the race. Mahmet started at dawn, when the sand was so

24

whirling around him, he didn't bother trying to prepare coffee; instead he chewed a few coffee beans. Mahmet began to think that the storm had moved down to him, on his direct route to Khassa, and that his competitors had perhaps not done too badly by stopping at Souk Mandela for water, then resuming a direct course to Khassa, because this would put them at the northern edge of the storm, not the middle.

It was difficult for Djemal to make good progress, since he had to keep his nostrils half shut against the sand, and consequently couldn't breathe well. Mahmet, riding on his shoulders and leaning over his neck, flogged him nervously to go ever faster. Djemal sensed that Mahmet was scared. If Djemal couldn't see or smell where he was going, how could Mahmet? Was Mahmet out of water? Maybe. Djemal's right shoulder became sore, then bleeding from Mahmet's whip. It hurt worse there, which was why Mahmet didn't try the other shoulder, Djemal supposed. Djemal knew Mahmet well by now. He knew that Mahmet intended to be paid somehow for his efforts, Djemal's efforts, or Mahmet wouldn't be putting himself to such discomfort. Djemal also had a vague notion that he was in competition with the other camels he had seen at Elu-Bana, because Djemal had been forced to do other 'races' in the form of running faster than other camels towards a group of tourists which Mahmet had spotted half a mile away.

'Hay-yee! Hay-yee!' Mahmet cried, bouncing up and down and wielding the whip.

At least they were getting out of the sandstorm. The pale haze of the sun could be seen now and then, still a long way above the horizon. Djemal stumbled and fell, tossing Mahmet off. Djemal got a mouthful of sand inadvertently, and would have loved to lie there for several minutes, recovering, but Mahmet flogged him up, shouting.

Mahmet had lost his transistor, and went scrambling

and scuffling about for it in the sand. When he found it, he kicked Djemal hard in the rump to no immediate avail, then kicked him unmercifully in the anus, because Djemal had lain down again.

Mahmet cursed.

Djemal did likewise, blowing his breath out and baring his two formidable front teeth before he gradually hauled himself up with a slow, bitter dignity. Stupefied by heat and thirst, Djemal saw Mahmet fuzzily, and was exasperated enough to attack him, except that he was weak from fatigue. Mahmet whacked him and gave him the command to kneel. Djemal knelt, and Mahmet mounted.

They were moving again. Djemal's feet became ever heavier, and dragged in the sand. But he could now smell people. Water. Then he heard music – the ordinary wailing music of Arabian transistors, but louder, as if several were playing in unison. Mahmet whacked Djemal again and again on the shoulder, shouting encouragement. Djemal saw no reason to exert himself, since the goal was plainly in sight, but he did his best to walk fast, hoping that this would make Mahmet ease up on the whip.

'Yeh-yah!' The cheers grew louder.

Djemal's mouth was now open and dry. Just before he reached the people, his eyesight failed him. So did his leg muscles. His knees, then his side hit the sand. The hump on his back sagged limp, empty like his mouth and his stomach.

And Mahmet beat him, yelling.

The crowd both moaned and yelled. Djemal didn't care. He felt he was dying. Why didn't someone bring him water? Mahmet was now lighting matches under Djemal's heels. Djemal barely twitched. He would have bitten through Mahmet's neck with pleasure, but he hadn't the strength. Djemal lost consciousness.

With fury and resentment, Mahmet saw a camel and its driver walk across the finish line. Then another. The camels looked tired, but they were not playing dead-tired like Djemal. There was no room for pity in Mahmet's mind. Djemal had failed him. Djemal who was supposed to be so strong.

When a couple of the camel drivers jeered at Mahmet and made nasty remarks about his not having given his camel water – a fact which was obvious – Mahmet cursed them back. Mahmet threw a bucket of water on to Djemal's head, and brought him to. Then Mahmet watched, grinding his teeth, as the winner of the race (a fat old swine who had always snubbed Mahmet in Elu-Bana) received his prize in the form of a paper cheque. Naturally the Government wasn't going to hand out that money in cash, because it might be stolen in the crowd.

Djemal drank water that night, and ate a bit also. Mahmet did not give him food, but there were bushes and trees where they spent the night. They were on the edge of the city of Khassa. The next day, having taken on provisions – bread, dates and water and a couple of dry sausages for himself – Mahmet started off with Djemal across the desert again. Djemal was still a little tired and could have rested for a day with profit. Was Mahmet going to stop somewhere for water this time? Djema hoped so. At least they weren't racing.

Near noon, when they had to rest under shade, Djemal's right front leg gave under him as he was kneeling for Mahmet to dismount. Mahmet tumbled on to the sand, then jumped up and struck Djemal a couple of times on the head with his whip handle.

'Stupid!' Mahmet shouted in Arabic.

Djemal bit at the whip and caught it. When Mahmet lunged for the whip, Djemal bit again and got Mahmet's wrist.

Mahmet shrieked.

Djemal got to his feet, inspired to further attack. How he hated this smelly little creature who considered himself his 'master'!

'Aaaah! Back! Down!' Mahmet yelled, and brandished the whip, retreating.

Djemal walked steadily towards Mahmet, teeth bared, and his eyes big and red with fury. Mahmet ran and took shelter behind the bending trunk of a date tree. Djemal circled the tree. He could smell the sharp stink of Mahmet's terror.

Mahmet was snatching off his old djellaba. He pulled off his turban also, and flung both these things towards Djemal.

Surprised, Djemal bit into the smelly clothes, shaking his head as if he had his teeth in Mahmet's neck and was shaking him to death. Djemal snorted and attacked the turban, now unwound in a long dirty length. He ate part of it, and stomped his big front feet on the rest.

Mahmet, behind his tree, began to breathe more easily. He knew that camels could vent their wrath on the clothes of the man they hated, and that was the end of it. He hoped so. He didn't fancy walking back to Khassa. He wanted to go to Elu-Bana, which he considered 'home'.

Djemal at last lay down. He was tired, almost too tired to bother putting himself in the patchy shade under the date tree. He slept.

Mahmet prodded him awake, carefully. The sun was setting. Djemal nipped at him, missing. Mahmet thought it wise to ignore it.

'Up, Djemal! Up – and we go!' said Mahmet.

Djemal plodded. He plodded on into the night, feeling the faint trail more than seeing it in the sand. The night was cool.

On the third day, they arrived at Souk Mandela, a busy market town, though small. Mahmet had decided to sell Djemal here. So he made for the open market where braziers, rugs, jewellery, camel saddles, pots and pans, hairpins and just about everything was for sale and on display on the ground. Camels were for sale too, at one corner. He led Djemal there, walking himself and being careful to look over his shoulder and to walk far enough ahead so that Djemal would not bite him.

'Cheap,' Mahmet said to the dealer. 'Six hundred dinars. He's a fine camel, you can see that. And he just won the Elu-Bana to Khassa race!'

'Oh yes? That's not the way we heard it!' said a turbaned camel driver who was listening, and a couple of others laughed. 'He collapsed!'

'Yes, we heard you didn't stop for water, you crooked old bastard!' said someone else.

'Even so—' Mahmet began, and dodged as Djemal's teeth came at him.

'Ha! Ha! Even his camel doesn't like this one!' said one old beard.

'Three hundred!' Mahmet screamed. 'With the saddle!'

A man pointed to Djemal's beaten shoulder, which was still bloody and on which flies had settled, as if it were a serious and permanent defect, and proposed two hundred and fifty dinars.

Mahmet accepted. Cash. The man had to go home to get it. Mahmet waited sullenly in some shade, watching the dealer and another man leading Djemal to the market water trough. He had lost a good camel — lost money, even more painful — but Mahmet was damned glad to be rid of Djemal. His life was worth more than money, after all.

That afternoon, Mahmet caught an uncomfortable bus to Elu-Bana. He was carrying his gear, empty watersacks, spirit lamp, cooking pot and blanket. He slept like the dead in an alley behind the restaurant where he often ate couscous. The next morning, with a clear vision of his bad luck, and the stinging memory of the low price he had got for one of the best camels in the country, Mahmet pilfered one of the tourists' cars. He got a plaid blanket and a bonus beneath it – a camera – a silver flask from the glove compartment, and a brown-paper-wrapped parcel which contained a small rug evidently just bought in the market. This theft took less than a minute, because the car was unlocked. It was in front of a shabby bar, and a couple of barefoot adolescent boys sitting at a table in the sand merely laughed when they saw Mahmet doing it.

Mahmet sold his loot before noon for seventy dinars (the camera was a good German one) which made him feel slightly better. With his own cache of dinars which he carried with him, sewn into a fold of blanket, Mahmet now had nearly five hundred. He could buy another camel of sorts, not as good as Djemal who had cost him four hundred dinars. And he would have enough to put something down on the house he wanted. The tourist season was on, and Mahmet needed a camel to earn money, because camel driving was the only thing he knew.

Meanwhile, Djemal had fallen into good hands. A poor but decent man called Chak had bought him to add to his string of three. Chak mainly hauled lemons and oranges and did other kinds of transport work with his camels, but in the tourist season, he gave camel rides too. Chak was delighted with Djemal's grace and willingness with the tourists. Because Djemal was so tall, he was often preferred by the tourists who wanted 'a view'.

Djemal was now quite healed of his sore shoulder, well fed, not overworked, and very content with his new master and his life. His memory of Mahmet was growing dimmer, because he never encountered him for one thing. Elu-Bana had many routes in and out of it. Djemal often worked miles away, and Chak's home was a few miles outside of town; there Djemal slept with the other camels under a shelter near the house where Chak lived with his family.

One day in early autumn, when the weather was a trifle cooler and most of the tourists had gone, Djemal picked up the scent of Mahmet. Djemal was just then entering the big fruit market in Elu-Bana, carrying a heavy load of grapefruit. Huge trucks were being loaded with boxes of dates and pineapples, and the scene was noisy with men talking and yelling and transistors everywhere blaring different programmes. Djemal didn't see Mahmet, but the hair on his neck rose a little, and he expected a blow out of nowhere. He knelt at Chak's command, and the burdens slipped from his sides.

Then he saw Mahmet just a camel's length in front of him. Djemal got to his feet. Mahmet saw Djemal also, took a second or two to make sure he was Djemal, then Mahmet jumped and stepped back. He pushed some paper dinars into his djellaba somewhere.

'So – your old camel, eh?' another camel driver said to Mahmet, jerking a thumb towards Djemal. 'Still afraid of him, Mahmet?'

'I never was afraid of him!' Mahmet came back.

'Ha-ha!'

A couple of other drivers joined the conversation.

Djemal saw Mahmet twitch, shrug his shoulders, talking all the while. Djemal could smell him well, and his hatred rose afresh. Djemal moved towards Mahmet.

'Ha! Ha! Watch out, Mahmet!' laughed a turbaned driver, who was a little drunk on wine.

Mahmet retreated.

Djemal followed, walking. He continued to walk, even though he heard Chak calling him. Then Djemal broke into a lope, as Mahmet vanished behind a truck. When Djemal reached the truck, Mahmet darted towards a small house, a shed of some kind for the market drivers.

To Mahmet's horror, the shed door was locked. He ran behind the shed.

Djemal bore down and seized Mahmet's djellaba and part of his spine in his teeth. Mahmet fell, and Djemal stomped him, stomped him again on the head.

'Look! It's a fight!'

'The old bastard deserves it!' cried someone.

A dozen men, then twenty gathered around to watch,

laughing, at first urging one another to go in and put a stop to it – but nobody did. On the contrary, someone passed a jug of red wine around.

Mahmet screamed. Djemal now came down with a foot in the middle of Mahmet's back. Then it was over really. Mahmet stopped moving, anyway. Djemal, just getting his strength up for the task, bit through the exposed calf of Mahmet's left leg.

The crowd howled. They were safe, the camel wasn't going to attack *them*, and to a man they detested Mahmet, who was not only stingy but downright dishonest, even with people whom he led to think were his friends.

'What a camel! What's his name?'

'Djemal! Ha-ha!'

'Used to be Mahmet's camel!' someone repeated, as if the whole crowd didn't know that.

At last Chak burst through. 'Djemal! Ho! Stop, Djemal!'

'Let him have his revenge!' someone yelled.

'This is terrible!' cried Chak.

The men surrounded Chak, telling him it wasn't terrible, telling him they would get rid of the body, somewhere. No, no, no, there was no need to call the police. Absurd! Have some wine, Chak! Even some of the truck drivers had joined them, smiling with sinister amusement at what had happened behind the shed.

Djemal, head high now, had begun to calm down. He could smell blood along with the stench of Mahmet. Haughtily he stepped over his victim, lifting each foot carefully, and rejoined his master Chak. Chak was still nervous.

'No, no,' Chak was saying, because the men, all a bit tipsy now, were offering Chak seven hundred and more dinars for Djemal. Chak was shaken by the events, but at the same time he was proud of Djemal, and wouldn't have parted with him for a thousand dinars at that moment.

Djemal smiled. He lifted his head and looked coolly

through his long-lashed eyes towards the horizon. Men patted his flanks, his shoulders. Mahmet was dead. His anger, like a poison, was out of his blood. Djemal followed Chak, without a lead, as Chak walked away, looking back and calling to him.

There I Was, Stuck with Bubsy

YES, here he was, stuck with Bubsy, a fate no living creature deserved. The Baron, aged sixteen – seventeen? – anyway aged, felt doomed to spend his last days with this plump, abhorrent beast whom the Baron had detested almost since he had appeared on the scene at least ten or twelve years ago. Doomed unless something happened. But what would happen, and what could the Baron make happen? The Baron racked his brain. People had said since he was a pup that his intelligence was extraordinary. The Baron took some comfort in that. It was a matter of strengthening Marion's hand, difficult for a dog to do, since the Baron didn't speak, though many a time his master Eddie had told him that he did speak. That was because Eddie had understood every bark and growl and glance that the Baron ever gave.

The Baron lay on a tufted polkadot cushion which lined his basket. The basket had an arched top, and even this was lined with tufted polkadot. From the next room, the Baron could hear laughter, jumbled voices, the *clink* of a glass or bottle now and then, and Bubsy's occasional 'Haw-ha-*haw*!' which in the days after Eddie's death had made the Baron's ears twitch with hostility. Now the Baron no longer reacted to Bubsy's guffaws. On the contrary, the Baron affected a languor, an unconcern (better for his nerves), and now he yawned mightily, showing yellowed lower canines, then he settled his chin on his paws. He wanted to pee. He'd gone into the noisy living-room ten minutes ago and indicated to Bubsy by approaching the door of the apartment that he wanted to go out.

But Bubsy had not troubled himself, though one of the young men (the Baron was almost sure) had offered to take him downstairs. The Baron got up suddenly. He couldn't wait any longer. He could of course pee straight on the carpet with a damn-it-all attitude, but he still had some decency left.

The Baron tried the living-room again. Tonight there was more than usually a sprinkling of women.

'O-o-o-oh!'

'Ah-h-h! There's the Baron!'

'Ah, the Baron!' said Bubsy.

'He wants to go out, Bubsy, for Christ's sake! Where's his leash?'

'I've just *had* him out!' shrieked Bubsy, lying.

'When? This morning? . . .'

A young man in thick, fuzzy tweed trousers took the Baron down in the elevator. The Baron made for the first tree at the kerb, and lifted a leg slightly. The young man talked to him in a friendly way, and said something about 'Eddie'. The name of his master made the Baron briefly sad, though he supposed it was nice of people, total strangers, to remember his master. They walked around the block. Near the delicatessen on Lexington Avenue, a man stopped them and in a polite tone asked a question with 'the Baron' in it.

'Yes,' said the young man who held the Baron's leash.

The strange man patted the Baron's head gently, and the Baron recognized his master's other name 'Brockhurst . . . Edward Brockhurst . . .'

They went on, back towards the awning of the apartment house, towards the awful party. Then the Baron's ears picked up a tread he knew, then his nose a scent he knew: Marion.

'Hello! Excuse me . . .' She was closer than the Baron had supposed, because his ears were not what they used to be, nor his eyes for that matter. She talked with the young man, and they all rode up in the elevator.

The Baron's heart was pounding with pleasure. Marion smelled nice. Suddenly the whole evening was better, even wonderful, just because Marion had turned up. His master had always loved Marion. And the Baron was well aware that Marion wanted to take him away to live with her.

There was quite a change in the atmosphere when the Baron and the young man and Marion walked in. The conversation died down, and Bubsy walked forward with a glass of his favourite bubble in his hand, champagne. The young man undid the Baron's leash.

'Good evening, Bubsy . . .' Marion was speaking politely, explaining something.

Some poeple had said hello to Marion, others were starting up their conversation again in little groups. The Baron kept his eyes on Marion. Could it be possible that she was going to take him away *tonight*? She was talking about him. And Bubsy looked flustered. He motioned for Marion to come into one of the other rooms, Bubsy's bedroom, and the Baron followed at Marion's heels. Bubsy would have shut the Baron out, but Marion held the door.

'Come in, Baron!' Marion said.

The Baron disliked this room. The bed was high, made higher still by pillows, and at the foot of it was the contraption Bubsy used when he had his fits of wheezing and gasping, usually at night. There were two chromium tanks from which a rubber pipe came out, flexible metal pipes also, and the whole thing could be wheeled up to Bubsy's pillows.

'. . . friend . . . vacation . . .' Marion was saying. She was pleading with Bubsy. The Baron heard his name two or three times, Eddie's name once, and Bubsy looked at the Baron with the angry, stubborn expression that the Baron knew well, knew since years, even when Eddie had been alive.

'Well, no . . .' Bubsy went on, making quite an elaborate speech.

39

Marion began again, not in the least discouraged.

Bubsy coughed, and his face darkened a little. He repeated his 'No . . . no . . .'

Marion dropped on her knees and looked into the Baron's eyes and talked to him. The Baron wagged his cropped tail. He trembled with joy, and could have flung his paws up on Marion's shoulders, but he didn't, because it was not the right thing to do. But his front paws kept dancing off the floor. He felt years younger.

Then Marion began talking about Eddie, and she grew angrier. She drew herself up a little when she talked about Eddie, as if he were something to be proud of, and it was evident to the Baron that she thought, she might even be saying, that Bubsy wasn't worth as much. The Baron knew that his master had been someone of importance. Strangers, coming to the house now and then, had treated Eddie as if he were their master, in a way, in those days when they had lived in another apartment, and Bubsy had served the drinks and cooked the meals like one of the servants on the ships the Baron had travelled on, or in the hotels where the Baron had stayed. Now suddenly Bubsy was claiming the Baron as his own dog. That was what it amounted to.

Bubsy kept saying 'No' in an increasingly firm voice. He walked towards the door.

Marion said something in a quietly threatening tone. The Baron wished very much that he knew exactly what she had said. The Baron followed her through the living-room towards the front door. He was prepared to sneak out with her, leap out leashless, and just stay with her. Marion paused to talk with the young man in the fuzzy tweed trousers who had come up to her.

Bubsy interrupted them, waving his hands, wanting to put an end to the conversation.

Marion said, 'Good night . . . good night . . .'

The Baron squeezed out with her, loped in the hall towards the elevators. A man laughed, not Bubsy.

'Baron, you can't . . . darling,' said Marion.

Someone caught the Baron by the collar. The Baron growled, but he knew he couldn't win, that someone would give him a warning slap, if he didn't do what *they* wanted. Behind him, the Baron heard the awful *clunk* that meant the elevator door had closed on Marion, and she was gone. Some people groaned as the Baron crossed the living-room, others laughed, as the din began again, louder and merrier than ever. The Baron made straight for his master's room which was across the hall from Bubsy's. The door was closed, but the Baron could open it by the horizontal handle, providing the door wasn't locked. The Baron couldn't manage the key, which stuck out below the handle, though he had often tried. Now the door opened. Bubsy had perhaps been showing the room to some of his guests tonight. The Baron went in and took a breath of the air that still smelled faintly of his master's pipe tobacco. On the big desk was his master's typewriter, now covered with a cloth of a sort of polkadot pattern like the lining of his basket-bed in the spare room. The Baron was just as happy, even happier, sleeping on the carpet here near the desk, as he had often done when his master worked, but Bubsy, nastily, usually kept the door of his master's room locked.

The Baron curled up on the carpet and put his head down, his nose almost touching a leg of his master's chair. He sighed, suddenly worn out by the emotions of the last ten minutes. He thought of Marion, recalled happy mornings when Marion had come to visit, and his master and Bubsy had cooked bacon and eggs, or hotcakes, and they had all gone for a walk in Central Park. The Baron had used to retrieve sticks that Marion threw into a lake there. And he remembered an especially happy cruise, sunlight on the decks, with his master and Marion (pre-Bubsy days), when the Baron had been young and spry and handsome, popular with the passengers, pampered by the stewards who brought whole steaks to his and

41

Eddie's cabin. The Baron remembered walks in a white-walled town full of white houses, with smells he had never known before or since . . . And a boat ride with the boat tossing, and spray in his face, to an island where the streets were paved with cobblestones, where he got to know the whole island and roamed where he wished. He heard again his master's voice talking calmly to him, asking him a question . . . The Baron heard the ghostly click of the typewriter . . . Then he fell asleep.

He awakened to Bubsy's coughing, then his strained intake of air, with a wheeze. The house was quiet now. Bubsy was walking about in his room. The Baron got to his feet and shook himself to wake up. He went out of the room, so as not to be locked in for the rest of the night, walked towards the living-room, but the smell of cigarette smoke turned him back. The Baron went into the kitchen, drank some water from his bowl, sniffed at the remains of some tinned dogfood, and turned away, heading for the spare room. He could have eaten something – a bit of left-over steak, or a lambchop bone would have been nice. Lately, Bubsy dined out a lot, didn't take the Baron with him, and Bubsy fed him mostly from tins. How his master would have put a stop to that! The Baron curled up in his basket.

Bubsy's machine was buzzing. Now and again it made a *click-click* sound. Bubsy blew his nose – a sign he was feeling better.

Bubsy didn't go to work, didn't work at all in the sense that Eddie had worked several hours a day at his typewriter, in some periods every day of the week. Bubsy got up in mid-morning, made tea and toast, and sat in his silk dressing gown reading the newspaper which was still delivered every morning at the door. It would be nearly noon before Bubsy took the Baron out for a walk. By this time Bubsy would have telephoned at least twice, and then he would go out for a long lunch, perhaps, or anyway he seldom came back before late afternoon. Bubsy had used to have something to do with the theatre, just what the

Baron didn't know. But when his master had met Bubsy, they had visited him a couple of times in the busy backstage part of a New York theatre. Bubsy had been nicer then, the Baron could remember quite well, always ready to take him out for a walk, to brush his ears and the clump of curly black hair on the top of his head, because Bubsy had been proud to show him off on the street in those days. Yes, and the Baron had won a prize or two at Madison Square Garden in his prime, so many years ago. Oh, happy days! His two silver cups and two or three medals occupied a place of honour on a bookshelf in the living-room, but the maid hadn't polished them in weeks now. Eddie had shown them sometimes to people who came to the apartment, and a couple of times, laughing, Eddie had served the Baron his morning biscuits and milk in one of the cups. The Baron recalled that at the moment there were no biscuits in the house.

Why did Bubsy hang on to him, if he didn't really like him? The Baron suspected it was because Bubsy was thus able to hang on to his master, who had been a more important man – which meant loved and respected by a lot more people – than Bubsy. In the awful days during his master's illness, and after his death, the person the Baron had clung to was Marion, not Bubsy. The Baron thought that his master wished, probably had made it clear, that he wanted the Baron to live with Marion after he died. Bubsy had always been jealous of the Baron, and the Baron had to admit that he had been jealous of Bubsy. But whether he lived with Bubsy or Marion, that was what the fight was about. He was no fool. Marion and Bubsy had been fighting ever since Eddie's death.

Down on the street, a car rattled over a manhole. From Bubsy's room, the Baron heard wheezing inhalations. The machine was unplugged now. The Baron was thirsty, thought of getting up to drink again, then felt too tired, and merely flicked his tongue over his nose and closed his eyes. A tooth was hurting. Old age was a terrible thing.

He'd had two wives, so long ago he scarcely remembered them. He'd had many children, maybe twelve, and the pictures of several of them were in the living-room, and one on his master's desk – the Baron with three of his offspring.

The Baron woke up, growling, from a bad dream. He looked around, dazed, in the darkness. It had *happened*. No, it was a dream. But it had happened, yes. Just a few days ago. Bubsy had waked him from a nap, leash in hand, to take him out, and the Baron – maybe ill-tempered at that moment because he'd been awakened – had growled in an ominous way, not raising his head. And Bubsy had slowly retreated. And later that day, again with the leash in his hand, doubled, Bubsy had reminded the Baron of his bad behaviour and slashed the air with the leash. The Baron had not winced, only watched Bubsy with a cool contempt. So they had stared at each other, and nothing had come of it, but Bubsy had been the first to move.

Would he be able to get anywhere by fighting? The Baron's old muscles grew tense at the thought. But he couldn't figure it out, couldn't see clearly into the future, and soon he was asleep again.

In the evening of that day, the Baron was surprised by a delicious meal of raw steak cut into convenient pieces, followed by a walk during which Bubsy talked to him in amiable tones. Then they got into a taxi. They rode quite a distance. Could they be going to Marion's apartment? Her apartment was a long way away, the Baron remembered from the days when Eddie had been alive. But Bubsy never went to Marion's house. Then when the taxi stopped and they got out, the Baron recognized the butcher's shop, still open, that smelled of spices as well as meat. They *were* at Marion's building! The Baron's tail began to wag. He lifted his head higher, and led Bubsy to the right door.

Bubsy pushed a bell, the door buzzed, then they went in

44

and climbed three flights, the Baron pulling Bubsy up, panting, happy.

Marion opened the door. The Baron stood on his hind legs, careful not to scratch her dress with his nails, and Marion took his paws.

'Hello, Baron! Hel-*lo*, hello! – Come in!'

Marion's apartment had a high ceiling and smelled of oil paint and turpentine. There were big comfortable sofas and chairs which the Baron knew he was allowed to lie on if he wished to. Now there was a strange man who stood up from a chair as they went in. Marion introduced Bubsy to him, and they shook hands. The men talked. Marion went into the kitchen and poured a bowl of milk for the Baron, and gave him a steak bone which had been wrapped in wax paper in the refrigerator. Marion said something which the Baron took to mean, 'Make yourself at home. Chew the bone anywhere.'

The Baron chose to chew it at Marion's feet, once she had sat down in a chair.

The conversation grew more heated. Bubsy whipped some papers out of his pocket, and now he was on his feet, his face pinker, his thin blond curls tossing.

'There is not a *thing* . . . No . . . *No*.'

Bubsy's favourite word, 'No'.

'That is not the *point*,' Marion said.

Then the other man said something more calmly than either Marion or Bubsy. The Baron chewed on his bone, sparing the sore tooth. The strange man made quite a long speech, which Bubsy interrupted a couple of times, but Bubsy finally stopped talking and listened. Marion was very tense.

'No . . . ?'

'No . . . now . . .'

That was a word the Baron knew. He looked up at Marion, whose face was a little flushed also, but nothing like Bubsy's. Only the other man was calm. He had papers in his hand, too. What was going to happen *now*? The

Baron associated the word with rather important commands to himself.

Bubsy spread his hands palm down and said, '*No.*' And many more words.

A very few minutes later, the Baron's leash was attached to his collar and he was dragged – gently but still dragged – towards the door by Bubsy. The Baron braced all four feet when he realized what was happening. He didn't want to go! He'd hardly begun to visit with Marion. The Baron looked over his shoulder and pled for her assistance. The strange man shook his head and lit a cigarette. Bubsy and Marion were talking to each other at the same time, almost shouting. Marion clenched her fists. But she opened one hand to pat the Baron, and said something kind to him before he was out in the hall, and the door shut.

Bubsy and the Baron crossed a wide street, and entered a bar. Loud music, awful smells, except for a whiff of freshly broiled steak. Bubsy drank, and twice muttered to himself. Then he yanked the Baron into a taxi, yanked him because the Baron missed his footing and sprawled in an undignified way, banging his jaw on the floor of the taxi. Bubsy was in the foulest of moods. And the Baron's heart was pounding with several emotions: outrage, regret he had not spent longer with Marion, hatred of Bubsy. The Baron glanced at the windows (both nearly closed) as if he might jump out of one of them, though Bubsy had the leash wrapped twice around his wrist, and the buildings on either side flashed by at great speed. Bubsy let out the leash a little for the benefit of the doormen who always greeted the Baron by name. Bubsy was so out of breath, he could hardly speak to the doormen. The Baron knew he was suffering, but had no pity for him.

In the apartment, Bubsy at once flopped into a chair, mouth open. The Baron's leash trailed, and he walked dismally down the hall, hesitated at his master's door, then went in. He collapsed on the carpet by the chair. Back again. How brief had been his pleasure at Marion's!

46

He heard Bubsy struggling to breathe, undressing in his room now – or at least removing his jacket and whipping off his tie. Then the Baron heard the machine being plugged in. *Buzz-zz* . . . *Click-click.* The groan of a chair. Bubsy was doubtless in the chair by his bed, holding the mask over his face.

Thirsty, the Baron got up to go to the kitchen. His leash, the hand loop part of it, caught under the door and checked him. The Baron patiently entered the room again, pulled the leash out, and went out with his shoulder near the right door jamb so the same accident wouldn't happen again. It reminded him of nasty tricks Bubsy had used to play when the Baron had been younger. Of course the Baron had played a few tricks, too, tripping Bubsy adroitly while he (the Baron) had been ostensibly only cavorting after a ball. Now the Baron was so tired, his hind legs ached and he limped. Several teeth were hurting. He had chewed too enthusiastically on that bone. The Baron drank all his bowl – it was only half full and stale – then on leaving the kitchen, the Baron caught his leash in the same manner under the kitchen door. Bubsy just then lurched out of his room, coughing, heading for the bathroom, and stepped hard on the Baron's front paw. The Baron gave an agonized cry, because it had really hurt, nearly broken his toes!

Bubsy kicked at him and cursed.

The Baron – as if a mysterious spring had been released – leapt and sank his teeth through Bubsy's trousers into his lower leg.

Bubsy screamed, and swatted the Baron on the head with his fist. This made the Baron turn loose, and Bubsy kicked at him again, missing. Bubsy was gasping. The Baron watched Bubsy go into the bathroom, knowing he was going to get a wet towel for his face.

The Baron was suddenly full of energy. Where had it come from? He stood with forelegs apart, his aching teeth bared, trapped by his leash which was stuck under the

47

kitchen door. When Bubsy emerged with the dripping towel clamped against his forehead, the Baron growled his deepest. Bubsy stumbled past him into his room, and the Baron heard him flop on the bed. Then the Baron went back into the kitchen slowly, so as not to make his leash predicament worse. The leather was tightly wedged this time, and there was not enough space, if the Baron moved towards the sink, to tug it out. The Baron caught the leash in his back teeth and pulled. The leash slipped through his teeth. He tried the other side of his jaw, and with one yank freed the leash. This was the worse side of his jaw, and the pain was awful. The Baron cringed on the floor, eyes shut for a moment, as he would never have cringed before Bubsy or anyone else. But pain was pain. Terrible. The Baron's very ears seemed to ring with his agony, but he didn't whine. He was remembering a similar pain inflicted by Bubsy. Or was that true? At any rate, the pain reminded him of Bubsy.

As the pain subsided, the Baron stood up, on guard against Bubsy who might come to life at any moment. The Baron carefully walked towards the living-room, dragging his leash straight behind him, then turned so that he was facing the hall. He sank down and put his chin on his paws and waited, listening, his eyes wide open.

Bubsy coughed, the kind of cough that meant the mask was off and he was feeling better. Bubsy was getting up. He was going to come into the living-room for some champagne, probably. The Baron's hind legs grew tense, and he really might have moved out of the way if not for a fear in the back of his mind that his leash would catch on something again. Bubsy approached coughing, pushing himself straight with a hand against a wall. Bubsy made a menacing gesture with his other hand, and ordered the Baron to get out of the way.

The Baron expected a foot in his face, and without thinking hurled himself at Bubsy's waistline and bit. Bubsy came down with a fist on the Baron's spine. They struggled on the floor, Bubsy hitting and missing most of his blows, the Baron snapping and missing also. But the Baron was still on the living-room side, and Bubsy retreated towards his room, the Baron after him. Bubsy grabbed a vase, and hit the Baron on the top of the head. The Baron's sight was knocked out, and he saw only silvery lights for a few seconds. As soon as his vision came back a little, he leapt for Bubsy whose legs now dangled over the side of the bed.

The Baron fell short, and his teeth clamped the rubber tube, not Bubsy's leg. The Baron bit and shook his head. The tube seemed as much Bubsy and Bubsy's own flesh. Bubsy loved that tube, depended on it, and the thick rubber was yielding slowly, just like flesh. Bubsy, with the mask over his face, kicked at the Baron, missing. Then the tube broke in two and the Baron slid to the floor.

Bubsy groped for the other end of the tube, started to put it in his mouth, but the end was frayed and full of holes. Bubsy gave it up, and lay back on the bed, panting like a dog himself. Blood was trickling through the hair above the Baron's eyes. The Baron staggered towards the door and turned, his tongue hanging out, his heart-beats shaking his body. The Baron lay down on the floor, and his eyes glazed until he could hardly see the bed and Bubsy's legs over the side, but the Baron kept his eyes open. The minutes passed. The Baron's breathing grew easier. He listened, and he could not hear anything. Was Bubsy asleep?

The Baron half-slept, instinctively saving every bit of strength that he had left. The Baron heard no sound from Bubsy, and finally the hackles on the Baron's neck told him that he was in the presence of something dead.

At dawn, the Baron withdrew from the room, and like a very old dog, head hanging, legs wobbling, made his way to the living-room. He lay on his side, more tired than ever. Soon the telephone began to ring. The Baron barely lifted his head at the first ring, then paid no more attention.

The telephone stopped, then rang again. This happened several times. The top of the Baron's head throbbed.

The woman who cleaned the apartment twice a week arrived in the afternoon – the Baron recognized her step in the hall – and rang the bell, although she had a key, the Baron knew. At the same time, another elevator opened its door, and some steps sounded in the hall, then voices. The apartment door opened, and the maid whose name was something like Lisa entered with two men friends of Bubsy's. They all seemed surprised to see the Baron standing in the living-room with his leash on. They were shocked by the patch of blood on the carpet, and the Baron was reminded vaguely of the first months of his life, when he had made what his master called mistakes in the house.

'Bubsy!'

'Bubsy, are you here?'

They found Bubsy in the next seconds. One man rushed back into the living-room and picked up the telephone. This man the Baron recognized as the one who had worn fuzzy trousers and had aired him at Bubsy's last party. No one paid any attention to the Baron, but when the Baron went into the kitchen, he saw that Lisa had put down some food for him and filled his water bowl. The Baron drank a little. Lisa undid his leash and said something kind to him. Another man arrived, a stranger. He went into Bubsy's bedroom. Then he looked at the Baron but didn't touch him, and he looked at the blood on the carpet. Then two men in white suits arrived and Bubsy was carried out, wrapped in a blanket, on a stretcher – just as his master had been carried out, the Baron recalled, but his master had been alive. Now the Baron felt no emotion at all on seeing Bubsy depart in the same manner. The young man made another telephone call. The Baron heard the name Marion, and his ears picked up.

Then the man put the telephone down, and he smiled at the Baron in a funny way: it was not really a happy smile. What was the man thinking of? He put the Baron's leash on. They went downstairs and took a taxi. Then they went into an office which the Baron knew at once was a vet's. The vet jabbed a needle into him. When the Baron woke up, he was lying on his side on a different table, and he tried to stand up, couldn't quite, and then he threw up the bit of water he had drunk. The friend of Bubsy's was still with him, and carried the Baron out, and they got into another taxi.

The Baron revived in the breeze through the window. The Baron took more interest as the ride went on and on. Could they possibly be going to Marion's?

They were! The taxi stopped. There was the butcher's shop again. And there was Marion on the sidewalk outside her door! The Baron wriggled from the man's arms and fell on the sidewalk outside the cab. Silly! Embarrassing! But the Baron got on his wobbly legs again, and was able to greet Marion with tail wagging, with a lick of her hand.

'Oh, Baron! Old Baron!' she said. And the Baron knew she was saying something reassuring about the cut on his head (now bandaged, the bandage going under his chin, too), which the Baron knew was not serious, was quite unimportant compared to the fact that he was with Marion, that he was going to stay with Marion, the Baron somehow felt sure. Marion and the man were talking – and sure enough, the man was taking his leave. He patted the Baron on the shoulder and said, 'Bye-bye, Baron,' but in a tone that was merely polite. After all, he was more a friend of Bubsy's than the Baron's. The Baron lifted his head, gave a lick of his tongue towards the man's hand, and missed.

Then Marion and the Baron walked into the butcher's shop. The butcher smiled and shook the Baron's paw, and said something about his head. The butcher cut a steak for Marion.

Marion and the Baron climbed the stairs, Marion going slowly for the Baron's sake. She opened the door into the apartment with the high ceiling, with the sharp smell of turpentine that he had come to love. The Baron ate a bit

51

of steak, and then had a sleep on one of the big sofas. He woke up and blinked his eyes. He'd just had a dream, a not so nice dream about Bubsy and a lot of noisy people, but he had already forgotten the dream. *This* was real: Marion standing at her worktable, glancing at him now because he had raised his head, but gazing back at her work – because for the moment she was thinking more about her work than about him. Like Eddie, the Baron thought. The Baron put his head down again and watched Marion. He was old, he knew, very old. People even marvelled about how old he was. But he sensed that he was going to have a second life, that he even had a fair amount of time before him.

Ming's Biggest Prey

MING was resting comfortably on the foot of his mistress's bunk, when the man picked him up by the back of the neck, stuck him out on the deck and closed the cabin door. Ming's blue eyes widened in shock and brief anger, then nearly closed again because of the brilliant sunlight. It was not the first time Ming had been thrust out of the cabin rudely, and Ming realized that the man did it when his mistress, Elaine, was not looking.

The sailboat now offered no shelter from the sun, but Ming was not yet too warm. He leapt easily to the cabin roof and stepped on to the coil of rope just behind the mast. Ming liked the rope coil as a couch, because he could see everything from the height, the cup shape of the rope protected him from strong breezes, and also minimized the swaying and sudden changes of angle of the *White Lark*, since it was more or less the centre point. But just now the sail had been taken down, because Elaine and the man had eaten lunch, and often they had a siesta afterward, during which time, Ming knew, that man didn't like him in the cabin. Lunchtime was all right. In fact, Ming had just lunched on delicious grilled fish and a bit of lobster. Now, lying in a relaxed curve on the coil of rope, Ming opened his mouth in a great yawn, then with his slant eyes almost closed against the strong sunlight, gazed at the beige hills and the white and pink houses and hotels that circled the bay of Acapulco. Between the *White Lark* and the shore where people plashed inaudibly, the sun twinkled on the water's surface like thousands of tiny electric lights going on and off. A water-skier went by, skimming up white spray behind him Such activity! Ming half dozed, feeling the heat of the sun sink into his fur. Ming was from New York, and he considered Acapulco a great improvement over his environment in the first weeks of his life. He remembered a sunless box with straw on the bottom, three or four other kittens in with him, and a window behind which giant forms paused for a few moments, tried to catch his attention by tapping, then passed on. He did not remember his mother at all. One day a young woman who smelled of something pleasant came into the place and took him away – away from the ugly, frightening smell of dogs, of medicine and parrot dung. Then they went on what Ming now knew was an aeroplane. He was quite used to aeroplanes now and rather liked them. On aeroplanes he sat on Elaine's lap, or slept on her lap, and there were always titbits to eat if he was hungry.

Elaine spent much of the day in a shop in Acapulco, where dresses and slacks and bathing suits hung on all the walls. This place smelled clean and fresh, there were flowers in pots and in boxes out front, and the floor was of cool blue and white tile. Ming had perfect freedom to wander out into the patio behind the shop, or to sleep in his basket in a corner. There was more sunlight in front of the shop, but mischievous boys often tried to grab him if he sat in front, and Ming could never relax there.

Ming liked best lying in the sun with his mistress on one of the long canvas chairs on their terrace at home. What Ming did not like were the people she sometimes invited to their house, people who spent the night, people by the score who stayed up very late eating and drinking, playing the gramophone or the piano – people who separated him from Elaine. People who stepped on his toes, people who sometimes picked him up from behind before he could do anything about it, so that he had to squirm and fight to get free, people who stroked him roughly, people who closed a door somewhere, locking him in. *People!* Ming detested people. In all the world, he liked only Elaine. Elaine loved him and understood him.

Especially this man called Teddie Ming detested now. Teddie was around all the time lately. Ming did not like the way Teddie looked at him, when Elaine was not watching. And sometimes Teddie, when Elaine was not near, muttered something which Ming knew was a threat. Or a command to leave the room. Ming took it calmly. Dignity was to be preserved. Besides, wasn't his mistress on his side? The man was the intruder. When Elaine was watching, the man sometimes pretended a fondness for him, but Ming always moved gracefully but unmistakably in another direction.

Ming's nap was interrupted by the sound of the cabin door opening. He heard Elaine and the man laughing and talking. The big red-orange sun was near the horizon.

'Ming!' Elaine came over to him. 'Aren't you getting *cooked*, darling? I thought you were *in*!'

'So did I!' said Teddie.

Ming purred as he always did when he awakened. She picked him up gently, cradled him in her arms, and took him below into the suddenly cool shade of the cabin. She was talking to the man, and not in a gentle tone. She set Ming down in front of his dish of water, and though he was not thirsty, he drank a little to please her. Ming did feel addled by the heat, and he staggered a little.

Elaine took a wet towel and wiped Ming's face, his ears and his four paws. Then she laid him gently on the bunk that smelled of Elaine's perfume but also of the man whom Ming detested.

Now his mistress and the man were quarrelling, Ming could tell from the tone. Elaine was staying with Ming, sitting on the edge of the bunk. Ming at last heard the splash that meant Teddie had dived into the water. Ming hoped he stayed there, hoped he drowned, hoped he never came back. Elaine wet a bathtowel in the aluminium sink, wrung it out, spread it on the bunk, and lifted Ming on to it. She brought water, and now Ming was thirsty, and drank. She left him to sleep again while she washed and put away the dishes. These were comfortable sounds that Ming liked to hear.

But soon there was another *plash* and *plop*, Teddie's wet feet on the deck, and Ming was awake again.

The tone of quarrelling recommenced. Elaine went up the few steps on to the deck. Ming, tense but with his chin still resting on the moist bathtowel, kept his eyes on the cabin door. It was Teddie's feet that he heard descending. Ming lifted his head slightly, aware that there was no exit behind him, that he was trapped in the cabin. The man paused with a towel in his hands, staring at Ming.

Ming relaxed completely, as he might do preparatory to a yawn, and this caused his eyes to cross. Ming then let his tongue slide a little way out of his mouth. The man started to say something, looked as if he wanted to hurl the wadded towel at Ming, but he wavered, whatever he had been going to say never got out of his mouth, and he threw the towel in the sink, then bent to wash his face. It was not the first time Ming had let his tongue slide out at Teddie. Lots of people laughed when Ming did this, if they were people at a party, for instance, and Ming rather enjoyed that. But Ming sensed that Teddie took it as a hostile gesture of some kind, which was why Ming did it deliberately to Teddie, whereas among other people, it was often an accident when Ming's tongue slid out.

The quarrelling continued. Elaine made coffee. Ming began to feel better, and went on deck again, because the sun had now set. Elaine had started the motor, and they were gliding slowly towards the shore. Ming caught the song of birds, the odd screams, like shrill phrases, of certain birds that cried only at sunset. Ming looked forward to the adobe house on the cliff that was his and his mistress's home. He knew that the reason she did not leave him at home (where he would have been more comfortable) when she went on the boat, was because she was afraid that people

58

might trap him, even kill him. Ming understood. People had tried to grab him from almost under Elaine's eyes. Once he had been suddenly hauled away in a cloth bag, and though fighting as hard as he could, he was not sure he would have been able to get out, if Elaine had not hit the boy herself and grabbed the bag from him.

Ming had intended to jump up on the cabin roof again, but after glancing at it, he decided to save his strength, so he crouched on the warm, gently sloping deck with his feet tucked in, and gazed at the approaching shore. Now he could hear guitar music from the beach. The voices of his mistress and the man had come to a halt. For a few moments, the loudest sound was the *chug-chug-chug* of the boat's motor. Then Ming heard the man's bare feet climbing the cabin steps. Ming did not turn his head to look at him, but his ears twitched back a little, involuntarily. Ming looked at the water just the distance of a short leap in front of him and below him. Strangely, there was no sound from the man behind him. The hair on Ming's neck prickled, and Ming glanced over his right shoulder.

At that instant, the man bent forward and rushed at Ming with his arms outspread.

Ming was on his feet at once, darting straight towards the man, which was the only direction of safety on the railless deck, and the man swung his left arm and cuffed Ming in the chest. Ming went flying backward, claws scraping the deck, but his hind legs went over the edge. Ming clung with his front feet to the sleek wood which gave him little hold, while his hind legs worked to heave him up, worked at the side of the boat which sloped to Ming's disadvantage.

The man advanced to shove a foot against Ming's paws, but Elaine came up the cabin steps just then.

'What's happening? *Ming!*'

Ming's strong hind legs were getting him on to the deck little by little. The man had knelt as if to lend a hand. Elaine had fallen on to her knees also, and had Ming by the back of the neck now.

59

Ming relaxed, hunched on the deck. His tail was wet.

'He fell overboard!' Teddie said. 'It's true, he's groggy. Just lurched over and fell when the boat gave a dip.'

'It's the sun. Poor *Ming!*' Elaine held the cat against her breast, and carried him into the cabin. 'Teddie – could you steer?'

The man came down into the cabin. Elaine had Ming on the bunk and was talking softly to him. Ming's heart was still beating fast. He was alert against the man at the wheel, even though Elaine was with him. Ming was aware that they had entered the little cove where they always went before getting off the boat.

Here were the friends and allies of Teddie, whom Ming detested by association, although these were merely Mexican boys. Two or three boys in shorts called 'Señor Teddie!' and offered a hand to Elaine to climb on to the dock, took the rope attached to the front of the boat, offered to carry *'Ming! – Ming!'* Ming leapt on to the dock himself and crouched, waiting for Elaine, ready to dart away from any other hand that might reach for him. And there were several brown hands making a rush for him, so that Ming had to keep jumping aside. There were laughs, yelps, stomps of bare feet on wooden boards. But there was also the reassuring voice of Elaine warning them off. Ming knew she was busy carrying off the plastic satchels, locking the cabin door. Teddie with the aid of one of the Mexican boys was stretching the canvas over the cabin now. And Elaine's sandalled feet were beside Ming. Ming followed her as she walked away. A boy took the things Elaine was carrying, then she picked Ming up.

They got into the big car without a roof that belonged to Teddie, and drove up the winding road towards Elaine's and Ming's house. One of the boys was driving. Now the tone in which Elaine and Teddie were speaking was calmer, softer. The man laughed. Ming sat tensely on his mistress's lap. He could feel her concern for him in the way she stroked him and touched the back of his neck. The man reached out to put his fingers on Ming's back, and Ming gave a low growl that rose and fell and rumbled deep in his throat.

'Well, well,' said the man, pretending to be amused, and took his hand away.

Elaine's voice had stopped in the middle of something she was saying. Ming was tired, and wanted nothing more than to take a nap on the big bed at home. The bed was covered with a red and white striped blanket of thin wool.

Hardly had Ming thought of this, when he found himself in the cool, fragrant atmosphere of his own home, being lowered gently on to the bed with the soft woollen cover. His mistress kissed his cheek, and said something with the word hungry in it. Ming understood, at any rate. He was to tell her when he was hungry.

Ming dozed, and awakened at the sound of voices on the terrace a couple of yards away, past the open glass doors. Now it was dark. Ming could see one end of the table, and could tell from the quality of the light that there were candles on the table. Concha, the servant who slept in the house, was clearing the table. Ming heard her voice, then the voices of Elaine and the man. Ming smelled cigar smoke. Ming jumped to the floor and sat for a moment looking out of the door towards the terrace. He yawned, then arched his back and stretched, and limbered up his muscles by digging his claws into the thick straw carpet. Then he slipped out to the right on the terrace and glided silently down the long stairway of broad stones to the garden below. The garden was like a jungle or a forest. Avocado trees and mango trees grew as high as the terrace itself, there were bougainvillaea against the wall, orchids in the trees, and magnolias and several camellias which Elaine had planted. Ming could hear birds twittering and stirring in their nests. Sometimes he climbed trees to get at their nests, but tonight he was not in the mood, though he was no longer tired. The voices of his mistress and the man disturbed him. His mistress was not a friend of the man's tonight, that was plain.

Concha was probably still in the kitchen, and Ming decided to go in and ask her for something to eat. Concha liked him. One maid who had not liked him had been dismissed by Elaine. Ming thought he fancied barbecued pork. That was what his mistress and the man had eaten tonight. The breeze blew fresh from the ocean, ruffling Ming's fur slightly. Ming felt completely recovered from the awful experience of nearly falling into the sea.

Now the terrace was empty of people. Ming went left, back into the bedroom, and was at once aware of the man's presence, though there was no light on and Ming could not see him. The man was standing by the dressing table, opening a box. Again involuntarily Ming gave a low growl which rose and fell, and Ming remained frozen in the position he had been in when he first became aware of the man, his right front paw extended for the next step. Now his ears were back, he was prepared to spring in any direction, although the man had not seen him.

'*Ssss-st!* Damn you!' the man said in a whisper. He stamped his foot, not very hard, to make the cat go away.

Ming did not move at all. Ming heard the soft rattle of the white necklace which belonged to his mistress. The man put it into his pocket, then moved to Ming's right, out of the door that went into the big living-room. Ming now heard the clink of a bottle against glass, heard liquid being poured. Ming went through the same door and turned left towards the kitchen.

Here he miaowed, and was greeted by Elaine and Concha. Concha had her radio turned on to music.

'Fish? – Pork. He likes pork,' Elaine said, speaking the odd form of words which she used with Concha.

Ming, without much difficulty, conveyed his preference for pork, and got it. He fell to with a good appetite. Concha was exclaiming 'Ah-eee-ee!' as his mistress spoke with her, spoke at length. Then Concha bent to stroke him, and

Ming put up with it, still looking down at his plate, until she left off and he could finish his meal. Then Elaine left the kitchen. Concha gave him some of the tinned milk, which he loved, in his now empty saucer, and Ming lapped this up. Then he rubbed himself against her bare leg by way of thanks, and went out of the kitchen, made his way cautiously into the living-room en route to the bedroom. But now Elaine and the man were out on the terrace. Ming had just entered the bedroom, when he heard Elaine call:

'Ming? Where are you?'

Ming went to the terrace door and stopped, and sat on the threshold.

Elaine was sitting sideways at the end of the table, and the candlelight was bright on her long fair hair, on the white of her trousers. She slapped her thigh, and Ming jumped on to her lap.

The man said something in a low tone, something not nice.

Elaine replied something in the same tone. But she laughed a little.

Then the telephone rang.

Elaine put Ming down, and went into the living-room towards the telephone.

The man finished what was in his glass, muttered something at Ming, then set the glass on the table. He got up and tried to circle Ming, or to get him towards the edge of the terrace, Ming realized, and Ming also realized that the man was drunk – therefore moving slowly and a little clumsily. The terrace had a parapet about as high as the man's hips, but it was broken by grills in three places, grills with bars wide enough for Ming to pass through, though Ming never did, merely looked through the grills sometimes. It was plain to Ming that the man wanted to drive him through one of the grills, or grab him and toss him over the terrace parapet. There was nothing easier for Ming than to elude him. Then the man picked up a chair and swung it suddenly, catching Ming on the hip. That had been quick, and it hurt. Ming took the nearest exit, which was down the outside steps that led to the garden.

The man started down the steps after him. Without reflecting, Ming dashed back up the few steps he had come, keeping close to the wall which was in shadow. The man hadn't seen him, Ming knew. Ming leapt to the terrace parapet, sat down and licked a paw once to recover and collect himself. His heart beat fast as if he were in the middle of a fight. And hatred ran in his veins. Hatred burned his eyes as he crouched and listened to the man uncertainly climbing the steps below him. The man came into view.

Ming tensed himself for a jump, then jumped as hard as he could, landing with all four feet on the man's right arm near the shoulder. Ming clung to the cloth of the man's white jacket, but they were both falling. The man groaned. Ming hung on. Branches crackled. Ming could not tell up from down. Ming jumped off the man, became aware of direction and of the earth too late, and landed on his side. Almost at the same time, he heard the thud of the man hitting the ground, then of his body rolling a little way, then there was silence. Ming had to breathe fast with his mouth open until his chest stopped hurting. From the direction of the man, he could smell drink, cigar, and the sharp odour that meant fear. But the man was not moving.

Ming could now see quite well. There was even a bit of moonlight. Ming headed for the steps again, had to go a long way through the bush, over stones and sand, to where the steps began. Then he glided up and arrived once more upon the terrace.

Elaine was just coming on to the terrace.

'Teddie?' she called. Then she went back into the bedroom where she turned on a lamp. She went into the kitchen. Ming followed her. Concha had left the light on, but Concha was now in her own room, where the radio played.

Elaine opened the front door.

The man's car was still in the driveway, Ming saw. Now Ming's hip had begun to hurt, or now he had begun to notice it. It caused him to limp a little. Elaine noticed this, touched his back, and asked him what was the matter. Ming only purred.

'Teddie? – Where are you?' Elaine called.

She took a torch and shone it down into the garden, down among the great trunks of the avocado trees, among the orchids and the lavender and pink blossoms of the bougainvillaeas. Ming, safe beside her on the terrace para-pet, followed the beam of the torch with his eyes and purred with content. The man was not below here, but below and to the right. Elaine went to the terrace steps and carefully, because there was no rail here, only broad steps, pointed the beam of the light downward. Ming did not bother looking. He sat on the terrace where the steps began.

'Teddie!' she said. '*Teddie!*' Then she ran down the steps.

Ming still did not follow her. He heard her draw in her breath. Then she cried:

'*Concha!*'

Elaine ran back up the steps.

Concha had come out of her room. Elaine spoke to Concha. Then Concha became excited. Elaine went to the telephone, and spoke for a short while, then she and Concha went down the steps together. Ming settled himself with his paws tucked under him on the terrace, which was still faintly warm from the day's sun. A car arrived. Elaine came up the steps, and went and opened the front door. Ming kept out of the way on the terrace, in a shadowy corner, as three or four strange men came out on the terrace and tramped down the steps. There was a great deal of talk below, noises of feet, breaking of bushes, and then the smell of all of them mounted the steps, the smell of tobacco, sweat, and the familiar smell of blood. The man's blood. Ming was pleased, as he was pleased when he killed a bird and created this smell of blood under his own teeth. This was big prey. Ming, unnoticed by any of the others, stood

65

up to his full height as the group passed with the corpse, and inhaled the aroma of his victory with a lifted nose.

Then suddenly the house was empty. Everyone had gone, even Concha. Ming drank a little water from his bowl in the kitchen, then went to his mistress's bed, curled against the slope of the pillows, and fell fast asleep. He was awakened by the *rr-rr-r* of an unfamiliar car. Then the front door opened, and he recognized the step of Elaine and then Concha. Ming stayed where he was. Elaine and Concha talked softly for a few minutes. Then Elaine came into the bedroom. The lamp was still on. Ming watched her slowly open the box on her dressing table, and into it she let fall the white necklace that made a little clatter. Then she closed the box. She began to unbutton her shirt, but before she had finished, she flung herself on the bed and stroked Ming's head, lifted his left paw and pressed it gently so that the claws came forth.

'Oh, Ming – Ming,' she said.

Ming recognized the tones of love.

In the Dead of Truffle Season

SAMSON, a large white pig in the prime of life, lived on a rambling old farm in the Lot region, not far from the grand old town of Cahors. Among the fifteen or so other pigs on the farm was Samson's mother Georgia (so named because of a song the farmer Emile had heard once on the television) but not Samson's grandmother, who had been hauled away, kicking and squealing, about a year ago, and not Samson's father, who lived many kilometres away and arrived on a pick-up car a few times a year for brief visits. There were also countless piglets, some from Samson's mother, some not, through whom Samson disdainfully waded, if they were between him and a feed trough. Samson never bothered shoving even the adult pigs, in fact, because he was so big himself, he had merely to advance and his way was clear.

His white coat, somewhat thin and bristly on his sides, grew fine and silky on the back of his neck. Emile often squeezed Samson's neck with his rough fingers when boasting about Samson to another farmer, then he would kick Samson gently in his larded ribs. Usually Samson's back and sides bore a grey crust of sun-dried mud, because he loved to roll in the mud of the unpaved farmyard court and in the thicker mud of the pig pen by the barn. Cool mud was pleasant in the southern summer, when the sun came boiling down for weeks on end, making the pig pen and the courtyard steam. Samson had seen two summers.

The greatest season of the year for Samson was the dead of winter, when he came into his own as truffle-hunter.

Emile and often his friend René, another farmer who sometimes took a pig, sometimes a dog with him, would stroll out with Samson on a rope lead of a Sunday morning, and walk for nearly two kilometres to where some oak trees grew in a small forest.

'*Vas-y!*' Emile would say as they entered the forest's edge, speaking however in the dialect of the region.

Samson, perhaps a bit fatigued or annoyed by the long promenade, would take his time, even if he did happen to smell truffles at once at the base of a tree. An old belt of Emile's served as his collar, very little of its end hanging, so big was Samson's neck, and Samson could easily tug Emile in any direction he chose.

Emile would laugh in anticipation, and say something cheery to René, or to himself if he were alone, then pull from a pocket of his jacket the bottle of Armagnac he took along to keep the cold out.

The main reason Samson took his time about disclosing any truffles was that he never got to eat any. He did get a morsel of cheese as a reward, if he indicated a truffle spot, but cheese was not truffles, and Samson vaguely resented this.

'Huh-*wan-nk!*' said Samson, meaning absolutely nothing by it, wasting time as he sniffed at the foot of a tree which was not an appropriate tree in the first place.

Emile knew this, and gave Samson a kick, then blew on his free hand: his woollen gloves were full of holes, and it was a damned freezing day. He threw down his Gauloise, and pulled the collar of his turtle-neck sweater up over his mouth and nose.

Then Samson's nostrils filled with the delicate, rare aroma of black truffles, and he paused, snorting. The hairs on his back rose a little with excitement. His feet of their own accord stomped, braced themselves, and his flat nose began to root at the ground. He drooled.

Emile was already tugging at the pig. He looped the rope a few times around a tree some distance away, then attacked the spot cautiously with the fork he had been carrying.

'Ah! A-hah!' There they were, a cluster of crinkly black fungus as wide as his hand. Emile put the truffles gently into the cloth knapsack that was swung over his shoulder. Such truffles were worth a hundred and thirty new francs the *livre* in Cahors on the big market days, which were every other Saturday, and Emile got just a trifle less where he usually sold them, at a Cahors delicacy shop which in turn sold the truffles to a pâté manufacturer called Compagnie de la Reine d'Aquitaine. Emile could have got a bit more by selling direct to La Reine d'Aquitaine, but their plant was the other side of Cahors, making the trip more expensive because of the cost of petrol. Cahors, where Emile went every fortnight to buy animal feed and perhaps a tool replacement, was only ten kilometres from his home.

Emile found with his fingers a bit of gruyère in his knapsack, and approached Samson with it. He tossed it on the ground in front of Samson, remembering Samson's teeth.

'*Us-ssh!*' Samson inhaled the cheese like a vacuum cleaner. He was ready for the next tree. The smell of truffles in the knapsack inspired him.

They found two more good spots that morning, before Emile decided to call it a day. They were hardly a kilometre from the Café de la Chasse, on the edge of Emile's home town Cassouac, and the bar-café was on the way home. Emile stomped his feet a few times as he walked, and tugged at Samson impatiently.

'Hey, fatso! Samson! – Get a move on! Of course you're not in a hurry with all that lard on you!' Emile kicked Samson on a back leg.

Samson pretended indifference, but condescended to trot for a few steps before he lapsed into his oddly dainty, I'll-take-my-time gait. Why should he hurry, why should he do everything to suit Emile? Also Samson knew where

71

they were heading, knew he'd have a long wait outside in the cold while Emile drank and talked with his friends. There was the café in view now, with a few dogs tied up outside it. Samson's blood began to course a little faster. He could hold his own with a dog, and enjoyed doing so. Dogs thought they were so clever, so superior, but one lunge from Samson and they flinched and drew back as far as their leads permitted.

'Bonjour, Pierre! . . . Ha-ha-ha!' Emile had encountered the first of his cronies outside the café.

Pierre was tying up his dog, and had made some risible remark about Emile's *chien de race*.

'Never mind, I've got nearly a *livre* of truffles today!' Emile countered, exaggerating.

The barks of more dogs sounded as Emile and Pierre went into the small café. Dogs were allowed in, but some dogs who might snarl at the others were always tied outside.

One dog nipped playfully at Samson's tail, and Samson turned and charged in a leisurely way, not going far enough to make his rope taut, but the dog rolled over in his effort to escape. All three dogs barked, and to Samson it sounded derogatory – towards him. Samson regarded the dogs with a sullen and calm antipathy. Only his pinkish little eyes were quick, taking in all the dogs, daring them or any one of them to advance. The dogs smiled uneasily. At last Samson collapsed by leaning back and letting his legs fold under him. He was in the sun and comfortable enough despite the cold air. But he was hungry again, therefore a bit annoyed.

Emile had found René in the café, drinking pastis at the bar. Emile meant to linger until there was just time to walk home and not annoy his wife Ursule, who liked Sunday dinner to start not later than a quarter past noon.

René wore high rubber boots. He'd been cleaning a drain of his cowbarn, he said. He talked about the truffle-hunting contest that was to take place in two weeks. Emile had not heard of it.

'Look!' said René, pointing to a printed notice at the right of the door. La Compagnie de la Reine d'Aquitaine offered a first prize of a cuckoo clock plus a hundred francs. a second prize of a transistor radio (one couldn't tell the size from the picture), a third prize of fifty francs to the finders of the most truffles on Sunday, January 27. Judges' decisions to be final. Local newspaper and television coverage was promised, and the town of Cassouac was to be the judges' base.

'I'm giving Lunache a rest this Sunday, maybe next too,' René said. 'That way she'll have time to work up a truffle appetite.'

Lunache was René's best truffling pig, a black and white female. Emile smiled a little slyly at his friend, as if to say, 'You know very well Samson's better than Lunache!' Emile said, 'That should be amusing. Let's hope it's not raining.'

'Or snowing! Another pastis? I invite you.' René put some money on the counter.

Emile glanced at the clock on the wall and accepted.

When he went out ten minutes later, he saw that Samson had chased the three tied-up dogs to the extremity of their leads, and was pretending to strain at his rope – a sturdy rope, but Samson might have been able to break it with a good tug. Emile felt rather proud of Samson.

'This monster! He needs a muzzle!' said a youngish man in muddy riding boots, a man Emile didn't recognize. He was patting one of the dogs in a reassuring way.

Emile was ready to return a spate of argument: hadn't the dog been annoying the pig first? But it crossed his mind that the young man might be a representative of La Reine d'Aquitaine come to look the scene over. Silence and a polite nod was best, Emile thought. Was one of the dogs bleeding a little on the hind leg? Emile didn't tarry to look more closely. He untied Samson and ambled off. After all, Emile was thinking, he'd had Samson's lower tusks sawed off three or four months ago. The tusks had

73

started to grow higher than his snout. His upper tusks were still with him, but they were less dangerous because they curved inward.

Samson, in a vaguer though angrier way, was also thinking about his teeth at that moment. If he hadn't been mysteriously deprived of his rightful lower tusks long ago, he could have torn that dog up. One upward sweep of his nose under the dog's belly, which in fact Samson had given ... Samson's breath steamed in the air. His four-toed feet, only the two middle toes on each foot touching the ground, bore him along as if his great bulk were light as a white balloon. Now Samson was leading like a thoroughbred dog straining at the leash.

Emile, knowing Samson was angry, gave him serious and firm tugs. Emile's hand hurt, his arms were growing tired, and as soon as they neared the open gate of the farm's court, Emile gladly released the rope. Samson went trotting directly towards the pig pen where the food was. Emile opened the low gate for him, followed Samson's galloping figure, and unbuckled the belt collar while Samson guzzled potato peelings.

'*Oink!* – Oink-oink!'

'Whuff-f!'

'*Hwon-nk!*'

The other pigs and piglets fell back from Samson.

Emile went into the kitchen. His wife was just setting a big platter of cold diced beets and carrots, sliced tomatoes and onions in the centre of the table. Emile gave a greeting which included Ursule, their son Henri and his wife Yvonne and their little one Jean-Paul. Henri helped a bit on the farm, though he was a full-time worker in a Cahors factory that made Formica sheets. Henri was not fond of farm work. But it was cheaper for him and his family to live here than to take an apartment or buy a house just now.

'Good truffling?' asked Henri, with a glance at the sack.

Emile was just emptying the contents of the sack into a pan of cold water in the sink. 'Not bad,' said Emile.

'Eat, Emile,' said Ursule. 'I'll wash them later.'

Emile sat down and began eating. He started to tell them about the truffle-hunting contest, then decided it might be bad luck to mention it. There were still two weeks in which to mention it, if he felt like it. Emile was imagining the cuckoo clock fixed on the wall in front of him, striking about now the quarter hour past twelve. And he would say a few words on the television (if it was true that there'd be television), and he'd have his picture in the local newspaper.

The main reason Emile did not take Samson truffling the following week-end was that he did not want to diminish the amount of truffles in that particular forest. This forest was known as 'the-little-forest-down-the-slope' and was owned by an old man who didn't even live on his land any more but in a near-by town. The old man had never objected to truffle-hunting on his land, nor had the current caretakers who lived in the farmhouse nearly a kilometre away from the forest.

So Samson had a leisurely fortnight of eating and of sleeping in the scoop of hard-packed hay in the pig shed, which was a lean-to against the main barn.

On the big day, January 27, Emile shaved. Then he made his way to the Café de la Chasse in his village, the meeting point. Here were René and eight or ten other men, all of whom Emile knew and nodded a greeting to. There were also a few boys and girls of the village come to watch. They were all laughing, smoking, pretending it was a silly game, but Emile knew that inside each man with a truffle-dog or truffle-pig was a determination to win first prize, and if not first then second. Samson showed a desire to attack Georges' dog Gaspar, and Emile had to tug at him and kick him. Just as Emile had suspected, the young man of two weeks ago, again in the riding boots, was master of ceremonies. He put on a smile, and spoke to the group from the front steps of the café.

'Gentlemen of Cassouac!' he began, then proceeded to announce the terms of the contest sponsored by La Reine d'Aquitaine, manufacturers of the best *pâté aux truffes* in all France.

'Where's the television?' a man asked, more to raise a laugh from his chums than to get an answer.

The young man laughed too. 'It'll be here when we all come back – a special crew from Toulouse – around eleven-thirty. I know all of you want to get home soon after noon so as not to annoy your wives!'

More good-natured 'Ha-ha's!' It was a frosty day, sharpening everyone's edge.

'Just for formality,' said the young man in riding boots, 'I'll take a look in your sacks to see that all's correct.' He stepped down and did so, and every man showed a clean bag or sack except for apples and bits of cheese or meat which were to be rewards for their animals.

One of the onlookers made a side bet: dogs against pigs. He had managed to find a pig man.

Final *petits rouges* were downed, then they were off, straggling with dogs and pigs down the unpaved road, fanning off into favourite fields, towards cherished trees. Emile and Samson, who was full of honks and oinks this morning, made for the-little-forest-down-the-slope. He was not the only man to do so: François with his black pig was going there too.

'Plenty of room for both of us, I think,' said François pleasantly.

That was true, and Emile agreed. He gave Samson a kick as they entered the forest, letting the cleats of his boot land solidly on Samson's backside, trying to convey that there was a greater urgency about the truffle-hunting today. Samson turned irritably and made a feint at Emile's legs, but bent to his work and snuffled at the foot of a tree. Then he abandoned the tree.

François, quite a distance away among the trees, was already digging with his fork, Emile saw. Emile gave Samson his head and the pig lumbered on, nose to the ground.

'Hwun-nf! – *Ha-wun-nf! Umpf!*' Samson had found a good cache and he knew it.

So did Emile. Emile tied Samson up, and dug as fast as he could. The ground was harder than a fortnight ago.

The aroma of truffles came stronger to Samson as Emile unearthed them. He strained at his rope, recoiled and charged forward again. There was a dull snap – and he was free! His leather collar had broken. Samson plunged his snout into the hollowed earth and began to eat with snorts of contentment.

'*Son of a bitch! – Merde!*' Emile gave Samson a mighty kick in his right ham. God damn the old belt! Emile had no choice but to waste precious minutes untying the rope from the tree and tying it again around the neck of Samson, who made every effort to evade him. That was to say, Samson rotated in a circle around the truffle hoard, keeping his muzzle on the same spot, eating. Emile got the rope tied, and at once tugged and cursed with all his might.

François' distant but loud laughter did not make Emile feel any more kindly towards Samson. Damn the beast, he'd eaten at least half the find here! Emile kicked Samson where his testicles would have been, if Emile had not had them removed at the same time as Samson's lower tusks.

Samson retaliated by charging Emile at knee level. Emile fell forward over the rushing pig, and barely had time to protect his face from the ground. The pain in his knees was agonizing. He was afraid for a few seconds that his legs had been broken. Then he heard François yelling with indignation. Samson was loose again and was invading François' digging place.

'Hey, Emile! You're going to be disqualified! Get this goddam pig away from me! Get him – or I'll *shoot* him!'

Emile knew that François had no gun. Emile got to his feet carefully. His legs were not broken, but his eyes felt awful from the shock, and he knew he'd have a pair of prize shiners by tomorrow. '*Damn* you, Samson, get the hell away!' Emile yelled, trudging towards François and the two pigs. François was now whacking at Samson with a tree branch he had found, and Emile couldn't blame François.

'A hell of a way to . . .' François' words were lost.

Emile had never been very chummy with François Malbert, and he knew François would try to disqualify him, if he possibly could, mainly because Samson was an excellent truffler and presented a threat. This thought, however, concentrated Emile's anger more on Samson for the moment than on François. Emile pulled at Samson's rope, yanked it hard, and François came down at the same time with the branch on Samson's head, and the branch broke.

Samson charged again, and Emile, suddenly nimble in desperation, looped the end of the rope a couple of times around a tree. Samson was jerked off his feet.

'No use digging any more here! That's not fair!' François said, indicating his half-eaten truffle bed.

'Ah, oui? It's an *accident*!' Emile retorted.

But François was trudging away, in the direction of the Café de la Chasse.

Emile now had the little forest to himself. He set about gathering what was left of François' truffle find. But he was afraid he was going to be disqualified. All because of Samson.

'Now get to work, you bastard!' Emile said to Samson, and hit him on the rump with a short piece of the branch that had broken.

Samson only stared at Emile, facing him, in case another blow was coming.

Emile groped for a piece of cheese in his sack, and tossed it on the ground as an act of appeasement, also to whet Samson's appetite, perhaps. Samson did look as angry as a pig could look.

Samson snuffed up the cheese.

'Let's go, boy!' Emile said.

Samson got moving, but very slowly. He simply walked.

He wasn't even sniffing the ground. Emile fancied that Samson's shoulders were hunched in anger, that he was ready to charge again. But that was absurd, he told himself. Emile pulled Samson towards a promising birch tree.

Samson smelled the truffles in Emile's sack. His saliva was still running from the truffles he had gobbled up from the hole in the ground. Samson turned with agility and pressed his nose against the sack at Emile's side. Samson had stood up a little on his hind legs, and his weight knocked Emile down. Samson poked his nose into the sack. What a blissful smell! He began to eat. There was cheese too.

Emile, on his feet now, jabbed at Samson with his fork, hard enough to break the skin in three places where the tines sank. *'Get away, you bastard!'*

Samson did leave the sack, but only to rush at Emile. *Crack!* He hit Emile's knees again. The man lay on the ground, trying to bring his fork into position for striking, and in a flash Samson charged.

Somehow the pig's belly hit Emile in the face, or the point of his chin, and Emile was knocked half unconscious. He shook his head, and made sure he still had a good grip on his fork. He had suddenly realized that Samson could and might kill him, if he didn't protect himself.

'Au secours!' Emile yelled. *'Help!'*

Emile brandished the fork at Samson, intending to scare the pig off while he got to his feet.

Samson had no intention, except to protect himself. He saw the fork as an enemy, a very clear challenge, and he blindly attacked it. The fork went askew and dropped as if limp. Samson's front hooves stood triumphant on Emile's abdomen. Samson snorted. And Emile gasped, but only a few times.

The awful pink and damp nose of the pig was almost in Emile's face, and he recalled from childhood many pigs he had known, pigs who had seemed to him as gigantic as this Samson now crushing the breath out of him. Pigs, sows, piglets of all patterns and colouring seemed to combine and become this one monstrous Samson who most certainly – Emile now knew it – was going to kill him, just by standing on him. The fork was out of reach. Emile flailed his arms with his last strength, but the pig wouldn't budge. And Emile could not gasp one breath of air. Not even an animal any longer, Emile thought, this pig, but an awful, evil force in a most hideous form. Those tiny, stupid eyes in the grotesque flesh! Emile tried to call out and found that he couldn't make as much noise as a small bird.

When the man became quiet, Samson stepped off his body and nuzzled him in the side to get at the truffle sack again. Samson was calming down a bit. He no longer held his breath, or panted, as he had done alternately for the last minutes, but began to breathe normally. The heavenly scent of truffles further soothed him. He snuffled, sighed, inhaled, ate, his snout and tongue seeking out the last morsels from the corners of the khaki sack. And all his own gleanings! But this thought came not at all clearly to Samson. In fact, he had a vague feeling that he was going to be shooed away from his banquet, yet who was there to shoo him away now? This very special sack, into which he had seen so many black truffles vanishing, out of which had come measly, contemptible crumbs of yellow cheese – all that was finished, and now the sack was his. Samson even ate some of the cloth.

Then, still chewing, he urinated. He listened, and looked around, and felt quite secure and in command of things – at least of himself. He could walk anywhere he chose, and he chose to walk away from the village of Cassouac. He trotted for a bit, then walked, and was sidetracked by the scent of still more truffles. It took Samson some time to dig them up, but it was glorious work, and his reward was his own, every gritty, superb crinkle. Samson came to a stream, a little crusty at the edges with ice, and drank. He went on, dragging his rope, not caring where he went. He was hungry again.

Hunger impelled him towards a group of low buildings, whence he smelled chicken dung and the manure of horses or cows. Samson strolled a little diffidently into the cobbled courtyard where some pigeons and chickens walked about. They made way for Samson. Samson was used to that. He was looking for a feed trough. He found a trough with some wet bread in it, a low trough. He ate. Then he collapsed against a stack of hay, half sheltered by a roof. It was now dark.

From the two lighted windows in the lower part of the house near by came music and voices, sounds of an ordinary household.

As dawn broke, the wandering, pecking chickens in the courtyard and near Samson did not really awaken him. He dozed on, and only opened one eye sleepily when he heard the gritty tread of a man.

'Ho-ha! What have we got here?' murmured the farmer, peering at the enormous pale pig lying in his hay. A rope dangled from the pig's neck, a good sturdy rope, he saw, and the pig was an even more splendid specimen of his kind. Whom did he belong to? The farmer knew all the pigs in the district, knew their types, anyway. This one must have come from a long way. The end of the rope was frayed.

The farmer Alphonse decided to keep his mouth shut. After more or less hiding Samson for a few days in a back field which was enclosed, Alphonse brought him forward once more and let him join the pigs he had, all black ones. He wasn't concealing the white pig, he reasoned, and if anyone came looking for such a pig, he could say the pig had simply wandered on to his land, which was true. Then he would give the pig back, of course, after being sure the inquirer knew that the pig's lower tusks had been sawn off, that he'd been castrated and so forth. Meanwhile Alphonse debated selling him on the market or trying him out at truffle-hunting before the winter was over. He'd try the truffling first.

Samson grew a little fatter, and dominated the other pigs, two sows and their piglets. The food was slightly different and more abundant than at the other farm. Then came the day – an ordinary working day, it seemed to Samson from the look of the farm – when he was taken on a lead to go to the woods for truffles. Samson trotted along in good spirits. He intended to eat a few truffles today, besides finding them for the man. Somewhere in his brain, Samson was already thinking that he must from the start show this man that he was not to be bossed.

The Bravest Rat in Venice

THE household at the Palazzo Cecchini on the Rio San Polo was a happy, lively one: husband and wife and six children ranging from two to ten years of age, four boys and two girls. This was the Mangoni family, and they were the caretakers. The owners of the Palazzo Cecchini, an English-American couple named Whitman, were away for three months, and probably longer, in London, staying at their townhouse there.

'It's a fine day! We'll open the windows and sing! And we'll *clean up* this place!' yelled Signora Mangoni from the kitchen as she untied her apron. She was eight months' pregnant. She had washed up the breakfast dishes, swept away the breadcrumbs, and was facing the crisp, sunny day with the joy of a proprietress. And why not? She and her family had the run of every room, could sleep in whatever beds they wished, and furthermore had plenty of money from the Whitmans to run things in a fine style.

'Can we play downstairs, mama?' asked Luigi, aged ten, in a perfunctory way. Mama would say '*No!*' he supposed, and he and a couple of brothers and maybe his sister Roberta would go anyway. Wading, slipping, falling in the shallow water down there was great fun. So was startling the passing gondoliers and their passengers just outside the canal door by suddenly opening the door and heaving a bucket of water – maybe on to a tourist's lap.

'No!' said mama. 'Just because today is a holiday—'

Luigi, Roberta and their two brothers Carlo and Arturo went to school officially. But they had missed a lot of days in the last month since the Mangoni family had full possession of the Palazzo Cecchini. It was more fun than school to explore the house, to pretend to own everything, to be able to open any door without knocking. Luigi was about to give a hail to Carlo to join him, when his mother said:

'Luigi, you promised to take Rupert for a walk this morning!'

Had he? The promise, if made, did not weigh much on Luigi's conscience. 'This afternoon.'

'No, this morning. Untie the dog!'

Luigi sighed and went in a waddling, irritated way to the kitchen corner where the Dalmatian was tied to the foot of a tile stove.

The dog was growing plump, and that was why his mother wanted him or Carlo to walk him a couple of times a day. The dog was plump because he was given risotto and pasta instead of the meat diet recommended by Signor Whitman, Luigi knew. Luigi had heard his parents discussing it, and the discussion had been brief: with the price of meat what it was, why feed a *dog* bistecca? It was an absurdity, even if they had been given the money for it. The dog could just as well eat stale bread and milk, and there was some fish and clam bits after all in the risotto leftovers. A dog was a dog, not a human being. The Mangoni family were now eating meat.

Luigi compromised by letting Rupert lift his leg in the narrow street outside the front door of the palazzo, summoned Carlo who was strolling homeward with a half-finished soda pop in hand, and together they went, with the dog, down the steps behind a door of the front hall.

The water looked half a metre deep. Luigi laughed in anticipation, pushed off his sandals and removed his socks on the steps.

Schluck-slosh! The dark water moved, blindly lapped into stone corners, rebounded. The big, empty square room was semi-dark. Two slits of sunlight showed on either side of the loose door. Beyond the door were more stone steps which went right down into the water of the rather wide canal called the Rio San Polo. Here for several hundred years, before the palazzo had sunk so much, gondolas had used to arrive, discharging well dressed ladies and gentlemen with dry feet into the marble-floored salon where Luigi and Carlo now splashed and slipped in water nearly up to their knees.

The dog Rupert shivered on one of the steps the boys had come down. He was not so much chilly as nervous and bored. He did not know what to do with himself. His routine of happy walks three times a day, milk and biscuits in the morning, a big meal of meat around 6 p.m. – all that was gone. His life now was a miserable chaos, and his days had lost their shape.

It was November, but not cold, not too cold for Luigi's and Carlo's informal game of push-the-other. First man down lost, but was rewarded by applause and laughter from the others – usually Roberta and little sister Benita were wading too, or watching from the steps.

'A rat!' Luigi cried, pointing, lying, and at that instant gave Carlo a good push behind his knees, causing Carlo to collapse on his back in the water with a great hollow-sounding splash that hit the walls and peppered Luigi with drops.

Carlo scrambled to his feet, soaked, laughing, making for the steps where the trembling dog stood.

'Look! There's a real one!' Luigi said, pointing.

'Ha-ha!' said Carlo, not believing.

'There it *is*!' Luigi slashed the surface of the water with his hand, trying to aim the water at the ugly thing swimming between him and the steps.

'Sissi!' Carlo shrieked with glee and waded towards a floating stick.

Luigi snatched the stick from him and came down with it on the rat's body – an unsatisfactory blow, rather sliding off the rat's back. Luigi struck again.

'Grab him by the tail!' giggled Carlo.

'Get a knife, we'll kill it!' Luigi spoke with bared teeth, excited by the fact the rat might dive and nip one of his feet with a fatal bite.

Carlo was already splashing up the stairs. His mother was not in the kitchen, and he at once seized a meat knife with a triangular blade, and ran back with it to Luigi.

Luigi had battered the rat twice more, and now with the knife in his right hand, he was bold enough to grab the rat's tail and whirl him up on to a marble ledge as high as Luigi's hips.

'Ah-i-i! Kill 'im!' Carlo said.

Rupert whined, lifting his head, thought of going up the steps, since his lead dangled, and could not come to any decision, because he had no purpose in going up.

Luigi made a clumsy stab at the rat's neck, while still holding its tail, missed the neck and struck an eye. The rat writhed and squealed, showing long front teeth, and Luigi was on the brink of releasing its tail out of fear, but came down once more with a blow he intended to be decapitating, but he cut off a front foot instead.

'Ha-ha-ha!' Carlo clapped his hands, and wildly splashed water, more on Luigi than the rat.

'*Bastard rat!*' cried Luigi.

For a few seconds the rat was motionless, with open mouth. Blood flowed from its right eye, and Luigi came down with the blade on the rat's right hind foot which was extended with splayed toes, vulnerable against the stone. The rat bit, caught Luigi in the wrist.

Luigi screamed and shook his arm. The rat fell off into the water, and began to swim wildly away.

'Oooh!' said Carlo.

'Ow!' Luigi swished his arm back and forth in the water and examined his wrist. It was merely a pink dot, like a pin-prick. He'd been wanting to exaggerate his prowess to his mother, have her nurse his wound, but he'd have to make do with this. 'It *hurts*!' he assured

Carlo, and made his way through the water towards the steps. Tears had already come to his eyes, though he felt no pain at all. '*Mama!*'

The rat scrabbled with one stump of a forepaw and his other good paw against a mossy stone wall, keeping his nose above water as best he could. Around him the water was pinkening with blood. He was a young rat, five months old and not fully grown. He had never been in this house before, and had come in at the street side via a dry alley or slit along one side of the wall. He had smelled food, or thought he had, rotting meat or some such. A hole had led through the wall, and he had tumbled into water before he knew it, water so deep he had had to swim. Now his problem was to find an exit. His left foreleg and right hind leg smarted, but his eye hurt worse. He explored a bit, but found no hole or slit of escape, and at last he clung to slimy threads of moss by the claws of his right forefoot and was still, rather in a daze.

Some time later, chill and numb, the rat moved again. The water had gone down a little, but the rat was not aware of this, because he still had to swim. Now a narrow beam of light showed in a wall. The rat made for this, squeezed through, and escaped from the watery dungeon. He was in a kind of sewer in semi-darkness. He found an exit from this: a crack in a pavement. His next hours were a series of short journeys to an ashcan's shelter, to a doorway, to a shadow behind a tub of flowers. He was, in a circuitous way, heading for home. The rat had no family as yet, but was indifferently accepted in the house or headquarters of several rat families where he had been born. It was dark when he got there – the cellar of an abandoned grocery store, long ago plundered of anything edible. The cellar's wooden door was falling apart, which made entry easy for the rats, and they were in such number no cat would have ventured to attack them in their lair, which had no escape route for a cat but the way the cat would have come.

Here the rat nursed his wounds for two days, unassisted by parents who did not even recognize him as offspring, or by relatives either. At least he could nibble on old veal bones, mouldy bits of potato, things that rats had brought in to chew in peace. He could see out of only one eye, but already this was making him more alert, quicker in darting after a crumb of food, quicker in retreating in case he was challenged. This period of semi-repose and recuperation was broken by a torrent of hose water early one morning.

The wooden door was kicked open and the blast of water sent baby rats flying up in the air, smashed a few against the wall, killing them by the impact or drowning them, while adult rats scrambled up the steps past the hose-holder to be met by clubs crashing on their heads and backs, huge rubber-booted feet stamping the life out of them.

The crippled rat remained below, swimming a bit finally. Men came down the steps with big nets on sticks, scooping up corpses. They dumped poison into the water which now covered the stone floor. The poison stank and hurt the rat's lungs. There was a back exit, a hole in a corner just big enough for him to get through, and he used it. A couple of other rats had used it also, but the rat did not see them.

It was time to move on. The cellar would never be the same again. The rat was feeling better, more self-assured and more mature. He walked and crept, sparing his two sore stumps. Before noon, he discovered an alley at the back of a restaurant. Not all the garbage had fallen into the bins. Pieces of bread, a long steakbone with meat on it lay on the cobblestones. It was a banquet! Maybe the best meal of his life. After eating, he slept in a dry drain-pipe, too small for a cat to enter. Best to keep out of sight in daylight. Life was safer at night.

The days passed. The rat's stumps grew less painful. Even his eye had ceased to hurt. He regained strength and even put on a little weight. His grey, slightly brownish coat became thick and sleek. His ruined eye was a half-closed, greyish splotch, a bit jagged because of the knife's thrust, but it was no longer running either with blood or lymph. He discovered that by charging a cat, he could make the cat retreat a bit, and the rat sensed that it was because he presented an unusual appearance, limping on two short legs, one eye gone. The cats too had their tricks, puffing their fur up to make themselves look bigger, making throaty noises. But only once had an old ginger tomcat, mangy and with one ear gone, tried to close his teeth on the back of the rat's neck. The rat had at once attacked a front leg of the cat, bitten as hard as he could, and the cat had never got a grip. When the rat had turned loose, the cat had been glad enough to run away and leap to a windowsill. That had been in a dark garden somewhere.

The days came and went and grew ever colder and wetter, days of sleep in a patch of sun if possible, more often not, because a hole somewhere was safer, nights of prowling and feeding. And day and night the dodging of cats and the upraised stick in the hands of a human being. Once a man had attacked him with a dustbin, slammed it down on the stones, catching the rat's tail but not cutting any of it off, only giving him *pain* such as he had not known since the stab in his eye.

The rat knew when a gondola was approaching. 'Ho! Aye!' the gondoliers would shout, or variations of this, usually when they were about to turn a corner. Gondolas were no threat. Sometimes the gondolier jabbed at him with an oar, more out of playfulness than to kill him. Not a chance had the gondolier! Just one stab that always missed, and the gondolier had glided past in his boat.

One night, smelling sausage from a tied-up gondola in a narrow canal, the rat ventured on board. The gondolier was sleeping under a blanket. The sausage smell came from a paper beside him. The rat found the remains of a sandwich, ate his fill, and curled up in a coarse, dirty rag. The gondola bobbed gently. The rat was an expert swimmer now. Many a time he had dived underwater to escape a cat that had been bold enough to pursue him into a canal. But cats didn't care to go below the surface.

The rat was awakened by a bumping sound. The man was standing up, untying a rope. The gondola moved away from the pavement. The rat was not alarmed. If the man saw him and came at him, he would simply jump overboard and swim to the nearest wall of stones.

The gondola crossed the Canale Grande and entered a widish canal between huge palaces which were now hotels. The rat could smell the aromas of fresh roasting pork, baking bread, orange peel and the sharper scent of ham. Some time later, the man manoeuvred the gondola to the steps of a house, got out and banged on a door with a round ring of a knocker. From the gunwale, the rat saw a decaying portion of the embankment that would offer foothold, jumped into the water and made for it. The gondola heard the splash and stomped towards him, yelling '*Aye*-yeh!' So the rat didn't climb up at that spot, but swam on, found another accessible place and got to dry pavement. The gondolier was back at the door, knocking again.

That day the rat met a female, a pleasant encounter in a rather damp alley behind a dress shop. It had just rained. Pushing on, the rat found a trail, almost, of sandwich ends, dropped peanuts, and hard corn kernels which he didn't bother with. Then he found himself in a large open area. It was the Piazza San Marco, where the rat had never been. He could not see all its vastness, but he sensed it. Pigeons in greater number than he had ever seen walked about on the pavement among people who were tossing grain to them. Pigeons sailed down, spread their wings and tails and landed on the backs of others. The smell of popcorn made the rat hungry. But it was broad daylight, and the rat knew he must be careful. He kept to the angle made by the pavement and the walls of the buildings, ready to duck into a passageway. He seized a peanut and nibbled it as he hobbled along, letting the shell fall, keeping the peanut in his mouth, retrieving the other half of the peanut which held a second morsel.

Tables and chairs. And music. Not many people sat in the chairs, and those who did wore overcoats. Here were all manner of croissant crumbs, bread crusts, even bits of ham on the stone pavement among the chairs.

A man laughed and pointed to the rat. 'Look, Helen!' he said to his wife. 'Look at that rat! At this time of day!'

'Oh! What a *creature!*' The woman's shock was genuine. She was nearly sixty, and from Massachusetts. Then she laughed, a laugh of relief, amusement, and with a little bit of fear.

'Good God, somebody's cut his feet off!' the man said in almost a whisper. 'And one eye's gone! Look at him!'

'Now *that's* something to tell the folks back home!' said the woman. 'Hand me the camera, Alden!'

The husband did so. 'Don't do it now, the waiter's coming.'

'*Altro, signor?*' asked the waiter politely.

'*No, grazie. Ah, si! Un caffe latte, per piacere.*'

'Alden—'

He wasn't supposed to have more than two coffees a day, one morning, one evening. Alden knew. He had only a few months to live. But the rat had given him a curious zest, a sudden joy. He watched the rat nosing nervously in the forest of chair legs just three feet away, peering with his good eye, darting for the crumbs, eschewing the small, the inferior, the already crushed. 'Do it now before he goes,' said Alden.

Helen lifted the camera.

The rat sensed the movement, one of potential hostility and glanced up.

Click!

'I think that'll be good!' Helen whispered, laughing with a gentle happiness as if she'd just taken the sunset at Sounion or Acapulco.

'In this rat,' Alden began, also speaking softly, and

93

interrupted himself to pick with slightly trembling fingers the end of a dainty frankfurter from the buttery little bun in front of him. He tossed it towards the rat, which drew back a little, then darted for the sausage and got it, chewed it with one foot – the stump – planted on it. Suddenly the sausage vanished from view, and the plump jowls worked. 'Now that rat has fortitude!' Alden said finally. 'Imagine what he's been through. Like Venice itself. And he's not giving up. Is he?'

Helen returned her husband's smile. Alden looked happier, better than he had in weeks. She was pleased. She felt grateful to the rat. Imagine being grateful to a rat, she thought. When she looked again, the rat had vanished. But Alden was smiling at her.

'We're going to have a splendid day,' he said.

'Yes.'

Daily the rat grew stronger, bolder about venturing out in the day-time, but he was also learning more about protecting himself, even against people. He might make a dash as if to attack a person who was lifting a broom, a stick, a crate to smash him, and the person, man or woman, would retreat a step, or hesitate, and in that instant the rat could run in any direction, even past the person, if that direction meant escape.

More female rats. When in the mood, the rat had his pick of the females, bcause other males were afraid of him, and their challenges, if any, never came to a real fight. The rat with his heavy, rolling gait and his evil, single eye had a menacing air, a look that said nothing would stop him but death. He thrust his way through the maze of Venice, at seven months rolling like an old sea captain, sure of himself and sure of his ground. Mothers pulled their small children away from him in horror. Older children laughed and pointed. Mange attacked his stomach and head. He rolled on cobblestones to relieve the itching sometimes, or plunged into water despite the cold. He ranged from the Rialto to San Trovaso, and was familiar with the warehouses on the Ponte Lungo which bordered the broad Canale della Giudecca.

The Palazzo Cecchini lay between the Rialto and the cusp of land which held the warehouses. One day Carlo was returning from the local grocery store with a big cardboard carton meant for the Dalmatian Rupert to sleep in. Rupert had caught a cold, and Carlo's mother was worried. Carlo spied the rat emerging from between two wooden crates of fish and ice outside a shop.

It was the same rat! Yes! Carlo remembered vividly the two feet cut off, the stabbed eye. Not hesitating more than a second, Carlo slammed the carton upside down on the rat, and sat on the carton. He had him! Carlo sat gently but firmly.

'Hey, Nunzio!' Carlo yelled to a chum who happened to be passing. 'Go call Luigi! Tell him to come! I've caught a rat!'

'A rat!' Nunzio had a fat loaf of bread under his arm. It was after six, getting dark.

'A special rat! Call Luigi!' Carlo yelled more forcefully, because the rat was hurling himself against the sides of the carton and soon he'd start chewing.

Nunzio ran.

Carlo got off the carton and pressed the bottom down hard, and kicked at the sides to discourage the rat from gnawing. His big brother would be impressed, if he could keep the rat till he got here.

'What're you doing there, Carlo, you're in the *way*!' yelled the fishmonger.

'I gotta rat! You oughta gimme a kilo of scampi for catching one of your rats!'

'*My* rats?' The fishmonger made a gesture of menace, but was too busy to shoo the boy off.

Luigi came on the run. He had picked up a piece of wood on the way, a square end of a crate. 'A rat?'

'Same rat we had before! The one with the feet off! I swear!'

Luigi grinned, set his hand on the carton and gave its side a good kick. He raised the carton a little at one side, his piece of wood at the ready. The rat darted out, and Luigi came down on its shoulders.

The rat was breathless, and hurt. Another blow fell on his ribs. The rat's legs moved, and he wanted frantically to escape, but he could not get to his feet. He heard the boys' laughter. He was being borne away, in the big carton.

'Let's throw him downstairs! Drown 'im!' said Carlo.

'I want to see him. If we found a cat, we could see a good fight. That black and white cat—'

'She's never around. The water's high. Drown 'im!' The downstairs room fascinated Carlo. He had fantasies of gondolas floating through the door, dumping passengers who would drown in that awful semi-darkness, and finally cover the marble floor with their corpses, which would be seen only when the tide ran out. The ground floor of the Palazzo Cecchini might become another gruesome attraction of Venice, like the dungeons past the Ponte dei Sospiri.

The boys climbed the front steps and entered the Palazzo Cecchini whose tall wooden doors were slightly ajar. Their mama was singing in the kitchen where the transistor played a popular song. Carlo kicked the door shut, and their mother heard it.

'Come and eat, Luigi, Carlo!' she called. 'We're going to the *cine*, don't forget!'

Luigi cursed, then laughed. '*Subito, mama!*'

He and Carlo went down the steps that led to the ground floor.

'You got the carton?' yelled their mother.

'*Si, si!* – Gimme the wood!' Luigi said to his brother. Luigi grabbed the square of wood and tipped the carton at the same time. Luigi remembered the bite on his wrist, and had a particular fear of this rat. The rat tumbled into the water. Yes, it was the same! Luigi saw the two

96

stumps of his legs. The rat sank at once, and barely felt the clumsy blow that Luigi gave with the edge of the wood.

'Where is he?' asked Carlo. He was ankle-deep in water, standing on the first step, not caring about sandals and socks.

'He'll be up!' Luigi, on the step above, held the wood poised, ready to throw it when he saw the rat surface for air. The boys scanned the dark water that now heaved because of some motor boat that had just passed beyond the door.

'Let's go down! Scare 'im up!' Carlo said, with a glance at his brother, and Carlo at once went down into water up to his knees, and began kicking to make sure the rat didn't come near him.

'Luigi!' their mother shrieked. 'Are you down below? You'll get a beating if you don't come up *now*!'

Luigi twisted around to shout a reply, mouth open, and at that instant saw the rat clumsily climbing the top step into the first floor of the house. 'Mama mia!' he whispered, pointing. 'The rat's gone up!'

Carlo grasped the situation at once, though he didn't see the rat, raised his eyebrows, and silently climbed the steps. They couldn't tell their mother. They'd have to follow the wet trail of the rat and get him out of the house. Both the boys understood this without speaking. When they entered the front hall, the rat had vanished. They peered about for a wet trail, but saw no sign of drops on the grey and white marble floor. Two salon doors were open. The downstairs toilet door was ajar. The rat could even have gone upstairs – maybe.

'Are you coming? The spaghetti is on the plates! Hurry!'

'*Sissi, subito, mama!*' Luigi pointed to Carlo's wet feet, and jerked a thumb to the upstairs, where Carlo's clothing mostly was.

Carlo dashed up the stairs.

Luigi took a quick look in the toilet. They couldn't tell their mother what had happened. She'd never leave the house or let them go to the film tonight, if she knew there was a rat loose. Luigi looked in one of the salons, where six chairs stood around an oval table, where more chairs stood beside wine tables near the walls of the room. He stopped, but still he saw no rat.

Carlo was back. They went down some steps into the kitchen. Papa had nearly finished his spaghetti. Then came bistecca. The plump dog watched with his muzzle on his paws. He salivated. He was tied again to a foot of the tile stove. Luigi looked around, covertly, for the rat in the corners of the kitchen. Before the meal was over, Maria-Teresa, the baby-sitter, arrived. She had two books under her arm. She smiled broadly, unbuttoned her coat and loosened the scarf that covered her head.

'I am early! I am sorry!' she said.

'No-no! Sit down! Have some torta!'

The dessert was a delicious open-faced pie with peach slices. Who could resist, especially with the appetite of a seventeen-year-old? Maria-Teresa sat and had a slice.

Papa Mangoni had a second piece. Like Rupert he was putting on weight.

Then the family was off, in a hurry, the smallest child in papa's arms, because they'd be four minutes late, by papa's calculations, even if they ran. Papa liked the advertisements that preceded the feature, and he liked saying hello to his chums.

The television set had been moved from the parents' bedroom into the room where the two-month-old Antonio lay as if in state in a cradle high off the ground and covered in white lace which hung nearly to the floor. The cradle was on wheels. Maria-Teresa, humming a song softly, saw that the baby was asleep, and rolled the cradle farther away from the television, which was in a corner, then switched the set on with the volume low. The programme didn't look interesting, so she sat down and opened one of her novels, a love story whose setting was the American West of the last century.

When Maria-Teresa looked at the television screen several minutes later, her eye was caught by a moving grey spot in the corner. She stood up. A rat! A big, horrible looking thing! She moved to the right, hoping to shoo it towards the door on her left, which was open. The rat advanced on her, slowly and steadily. It had one eye only. One of its front feet had been cut off. Maria-Teresa gave a little cry of panic, and ran out of the door herself.

She had no intention of attempting to kill the thing. She hated rats! They were the curse of Venice! Maria-Teresa went at once to the telephone in the downstairs hall. She dialled the number of a bar-café not far away, where her boy friend worked.

'Cesare,' she said. 'I want to speak with Cesare.'

Cesare came on. He heard the story and laughed.

'But can you *come*? The Mangonis went to the cinema. I'm all alone! I'm so scared I want to run out of the house!'

'Okay, I'll come!' Cesare hung up. He swung a napkin over his shoulder, grinning, and said to one of his colleagues, a bar-man, 'My girl friend's baby-sitting and there's a rat in the house. I'm supposed to go over and kill it!'

'Ha-ha!'

'That's a new one! What time you coming back, Ces?' asked a customer.

More laughter.

Cesare didn't bother telling his boss he was leaving for a few minutes, because the Palazzo Cecchini was one minute away if he trotted. From the pavement outside, Cesare picked up an iron bar four feet long which went across the inside of the door when they closed up. It was heavy. He trotted, and imagined stabbing the bar at a cornered rat, killing it, and imagined the gratitude, the rewarding kisses he would get from Maria-Teresa.

Instead of the door being opened by an anxious girl, his beloved whom he would comfort with a firm embrace, words of courage before he tackled the little beast – instead of this, Cesare was met by a girl crumpled in tears, trembling with terror.

'The rat has eaten the baby!' she said.

'What?'

'Upstairs—'

Cesare ran up with the iron bar. He looked around in the nearly empty, formally furnished room for the rat, looked under a double bed which had a canopy.

Maria-Teresa came in. 'I don't know where the rat is. Look at the baby! We've got to get a doctor! It just happened – while I was telephoning you!'

Cesare looked down at the shockingly red, blood-covered pillow of the baby. All the baby's nose – It was horrible! There *wasn't* any nose! And the cheek! Cesare murmured an invocation of aid from a saint, then turned quickly to Maria-Teresa. 'The baby's *alive*?'

'I don't know! *Yes*, I think!'

Cesare timidly stuck a forefinger into the baby's curled hand. The baby twitched, gave a snuffling sound, as if he were having trouble breathing through blood. 'Shouldn't we turn him over? Turn him on his side! I'll – I'll telephone. Do you know any doctor's number?'

'No!' said Maria-Teresa who was already imagining concretely the blame she was going to get for letting this happen. She knew she should have fought the rat out of the room instead of telephoning Cesare.

Cesare after one vain attempt to reach a doctor whose name he knew and whose number he looked up in the telephone book, rang the main hospital of Venice, and they promised to arrive at once. They came via a hospital boat which docked on the Canale Grande some fifty yards away. Cesare and Maria-Teresa even heard the noise of the fast motor. By this time Maria-Teresa had wiped the baby's face gently with a damp face towel, mainly with an idea of facilitating the baby's breathing. The nose was gone, and she could even see a bit of bone there.

Two young men in white gave the baby two injections, and kept murmuring '*Orribile!*' They asked Maria-Teresa to make a hot water bottle.

The blood had gone from Cesare's usually ruddy cheeks, and he felt about to faint. He sat down on one of the formal chairs. Gone was his idea of a passionate embrace with Maria-Teresa. He couldn't even stand on his legs.

The interns took the baby away in the boat, the baby wrapped in a blanket with the hot water bottle.

Cesare recovered a bit of strength, went down to the kitchen and after a search found half a bottle of Strega. He poured two glasses. He was keeping an eye out for the rat, but didn't see it. The Mangonis were due back soon, and he would have preferred to be elsewhere – back at his job – but he reasoned that he ought to stand by Maria-Teresa, and that this excuse would be a good one for his boss. A baby nearly killed, maybe dead now – who knew?

The Mangoni family arrived at 10.40 p.m., and there was intant chaos.

Mama screamed. Everyone talked at once. Mama went up to see the bloody cradle, and screamed again. Papa was told to telephone the hospital. Cesare and the oldest three of the brothers and one of the sisters went on a complete search of the house, armed with empty wine bottles for bashing, knives, a wooden stool from the kitchen, a flat iron, and Cesare had his iron bar. No one saw a rat, but several pieces of furniture received nicks inadvertently.

Maria-Teresa was forgiven. Or was she? Papa could understand her telephoning for help to her boy friend who was near. The hospital reported that the baby had a fifty-fifty chance to live, but could the mother come at once?

The rat had escaped via a square drain in the kitchen wall at floor level. His jump had put him in the Rio San Polo nearly three metres below, but that was no problem. He swam with powerful thrusts of his two good legs, all his legs, plus sheer will power, to the nearest climbing point, and got on to dry land feeling no diminution of his energy. He shook himself. The taste of blood was still in his mouth. He had attacked the baby out of panic, out of fury also, because he hadn't at that point found an exit from the accursed house. The baby's arms and fists had flailed feebly against his head, his ribs. The rat had taken some pleasure in attacking a member of the human race, one with the same smell as the big ones. The morsels of tender flesh had filled his belly somewhat, and he was now deriving energy from them.

He made his way in the darkness with a rolling gait, pausing now and then to sniff at a worthless bit of food, or to get his bearings with an upward glance, with a sniff at the breeze. He was making for the Rialto, where he could cross by means of the arched bridge, pretty safe at night. He thought to make informal headquarters around San Marco, where there were a lot of restaurants in the area. The night was very black, which meant safety for him. His strength seemed to increase as he rolled along, belly nearly touching the dampish stones. He stared at, then sprang at a curious cat which had dared to come close and size him up. The cat leapt a little in the air, then retreated.

Engine Horse

WHEN the big mare, Fanny, heard the rustle in the hay, she turned her head slowly, still chomping with unbroken rhythm, and her eyes, which were like large soft brown eggs, tried to look behind her and down. Fanny supposed it was one of the cats, though they seldom came close. There were two cats on the farm, one ginger, one black and white. Fanny's looking back had been casual. A cat often came into the stable in search of a quiet spot to nap in.

Still munching hay from her trough, Fanny looked for a second time and saw the little grey thing near her front foot. A tiny cat it was. Not one of the household, not one of the small cats belonging to either of the larger cats, because there weren't any just now.

It was sunset in the month of July. Gnats played around Fanny's eyes and nose, and made her snort. A small square window, closed in winter, was now open and the sun flooded directly into Fanny's eyes. She had not done much work that day, because the man called Sam, whom Fanny had known all her twelve years, had not come, either today or yesterday. Fanny had not done anything that she could remember except walk with the woman Bess to the water tank and back again. Fanny had a long period of munching in daylight, before she lay down with a grunt to sleep. Her vast haunch and rib cage, well covered with fat and muscle, hit the bed of hay like a carefully lowered barrel. It became cooler. The little grey kitten, which Fanny could now see more clearly, came and curled herself up in the reddish feathers behind Jenny's left hoof.

The little cat was not four months, an ash-grey and

black brindle, with a tail only the length of a king-sized cigarette, because someone had stepped in the middle of it when she was younger. She had wandered far that day, perhaps three or four miles, and turned in at the first shelter she had seen. She had left home, because her grandmother and great-grandmother had attacked her for an uncountable time, one time too many. Her mother had been killed by a car just a few days ago. The little cat had seen her mother's body on the road and sniffed it. So the little kitten, with an instinct for self-preservation, had decided that the great unknown was better than what she knew. She was already wiry of muscle, and full of pluck, but now she was tired. She had investigated the farmyard and found only some muddy bread and water to eat in the chicken's trough. And even at that hour in July the little cat was chilly. She had felt the warmth coming from the huge bulk of the red-brown mare, and when the horse lay down, the kitten found a nook, and collapsed.

The mare was somehow pleased. Such a dainty little creature! That size, that weight that was nothing at all!

The horse and the kitten slept.

And in the white, two-storey farmhouse, the people argued.

The house belonged to Bess Gibson, a widow for the last three years. Her grandson Harry had come with his bride Marylou a few days ago, for a visit, Bess had thought, and to introduce Marylou. But Harry had plans also. He wanted some money. His mother hadn't enough, or had refused him, Bess gathered. Bess's son Ed, Harry's father, was dead, and Harry's mother in California had remarried.

Now Harry sat in the kitchen, dressed in cowboy clothes, a toothpick alternating with a cigarette between his lips, and talked about the restaurant-drive-in-bar-and-café that he wanted to buy his way into.

'If you could only see, Gramma, that this farm isn't even paying its way, that the money's sitting here doing nothing! What've you got here?' He waved a hand. 'You could get a hundred and twenty thousand for the house and land, and think for a minute what kind of apartment in town you could have for a fraction of that!'

'That's true, you know?' Marylou parroted. She was dawdling over her coffee, but she'd whipped out a nailfile and was sawing away now.

Bess shifted her weight in the wooden chair, and the chair gave a creak. She wore a blue and white cotton dress and white sandals. She suffered from dropsy. Her hair had gone completely white in the last couple of years. She realized that Harry meant an apartment in town, and town was Danville, thirty miles away. Some poky little place with two flights of stairs to climb, probably belonging to someone else to whom she'd have to pay rent. Bess didn't want to think about an apartment, no matter how many modern conveniences it might have. 'This place pays its way,' Bess said finally. 'It's not losing money. There's the chickens and ducks – people come to buy them or their eggs. There's the corn and the wheat. Sam manages it very well – I don't know about the immediate future, with Sam gone,' she added with an edge in it, 'but it's home to me and it's yours when I'm gone.'

'But not even a tractor? Sam still uses a plough. It's ridiculous. That one horse. What century are you living in, Gramma? – Well, you could *borrow* on it,' Harry said not for the first time, 'if you really want to help me out.'

'I'm not going to leave you or anybody a mortgaged house,' Bess replied.

That meant she was not completely convinced of the safety of what he wanted to do. But since Harry had been over this ground, he was too bored to go over it again. He merely exchanged a glance with Marylou.

Bess felt her face grow warm. Sam, their handyman – hers and her husband Claude's for seventeen years, a real member of the family – had left two days ago. Sam had made a speech and said he just couldn't stand Harry, he was sorry. Sam was getting on in years, and Harry had tried to boss him around, as if he were a hired hand, Bess supposed. She wasn't sure, but she could imagine. Bess hoped Sam would write to her soon, let her know where he was, so she could ask him back when Harry left. When she remembered old Sam with his best jacket on and his suit-case beside him, hailing the bus on the main road, Bess almost hated her grandson.

'Gramma, it's as simple as this,' Harry began in the slow, patient voice in which he always presented his case. 'I need sixty thousand dollars to buy my half with Roscoe. I told you Roscoe's just a nickname for laughs. His name is Ross Levitt.'

I don't care what his name is, Bess thought, but she said a polite 'Um-hm.'

'Well – with sixty thousand dollars each, it's a sure thing for both of us. It's part of a chain, you know, twelve other places already, and they're all coining money. But if I can't put up my part in a few days, Gramma – or can't give a promise of the money, my chances are gone. I'll pay you back, Gramma, naturally. But this is the chance of a lifetime!'

To use such words, Bess was thinking, and to be only twenty-two! Harry had a lot to learn.

'Ask your lawyer if you're in doubt, Gramma,' Harry said. 'Ask any banker. I'm not afraid of the facts.'

Bess recrossed her thick ankles. Why didn't his mother advance the money, if it was so safe? His mother had married a well-to-do man. And here was her grandson, married, at twenty-two. Too early for Harry, Bess thought, and she didn't care for Marylou or her type. Marylou was pretty and silly. Might as well be a highschool crush, not a wife. Bess knew she had to keep her thoughts to herself, however, because there was nothing worse than meddling.

'Gramma, what fun is it here for you any more, all alone in the country? Both the Colmans dead in the last year, you told me. In town, you'd have a nice circle of friends who could . . .'

Harry's voice became a drone to Bess. She had three or four good friends, six or eight even in the district. She'd known them all a long time, and they rang up, they came to see her, or Sam drove her to see them in the pick-up. Harry was too young to appreciate what a home meant, Bess thought. Every high-ceilinged bedroom upstairs was handsome, everyone said, with curtains and quilts that Bess or her own mother had made. The local newspaper had even come to take photographs, and the article had been reprinted in the . . .

Bess was stirred out of her thoughts by Harry's getting up. 'Guess we'll be turning in, Gramma,' he said.

Marylou got up with her coffee cup and took it to the sink. All the other dishes were washed. Marylou hadn't much to say, but Bess sensed a terrible storm in her, some terrible wish. And yet, Bess supposed, it probably wasn't any worse or any different from Harry's wish, which was simply to get his hands on a lot of money. They could live on the grounds behind the restaurant, Harry had said. A fine house with swimming pool all their own. Bess could imagine Marylou looking forward to that.

The young people had gone up to the front bedroom. They'd taken the television set up there, because Bess had said she didn't often watch it. She did look at it nearly every night, but she'd wanted to be polite when Harry and Marylou first arrived. Now she wished she had the set, because she could have done with a little change of thoughts, a laugh may be. Bess went to her own sleeping quarters, which in summer was a room off the back porch with screened windows against mosquitoes, though there weren't ever many in this region. She turned on her transistor radio, low.

Upstairs, Harry and Marylou talked softly, glancing now and then at the closed door, thinking Bess might knock with a tray of milk and cake, as she had done once since they'd been here.

'I don't think she'll be coming up tonight,' Marylou said. 'She's sort of mad at us.'

'Well, that's too bad.' Harry was undressing. He blew on the square toes of his cowboy boots and passed them once across the seat of his levis to see if the shine came up. 'God damn it, I've heard of these situations before, haven't you? Some old person who won't turn loose of the dough – which is really *coming* to me – just when the younger people damn well need it.'

'Isn't there someone else you know who could persuade her?'

'Hell – around here?' They'd all be on his grandmother's side, Harry was thinking. Other people were the last thing they needed. 'I'm for a small snort. How about you?' Harry pulled from a back corner of the closet a big half-empty bottle of bourbon.

'No, thanks. I'll have a sip of yours, if you're going to put water in it.'

Harry splashed some water from the porcelain pitcher into his glass, handed the glass to Marylou for a sip, then added more bourbon for himself, and drank it almost off. 'You know Roscoe wanted me to call him up yesterday or today? With an answer?' Harry wiped his mouth. He wasn't expecting a reply from Marylou and didn't get one. *I damn well wish she was dead now*, Harry thought, like a curse that he might have said aloud to get the resentment and anger out of his system. Then suddenly it came to him. An idea. Not a bad idea, not a horrible idea. Not too horrible. And safe. Well, ninety per cent safe, if he did it wisely, carefully. It was even a simple idea.

'What're you thinking?' Marylou asked, propped up in bed now with the sheet pulled up to her waist. Her curly reddish hair glowed like a halo in the light of the reading lamp fixed to the bed.

'I'm thinking – if Gramma had something like a hip injury, you know – those things old people always get. She'd—' He came closer to the bed and spoke even more softly, knowing already that Marylou would be with him, even if his idea were more dangerous. 'I mean, she'd have to stay in a town, wouldn't she – if she couldn't get around?'

Marylou's eyes swam in excited confusion, and she blinked. 'What're you talking about?' she asked in a whisper. 'Pushing her down the stairs?'

Harry shook his head quickly. 'That's too obvious. I was thinking of – maybe going on a picnic, the way she says she does, you know? With the horse and wagon. A watermelon, sandwiches and all and—'

'And beer!' Marylou said, giggling nervously knowing the climax was coming.

'Then the wagon turns over somewhere,' Harry said simply, shrugging. 'You know, there's that ford by the stream. Well, *I* know it, anyway.'

'Wagon turns over. What about us? If we're in it?'

'You don't have to be in it. You could've jumped off to lay the cloth, some damn thing. I'll do it.'

A pause.

'You're serious?' Marylou asked.

Harry was thinking, with his eyes almost closed. Finally he nodded. 'Yes. If I can't think of anything else. Anything better. Time's getting short, even for promises to Roscoe. Sure. I'm serious.' Then abruptly Harry went and switched on the television.

To the little grey cat, Fanny the horse had become a protectress, a fortress, a home. Not that Fanny did anything. Fanny merely existed, giving out warmth in the cold of the night before dawn. The grey kitten's only enemies were the two older cats, and fortunately these chose to be simply huffy, ready with a spit, a swipe of a paw full of claws. They made life unpleasant, but they were not out for the kill, or even to drive her off the premises, which was something.

The kitten spent not much time in the stable, however. She liked to play in the ducks' and the chicken's yard, to canter towards a chick as if with evil intent, then to dodge the lunge, the terrible beak of the mother hen. Then the kitten would leap to an upright of the wooden fence and sit, washing a paw, surveying alertly the area in front of her and the meadow behind her. She was half-wild. She was not tempted to approach the back door of the house. She sensed that she wouldn't be welcome. She had never had anything but ill-treatment or indifference at best from the creatures that walked on two legs. With her grandmother and great-grandmother, she had eaten the remains of their kills, what was left of rats, birds, now and then a small rabbit, when her elders had eaten their fill. From the two-legged creatures came nothing reliable or abundant, maybe a pan of milk and bread, not every day, not to be counted on.

But the big red horse, so heavy, so slow, the grey kitten had come to recognize as a reliable friend. The kitten had seen horses before, but never any as huge as this. She had never come close to a horse, never touched one before. The kitten found it both amusing and dangerous. The kitten loved to feel amused, to feel as if she were playing tricks on other creatures (like the chickens) and on herself, because it eased the realities of existence, the fact that she could be killed – in a flash, as her mother had been – if the gigantic horse happened to step on her, for instance. Even the horse's big feet had metal bottoms: the kitten had noticed this one evening when the horse was lying down. Not soft, like the horse's long hair there, but hard, able to hurt.

Yet the kitten realized that the horse played with her too. The horse turned its great head and neck to look at her, and was careful not to step on her. Once when the horse was lying down, the kitten in a nervous rush of anxiety and mischief dashed up the horse's soft nose, up the bony front, and seized an ear and nipped it. Then at once the kitten had leapt down and crouched, fearing the worst in retaliation. But the horse had only tossed its head a little, showed its teeth and snorted – disturbing some near-by wisps of hay – as if it were amused also. Therefore the grey kitten pranced without fear now on the horse's side and haunch, leapt to tackle the coarse hair of the horse's tail, and dodged the tail's slow flick with ease. The horse's eyes followed her. The kitten felt those eyes a kind of protection, like her mother's eyes which the kitten remembered. Now the kitten slept in the warm place under the horse's shoulder, next to the great body which radiated heat.

One day the fat woman caught sight of the little kitten. Usually the kitten hid at the first glimpse of a human figure coming from the house, but the kitten was caught unawares while investigating a well-pecked chicken bone outside the stable. The kitten crouched and stared at the woman, ready to run.

'Well, well! Where'd you come from!' said Bess, bending to see better. 'And what's happened to your tail? You're a tiny little thing!' When Bess moved closer, the kitten dashed into the raspberry bushes and disappeared.

Bess carried the bucket of oats into Fanny's stable – poor Fanny was standing and doing nothing now – set the oats on the corner of the trough, and led Fanny out for water. When Fanny had drunk, Bess opened a fence gate, and led Fanny into an enclosed meadow.

'You're having a fine holiday, aren't you, Fanny? But we're going on a picnic today. You'll pull the wagon. Down to the old brook where you can cool your feet.' She patted the mare's side. The top of Fanny's back was on a level with Bess's eyes. A huge creature she was, but she didn't eat a lot, and she worked willingly. Bess remembered Harry at thirteen or so, sitting astride Fanny for his picture to be taken, legs all bowed out as if he were sitting on a barrel. Bess didn't like to recall those days. Harry had been a nicer boy then. Engine Horse, Harry had called Fanny, impressed by her strength, as who wouldn't be, seeing her pull a wagon-load of wheatsacks.

Bess went into the stable, poured the oats into Fanny's trough, then went back to the house, where she had a peach pie in the oven. She turned the oven off, and opened the oven door so it stayed ajar about four inches. Bess never measured or timed things, but her baking came out right. She ought to give the little kitten a roast beef rib to chew on, Bess thought. She knew the type this kitten was, half-wild, full of beans, and she – or maybe it was a he – would make a splendid mouser, if it could hold its own against the pair of cats here till it grew up a little. Bess took the plate of left-over roast beef from the refrigerator and with a sharp knife cut off a rib about fourteen inches long. If she could manage to give it to the kitten without the other cats noticing and stealing it, it would do the kitten a power of good.

The ham and cheese sandwiches were already made, and it was only a quarter to 12. Marylou had devilled half a dozen eggs this morning. Where was she now? They were both upstairs talking, Bess supposed. They did a lot of talking. Bess heard a floorboard squeak. Yes, they were upstairs, and she decided to go out now and see if she could find the kitten.

Bess approached the chicken yard in her waddling gait, calling, 'Here kitty-kitty-kitty!' and holding the bone out. Her own two cats were away hunting now, probably, and just as well. Bess even looked in the stable for the little one, but didn't see her. Then when she glanced at Fanny in the meadow – Fanny with her head down, munching clover – Bess caught sight of the little kitten, gambolling and darting in the sunlight around Fanny's hooves, like a puff of smoke blown this way and that. The kitten's lightness and energy held Bess spellbound for a few moments. What a contrast, Bess was thinking, with her own awful weight, her slowness, her *age*! Bess smiled as she walked towards the gate. The kitten was going to be pleased with the bone.

'Puss-puss?' she called. 'What'll we name you – if you stay?' Bess breathed harder, trying to walk and talk at the same time.

The kitten drew back and stared at Bess, her ears erect,

yellow-green eyes wary, and she moved nearer the horse as if for protection.

'Brought you a bone,' Bess said, and tossed it.

The kitten leapt backward, then caught the smell of meat and advanced, nose down, straight towards her objective. An involuntary, primal growl came from her small throat, a growl of warning, triumph and voraciousness. With one tiny foot on the great bone, in case an intruder would snatch it, the kitten tore at the meat with baby teeth. Growling and eating at the same time, the kitten circled the bone, glancing all around her to see that no enemy or rival was approaching from any direction.

Bess chuckled with amusement and gratification. Certainly old Fanny wasn't going to bother the little cat with her bone!

Marylou was already loading the wagon with baskets and thermoses and the blankets to sit on. Bess pulled a fresh tablecloth out of the kitchen cabinet.

Harry went out to hitch up Fanny. He strode like a cowboy in his highheeled boots, grabbed the curved brim of his Stetson and readjusted it to reassure himself, because he was not an expert at throwing a collar over a horse's head.

'*Whoa*, Fanny!' he yelled, when the mare drew back. He'd missed. Dammit, he wasn't going to call for Bess to help him, that'd be ridiculous. The mare circled Harry, facing him, but drawing back every time he tried to slip the heavy collar on. Harry jumped about like a bull-fighter – except that the collar was getting damned heavy in his hands, not like something a bull-fighter had to carry. He might have to tie up the beast, he thought. He seized the bridle, which dangled from a halter. She hadn't even a bit in as yet. 'Engine hoss! *Whoa*, girl!'

Fortified and exhilarated by her half-eaten banquet, the little grey kitten leapt about also, playing, pretending she had to guard her bone, though she knew the man hadn't even seen her.

'Whoa, I *said*!' Harry yelled, and lunged at Fanny and this time made it with the collar. Harry turned his ankle and fell to the ground. He got up, not at all hurt by the fall, and then he heard a cry, a rhythmic cry like something panting.

Harry saw the little grey animal, thought at first it was a rat, then realized it was a kitten with half its bowels out. He must have stepped on it, or the horse had. Or maybe he'd fallen on it. He'd have to kill it, that he saw right away. Annoyed and suddenly angry, Harry stepped hard on the kitten's head with the heel of his cowboy boot. Harry's teeth were bared. He was still getting his own breath back. His Gramma probably wouldn't miss the kitten, he thought. She usually had too many of them. But Harry picked the kitten up by its oddly short tail, swung it once and hurled it as far as he could across the meadow, away from the house.

The mare followed the movement with her eyes, until the kitten – even before it landed on the ground – was lost to her vision. But she had seen the kitten smashed by the man falling on it. Fanny followed docilely as Harry led her towards the gate, towards the house. Fanny's awareness of what had happened came slowly and ponderously, even more slowly than she plodded across the meadow. Involuntarily, Fanny turned her head and tried to look behind her, almost came to a stop, and the man jerked her bridle.

'Come on, come on, Engine!'

The brook, sometimes called Latham's Brook, was about two miles from Bess's farm. Harry knew it from his childhood visits with his grandmother. It crossed his mind that the wooden bridge might be different – wider, maybe with a rail now – and was relieved to see that it was the same: a span of hardly twenty feet, and maybe eight or nine feet wide, not wide enough for two cars, but a car seldom came here, probably. The road was a single-lane, unpaved, and there were lots of better roads around for cars.

'There's the old spot,' said Bess, looking across the brook at the green grass, pleasantly sheltered by a few trees, where the family had come for years to picnic. 'Hasn't changed, has it, Harry?' Bess was seated on a bench that let down from a side of the wagon, the right side.

Harry had the reins. 'Nope. Sure hasn't.'

This was where Marylou was to get down, and according to plan, she said, 'Let me walk across, Harry! Is it shallow enough to wade?'

Harry tugged Fanny to a halt, sawing on her bit, and Fanny even backed a little, thinking that was what he wanted. 'I dunno,' said Harry in a frozen tone.

Marylou jumped down. She was in blue jeans, espadrilles, and a red-checked shirt. She trotted across the bridge, as if feeling happy and full of pep.

Harry clucked up Fanny again. He'd go over the right side of the bridge. He tugged Fanny to the right.

'Careful, Harry!' said Bess. '*Harry*, you're—'

The horse was on the bridge, the two right wheels of the wagon were not. There was a loud bump and scrape, a terrible jolt as the axles hit the edge of the bridge. Bess was thrown backward, balanced for a second with the wagon side in the small of her back, then she fell off into the water. Harry crouched, prepared to spring to safety, to jump towards the bank, but the falling wagon gave him nothing solid to leap from. Fanny, drawn backward and sideways by the weight of the wagon, was suddenly over the edge of the bridge, trapped in her shafts. She fell on Harry's shoulders, and Harry's face was suddenly smashed against stones, under water.

Fanny threshed about on her side, trying to regain her feet.

'*Har-ry!*' Marylou screamed. She had run on to the bridge. She saw a red stream coming from Harry's head, and she ran to the bank and waded into the water. '*Harry!*'

The crazy horse was somehow sideways in the wagon shafts, trampling all over Harry's legs now. Marylou raised her fists and shouted.

'*Back*, you idiot!'

Fanny, dazed with shock and fear, raised her front feet, not high, and when they came down, they struck Marylou's knees.

Marylou screamed, gave a panic-stricken, brandishing movement of her right fist to drive the horse off, then sank into the water up to her waist, gasping. Blood, terrifying blood, poured from her knees, through her torn blue jeans. And the stupid horse was now pitching and stomping, trying to get out of the shafts. Again the hooves came down on Harry, on his body.

It all happened so slowly. Marylou felt paralysed. She couldn't even cry out. The horse looked like something in a slow-motion film, dragging now the broken wagon right across Harry. My God! And was it Bess yelling something now? Was it? Where? Marylou lost consciousness.

Bess was struggling to get to her feet. She'd been knocked out for a few minutes, she realized. What on earth had happened? Fanny was trying to climb the bank opposite, and the wagon was wedged between two trees. When Bess's eyes focused a bit better, she saw Harry almost covered by water, and then Marylou, who was nearer. Clumsily Bess waded into the deeper water of the brook, siezed Marylou by one arm, and dragged her slowly, slowly over the stones, until her head was on the bank, clear of water.

But Harry was face down and underwater! Bess had a horrible moment, had a desire to scream as loudly as she could for help. But all she did was wade towards Harry, hands outstretched, and when she reached him, she took as hard a grip as she could on his shirt, under his arm, and tugged with all her strength. She could not move him, but she turned him over, held his head in the air. His face was a pink and red blur, no longer a face. There was something wrong with his chest. It was crushed.

'*Help!*' Bess yelled. 'Please! – *Help!*'

She waited a minute, and shouted again. She sat down finally on the grass of the bank. She was in shock, she realized. She shivered then she began to tremble violently. A chill. She was soaking wet. Even her hair was wet. See about Marylou, she told herself, and she got up again and went to Marylou who was on her back, her legs twisted in an awful way, as if they were broken. But Marylou was breathing.

Bess made herself move. She unhitched Fanny. Bess had no purpose. She felt she was in some kind of nightmare, yet she knew she was awake, that it had all happened. She held on to a brass ring of Fanny's collar, and Fanny pulled her up the slope, on to the bridge. They walked slowly, the woman and the horse, back the way they had come. It was easily nearly a mile to any house, Bess thought. The Poindexter place, wasn't that the next?

When the Poindexter house was in sight, Bess saw a car approaching. She raised her arm, but found she hadn't strength to yell out loudly enough. Still, the car was coming, slowing down.

'Go to the bridge. The brook,' Bess told the bewildered looking man who was getting out of his car. 'Two people—'

'You're hurt? You're bleeding,' said the man, pointing to Bess's shoulder. 'Get in the car. We'll go to the Poindexters' house. I know the Poindexters.' He helped Bess into the car, then he took Fanny's dangling reins and pulled her into the long driveway of the Poindexters' property, so the horse would be off the road. He went back and drove the car into the driveway, past the horse, on to the house.

Bess knew the Poindexters too. They were not close friends, but good neighbours. Bess had enough of her wits about her to refuse to lie down on the sofa, as Eleanor Poindexter wished her to do, until they'd put newspapers down on it. Her clothes were still damp. Eleanor made her some tea. The man was already on the telephone. He came back and said he'd asked for an ambulance to go at once to the ford.

Eleanor, a gentle, rather pretty woman of fifty, saw to Bess's shoulder. It was a cut, not serious. 'Whatever made your grandson go over the edge?' she said for the second time, as if in wonderment. 'That bridge isn't all that narrow.'

It was two or three days before Bess felt anything like her usual self. She hadn't needed to go into a hospital, but the doctor had advised her to rest a lot at home, which she had done. And Eleanor Poindexter had been an angel, and driven Bess twice to visit Marylou in the Danville hospital. Marylou's legs had been broken, and she'd need an operation on both knees. She might always walk with a limp, one doctor told Bess. And Marylou was strangely bitter about Harry – that shocked Bess the most, considering they were newlyweds, and Bess assumed much in love.

'Stupid – selfish – so-and-so,' Marylou said. Her voice was bitter.

Bess felt Marylou might have said more, but didn't want to or didn't dare. Harry's body had been sent to California, to Harry's mother. After the brook, Bess had never seen Harry.

One day that same week, Bess took Fanny into the meadow for grazing. Bess was feeling a little happier. She'd had a letter from Sam, and he was willing to come back, providing Harry's visit was over (Sam didn't mince words), and Bess had just replied to him in a letter which the mailman would take away tomorrow morning.

Then Bess saw the dry and half-eaten body of the little grey cat, and a shock of pain went through her. She'd supposed the kitten had wandered on somewhere. What had happened to it? Crushed somehow. By what? A car or tractor never came into this meadow. Bess turned and looked at Fanny, whose thick neck was bent towards the ground. Fanny's lips and teeth moved in the grass. Fanny couldn't have stepped on the little thing, the kitten was much too quick, had been. Fanny had liked the kitten, Bess had seen that the morning she'd given the kitten the rib bone. And there, just a few feet away, was the long bone, stripped clean now by birds. Bess bent and picked it up. How the little kitten had loved this bone! Bess, after bracing herself, lifted the kitten's body up too. Hadn't Harry harnessed Fanny in the meadow that day? What had happened? What had happened to make Fanny so angry that day at the brook? It was Harry's hands that had driven the wagon over the edge. Bess had seen it. Fanny would never have gone so near the edge, if she hadn't been tugged that way.

In the afternoon, Bess buried the kitten in an old, clean dishtowel in a grave she dug in the far meadow, beyond the chickens' and the ducks' yard. It hadn't seemed right to dispose of the kitten in the garbage, even if she'd wrapped the body well. The kitten had been so full of life! Harry had somehow killed the kitten, Bess felt sure. And Fanny had seen it. Bess knew too that Harry had meant to kill her. It was horrid, too horrid to think about.

The Day of Reckoning

JOHN took a taxi from the station, as his uncle had told him to do in case they weren't there to meet him. It was less than two miles to Hanshaw Chickens, Inc. as his Uncle Ernie Hanshaw now called his farm. John knew the white two-storey house well, but the long grey barn was new to him. It was huge, covering the whole area where the cow barn and the pigpens had been.

'Plenty of wishbones in that place!' the taxi driver said cheerfully as John paid him.

John smiled. 'Yes, and I was just thinking – not a chicken in sight!'

John carried his suitcase towards the house. 'Anybody home?' he called, thinking Helen would probably be in the kitchen now, getting lunch.

Then he saw the flattened cat. No, it was a kitten. Was it real or made of paper? John set his suitcase down and bent closer. It was real. It lay on its side, flat and level with the damp reddish earth, in the wide track of a tyre. Its skull had been crushed and there was blood there, but not on the rest of the body which had been enlarged by pressure, so that the tail looked absurdly short. The kitten was white with patches of orange, brindle and black.

John heard a hum of machinery from the barn. He put his suitcase on the front porch, and hearing nothing from the house, set off at a trot for the new barn. He found the big front doors locked, and went round to the back, again at a trot, because the barn seemed to be a quarter of a mile long. Besides the machine hum, John heard a high-pitched sound, a din of cries and peeps from inside.

'Ernie?' John yelled. Then he saw Helen. '*Hello*, Helen!'

'John! Welcome! You took a taxi? We didn't hear any car!' She gave him a kiss on the cheek. 'You've grown another three inches!'

His uncle climbed down from a ladder and shook John's hand. 'How're you, boy?'

'Okay, Ernie. What's going on here?' John looked up at moving belts which disappeared somewhere inside the barn. A rectangular metal container, nearly as big as a boxcar, rested on the ground.

Ernie pulled John closer and shouted that the grain, a special mixture, had just been delivered and was being stored in the factory, as he called the barn. This afternoon a man would come to collect the container.

'Lights shouldn't go on now, according to schedule, but we'll make an exception so you can see. Look!' Ernie pulled a switch inside the barn door, and the semi-darkness changed to glaring light, bright as full sun.

The cackles and screams of the chickens augmented like a siren, like a thousand sirens, and John instinctively covered his ears. Ernie's lips moved, but John could not hear him. John swung around to see Helen. She was standing farther back, and waved a hand, shook her head and smiled, as if to say she couldn't bear the racket. Ernie drew John farther into the barn, but he had given up talking and merely pointed.

The chickens were smallish and mostly white, and they all shuffled constantly. John saw that this was because the platforms on which they stood slanted forward, inclining them towards the slowly moving feed troughs. But not all of them were eating. Some were trying to peck the chickens next to them. Each chicken had its own little wire coop. There must have been forty rows of chickens on the ground floor, and eight or ten tiers of chickens went up to the ceiling. Between the double rows of back-to-back chickens were aisles wide enough for a man to pass and sweep the floor, John supposed, and just as he thought this, Ernie

turned a wheel, and water began to shoot over the floor.
The floor slanted towards various drain holes.

'*All automatic! Somethin', eh?*'

John recognized the words from Ernie's lips, and nodded
appreciatively. 'Terrific!' But he was ready to get away
from the noise.

Ernie shut off the water.

John noticed that the chickens had worn their beaks
down to blunt nubs, and their white breasts dripped blood
where the horizontal bar supported their weight. What else
could they do but eat? John had read a little about battery
chicken farming. These hens of Ernie's, like the hens he had
read about, couldn't turn around in their coops. Much of
the general flurry in the barn was caused by chickens trying
to fly upward. Ernie cut the lights. The doors closed after
them, apparently also automatically.

'Machine farming has really got me over the hump,'
Ernie said, still talking loudly. 'I'm making good money now.
And just imagine, one man – me – can run the whole show!'

John grinned. 'You mean you won't have anything for
me to do?'

'Oh, there's plenty to do. You'll see. How about some
lunch first? Tell Helen I'll be in in about fifteen minutes.'

John walked towards Helen. 'Fabulous.'

'Yes. Ernie's in love with it.'

They went on towards the house, Helen looking down at
her feet, because the ground was muddy in spots. She wore
old tennis shoes, black corduroy pants, and a rust-coloured
sweater. John purposely walked between her and where the
kitten lay, not wanting to mention it now.

He carried his suitcase up to the square, sunny corner
room which he had slept in since he was a boy of ten, when
Helen and Ernie had bought the farm. He changed into
blue jeans, and went down to join Helen in the kitchen.

'Would you like an old-fashioned? We've got to celebrate
your arrival,' Helen said. She was making two drinks at
the wooden table.

'Fine. – Where's Susan?' Susan was their eight-year-old daughter.

'She's at a— Well, sort of summer school. They'll bring her back around four-thirty. Helps fill in the summer holidays. They make awful clay ashtrays and fringed money-purses – you know. Then you've got to praise them.'

John laughed. He gazed at his aunt-by-marriage, thinking she was still very attractive at – what was it? Thirty-one, he thought. She was about five feet four, slender, with reddish blond curly hair and eyes that sometimes looked green, sometimes blue. And she had a very pleasant voice. 'Oh, thank you.' John accepted his drink. There were pineapple chunks in it, topped with a cherry.

'Awfully good to see you, John. How's college? And how're your folks?'

Both those items were all right. John would graduate from Ohio State next year when he would be twenty, then he was going to take a post-graduate course in government. He was an only child, and his parents lived in Dayton, a hundred and twenty miles away.

Then John mentioned the kitten. 'I hope it's not yours,' he said, and realized at once that it must be, because Helen put her glass down and stood up. Who else could the kitten have belonged to, John thought, since there was no other house around?

'Oh, Lord! Susan's going to be—' Helen rushed out of the back door.

John ran after her, straight for the kitten which Helen had seen from a distance.

'It was that big truck this morning,' Helen said. 'The driver sits so high up he can't see what's—'

'I'll help you,' John said, looking around for a spade or a trowel. He found a shovel and returned, and prised the flattened body up gently, as if it were still alive. He held it in both his hands. 'We ought to bury it.'

'Of course. Susan mustn't see it, but I've got to tell her. – There's a fork in back of the house.'

John dug where Helen suggested, a spot near an apple tree behind the house. He covered the grave over, and put some tufts of grass back so it would not catch the eye.

'The times I've brought that kitten in the house when the damned trucks came!' Helen said. 'She was barely four months, wasn't afraid of anything, just went trotting up to cars as if they were something to play with, you know? She gave a nervous laugh. 'And this morning the truck came at eleven, and I was watching a pie in the oven, just about to take it out.'

John didn't know what to say. 'Maybe you should get another kitten for Susan as soon as you can.'

'What're you two doing?' Ernie walked towards them from the back door of the house.

'We just buried Beansy,' Helen said. 'The truck got her this morning.'

'Oh.' Ernie's smile disappeared. 'That's too bad. That's really too bad, Helen.'

But at lunch Ernie was cheerful enough, talking of vitamins and antibiotics in his chicken feed, and his produce of one and a quarter eggs per day per hen. Though it was July, Ernie was lengthening the chicken's 'day' by artificial light.

'All birds are geared to spring,' Ernie said. 'They lay more when they think spring is coming. The ones I've got are at peak. In October they'll be under a year old, and I'll sell them and take on a new batch.'

John listened attentively. He was to be here a month. He wanted to be helpful. 'They really do eat, don't they? A lot of them have worn off their beaks, I noticed.'

Ernie laughed. 'They're de-beaked. They'd peck each other through the wire, if they weren't. Two of 'em got loose in my first batch and nearly killed each other. Well, one did kill the other. Believe me, I de-beak 'em now, according to instructions.'

'And one chicken went on eating the other,' Helen said. 'Cannibalism.' She laughed uneasily. 'Ever hear of cannibalism among chickens, John?'

'No.'

'Our chickens are insane,' Helen said.

Insane. John smiled a little. Maybe Helen was right. Their noises had sounded pretty crazy.

'Helen doesn't much like battery farming,' Ernie said apologetically to John. 'She's always thinking about the old days. But we weren't doing so well then.'

That afternoon, John helped his uncle draw the conveyor belts back into the barn. He began learning the levers and switches that worked things. Belts removed eggs and deposited them gently into plastic containers. It was nearly 5 p.m. before John could get away. He wanted to say hello to his cousin Susan, a lively little girl with hair like her mother's.

As John crossed the front porch, he heard a child's weeping, and he remembered the kitten. He decided to go ahead anyway and speak to Susan.

Susan and her mother were in the living-room – a front room with flowered print curtains and cherrywood furniture. Some additions, such as a bigger television set, had been made since John had seen the room last. Helen was on her knees beside the sofa on which Susan lay, her face buried in one arm.

'Hello, Susan,' John said. 'I'm sorry about your kitten.'

Susan lifted a round, wet face. A bubble started at her lips and broke. 'Beansy—'

John embraced her impulsively. 'We'll find another kitten. I promise. Maybe tomorrow. Yes?' He looked at Helen.

Helen nodded and smiled a little. 'Yes, we will.'

The next afternoon, as soon as the lunch dishes had been washed, John and Helen set out in the station wagon for a farm eight miles away belonging to some people called Ferguson. The Fergusons had two female cats that frequently had kittens, Helen said. And they were in luck this time. One of the cats had a litter of five – one black, one white, three mixed – and the other cat was pregnant.

'White?' John suggested. The Fergusons had given them a choice.

'Mixed,' Helen said. 'White is all good and black is – maybe unlucky.'

They chose a black and white female with white feet.

'I can see this one being called Bootsy,' Helen said, laughing.

The Fergusons were simple people, getting on in years, and very hospitable. Mrs Ferguson insisted they partake of a freshly baked coconut cake along with some rather powerful home-made wine. The kitten romped around the kitchen, playing with grey rolls of dust that she dragged out from under a big cupboard.

'That ain't no battery kitten!' Frank Ferguson remarked, and drank deep.

'Can we see your chickens, Frank?' Helen asked. She slapped John's knee suddenly. 'Frank has the most *wonderful* chickens, almost a hundred!'

'What's wonderful about 'em?' Frank said, getting up on a stiff leg. He opened the back screen door. 'You know where they are, Helen.'

John's head was buzzing pleasantly from the wine as he walked with Helen out to the chicken yard. Here were Rhode Island Reds, big white Leghorns, roosters strutting and tossing their combs, half-grown speckled chickens, and lots of little chicks about six inches high. The ground was covered with claw-scored watermelon rinds, tin bowls of grain and mush, and there was much chicken dung. A wheelless wreck of a car seemed to be a favourite laying spot: three hens sat on the back of the front seat with their eyes half closed, ready to drop eggs which would surely break on the floor behind them.

'It's such a wonderful *mess*!' John shouted, laughing.

Helen hung by her fingers in the wire fence, rapt. 'Like

the chickens I knew when I was a kid. Well, Ernie and I had them too, till about—' She smiled at John. 'You know – a year ago. Let's go in!'

John found the gate, a limp thing made of wire that fastened with a wooden bar. They went in and closed it behind them.

Several hens drew back and regarded them with curiosity, making throaty, sceptical noises.

'They're such stupid darlings!' Helen watched a hen fly up and perch herself in a peach tree. 'They can see the sun! They can fly!'

'And scratch for worms – and eat watermelon!' John said.

'When I was little, I used to dig worms for them at my grandmother's farm. With a hoe. And sometimes I'd step on their droppings, you know – well, on purpose – and it'd go between my toes. I loved it. Grandma always made me wash my feet under the garden hydrant before I came in the house.' She laughed. A chicken evaded her outstretched hand with an '*Urrr-rrk!*' 'Grandma's chickens were so tame, I could touch them. All bony and warm with the sun, their feathers. Sometimes I want to open all the coops in the barn and open the doors and let ours loose, just to see them walking on the grass for a few minutes.'

'Say, Helen, want to buy one of these chickens to take home? Just for fun? A couple of 'em?'

'No.'

'How much did the kitten cost? Anything?'

'No, nothing.'

Susan took the kitten into her arms, and John could see that the tragedy of Beansy would soon be forgotten. To John's disappointment, Helen lost her gaiety during dinner. Maybe it was because Ernie was droning on about his profit and loss – not loss really, but outlay. Ernie was obsessed, John realized. That was why Helen was bored.

Ernie worked hard now, regardless of what he said about machinery doing everything. There were creases on either side of his mouh, and they were not from laughing. He was starting to get a paunch. Helen had told John that last year Ernie had dismissed their handyman Sam, who'd been with them seven years.

'Say,' Ernie said, demanding John's attention. 'What d'you think of the idea? Start a battery chicken farm when you finish school, and hire *one man* to run it. You could take another job in Chicago or Washington or wherever, and you'd have a steady *separate* income for life.'

John was silent. He couldn't imagine owning a battery chicken farm.

'Any bank would finance you – with a word from Clive, of course.'

Clive was John's father.

Helen was looking down at her plate, perhaps thinking of something else.

'Not really my life-style, I think,' John answered finally. 'I know it's profitable.'

After dinner, Ernie went into the living-room to do his reckoning, as he called it. He did some reckoning almost every night. John helped Helen with the dishes. She put a Mozart symphony on the record-player. The music was nice, but John would have liked to talk with Helen. On the other hand, what would he have said, exactly? *I understand why you're bored. I think you'd prefer pouring slop for pigs and tossing grain to real chickens, the way you used to do.* John had a desire to put his arms around Helen as she bent over the sink, to turn her face to his and kiss her. What would Helen think if he did?

That night, lying in bed, John dutifully read the brochures on battery chicken farming which Ernie had given him.

'. . . The chickens are bred small so that they do not eat so much, and they rarely reach more than 3½ pounds

... Young chickens are subjected to a light routine which tricks them into thinking that a day is 6 hours long. The objective of the factory farmer is to increase the original 6-hour day by leaving the lights on for a longer period each week. Artificial Spring Period is maintained for the hen's whole lifetime of 10 months ... There is no real falling off of egg-laying in the natural sense, though the hen won't lay quite so many eggs towards the end ...' (Why, John wondered. And wasn't 'not quite so many' the same as 'falling off'?) 'At 10 months the hen is sold for about 30¢ a pound, depending on the market ...'

And below:

'Richard K. Schultz of Poon's Cross, Pa., writes: "I am more than pleased and so is my wife with the modernization of my farm into a battery chicken farm operated with Muskeego-Ryan Electric equipment. Profits have quadrupled in a year and a half and we have even bigger hopes for the future ..."'

'Writes Henry Vliess of Farnham, Kentucky: "My old farm was barely breaking even. I had chickens, pigs, cows, the usual. My friends used to laugh at my hard work combined with all my tough luck. Then I ..."'

John had a dream. He was flying like Superman in Ernie's chicken barn, and the lights were all blazing brightly. Many of the imprisoned chickens looked up at him, their eyes flashed silver, and they were struck blind. The noise they made was fantastic. They wanted to escape, but could no longer see, and the whole barn heaved with their efforts to fly upward. John flew about frantically, trying to find the lever to open the coops, the doors, anything, but he couldn't. Then he woke up, startled to find himself in bed, propped on one elbow. His forehead and chest were damp with sweat. Moonlight came strong through the window. In the night's silence, he could hear the steady high-pitched din of the hundreds of chickens in the barn, though Ernie had said the barn was absolutely sound-proofed. Maybe it was 'day-time' for the chickens now. Ernie said they had three more months to live.

John became more adept with the barn's machinery and the fast artificial clocks, but since his dream he no longer looked at the chickens as he had the first day. He did not look at them at all if he could help it. Once Ernie pointed out a dead one, and John removed it. Its breast, bloody from the coop's barrier, was so distended, it might have eaten itself to death.

Susan had named her kitten 'Bibsy', because it had a white oval on its chest like a bib.

'Beansy and now Bibsy,' Helen said to John. 'You'd think all Susan thinks about is food!'

Helen and John drove to town one Saturday morning. It was alternately sunny and showery, and they walked close together under an umbrella when the showers came. They bought meat, potatoes, washing powder, white paint for a kitchen shelf, and Helen bought a pink-and-white striped blouse for herself. At a pet shop, John acquired a basket with a pillow to give Susan for Bibsy.

When they got home, there was a long dark grey car in front of the house.

'Why, that's the doctor's car!' Helen said.

'Does he come by just to visit?' John asked, and at once felt stupid, because something might have happened to Ernie. A grain delivery had been due that morning, and Ernie was always climbing about to see that everything was going all right.

There was another car, dark green, which Helen didn't recognize beside the chicken factory. Helen and John went into the house.

It was Susan. She lay on the living-room floor under a plaid blanket, only one sandalled foot and yellow sock visible under the fringed edge. Dr Geller was there, and a man Helen didn't know. Ernie stood rigid and panicked beside his daughter.

Dr Geller came towards Helen and said, 'I'm sorry, Helen. Susan was dead by the time the ambulance got here. I sent for the coroner.'

'What *happened*?' Helen started to touch Susan, and instinctively John caught her.

'Honey, I didn't see her in time,' Ernie said. 'She was chasing under that damned container after the kitten just as it was lowering.'

'Yeah, it bumped her on the head,' said a husky man in tan workclothes, one of the delivery men. 'She was running out from under it, Ernie said. My *gosh*, I'm sorry, Mrs Hanshaw!'

Helen gasped, then she covered her face.

'You'll need a sedative, Helen,' Dr Geller said.

The doctor gave Helen a needle in her arm. Helen said nothing. Her mouth was slightly open, and her eyes stared straight ahead. Another car came and took the body away on a stretcher. The coroner took his leave then too.

With a shaky hand, Ernie poured whiskies.

Bibsy leapt about the room, and sniffed at the red splotch on the carpet. John went to the kitchen to get a sponge. It was best to try to get it up, John thought, while the others were in the kitchen. He went back to the kitchen for a saucepan of water, and scrubbed again at the abundant red. His head was ringing, and he had difficulty keeping his balance. In the kitchen, he drank off his whisky at a gulp and it at once burnt his ears.

'Ernie, I think I'd better take off,' the delivery man said solemnly. 'You know where to find me.'

Helen went up to the bedroom she shared with Ernie, and did not come down when it was time for dinner. From his room, John heard floorboards creaking faintly, and knew that Helen was walking about in the room. He wanted to go in and speak to her, but he was afraid he would not be capable of saying the right thing. Ernie should be with her, John thought.

John and Ernie gloomily scrambled some eggs, and John went to ask Helen if she would come down or would prefer him to bring her something. He knocked on the door.

'Come in,' Helen said.

He loved her voice, and was somehow surprised to find that it wasn't any different since her child had died. She was lying on the double bed, still in the same clothes, smoking a cigarette.

'I don't care to eat, thanks, but I'd like a whisky.'

John rushed down, eager to get something that she wanted. He brought ice, a glass, and the bottle on a tray. 'Do you just want to go to sleep?' John asked.

'Yes.'

She had not turned on a light. John kissed her cheek, and for an instant she slipped her arm around his neck and kissed his cheek also. Then he left the room.

Downstairs the eggs tasted dry, and John could hardly swallow even with sips of milk.

'My God, what a day,' Ernie said. 'My God.' He was evidently trying to say more, looked at John with an effort at politeness, or closeness.

And John, like Helen, found himself looking down at his plate, wordless. Finally, miserable in the silence, John got up with his plate and patted Ernie awkwardly on the shoulder. 'I am sorry, Ernie.'

They opened another bottle of whisky, one of the two bottles left in the living-room cabinet.

'If I'd known this would happen, I'd never have started this damned chicken farm. You know that. I meant to earn something for my family – not go limping along year after year.'

John saw that the kitten had found the new basket and gone to sleep in it on the living-room floor. 'Ernie, you probably want to talk to Helen. I'll be up at the usual time to give you a hand.' That meant 7 a.m.

'Okay. I'm in a daze tonight. Forgive me, John.'

John lay for nearly an hour in his bed without sleeping. He heard Ernie go quietly into the bedroom across the hall, but he heard no voices or even a murmur after that. Ernie was not much like Clive, John thought. John's father might have given way to tears for a minute, might have cursed. Then with his father it would have been all over, except for comforting his wife.

A raucous noise, rising and falling, woke John up. The chickens, of course. What the hell was it now? They were louder than he'd ever heard them. He looked out of the front window. In the pre-dawn light, he could see that the barn's front doors were open. Then the lights in the barn came on, blazing out on to the grass. John pulled on his tennis shoes without tying them, and rushed into the hall.

'*Ernie! – Helen!*' he yelled at their closed door.

John ran out of the house. A white tide of chickens was now oozing through the wide front doors of the barn. What on earth had happened? 'Get *back*!' he yelled at the chickens, flailing his arms.

The little hens might have been blind or might not have heard him at all through their own squawks. They kept on flowing from the barn, some fluttering over the others, and sinking again in the white sea.

John cupped his hands to his mouth. 'Ernie! The *doors*!' He was shouting into the barn, because Ernie must be there.

John plunged into the hens and made another effort to shoo them back. It was hopeless. Unused to walking, the chickens teetered like drunks, lurched against each other, stumbled forward, fell back on their tails, but they kept pouring out, many borne on the backs of those who walked. They were pecking at John's ankles. John kicked some aside and moved towards the barn doors again, but the pain of the blunt beaks on his ankles and lower legs made him stop. Some chickens tried to fly up to attack him, but had no strength in their wings. *They are insane*, John remembered. Suddenly frightened, John ran towards the clearer area at the side of the barn, then on towards the back door. He knew how to open the back door. It had a combination lock.

Helen was standing at the corner of the barn in her bathrobe, where John had first seen her when he arrived. The back door was closed.

'What's *happening*?' John shouted.

'I opened the coops,' Helen said.

'Opened them – why? – Where's Ernie?'

'He's in there.' Helen was oddly calm, as if she were standing and talking in her sleep.

'Well, what's he *doing*? Why doesn't he close the place?' John was shaking Helen by the shoulders, trying to wake her up. He released her and ran to the back door.

'I've locked it again,' Helen said.

John worked the combination as fast as he could, but he could hardly see it.

'Don't open it! Do you want them coming *this* way?' Helen was suddenly alert, dragging John's hands from the lock.

Then John understood. Ernie was being killed in there, being pecked to death. Helen wanted it. Even if Ernie was screaming, they couldn't have heard him.

A smile came over Helen's face. 'Yes, he's in there. I think they will finish him.'

John, not quite hearing over the noise of chickens, had read her lips. His heart was beating fast.

Then Helen slumped, and John caught her. John knew it was too late to save Ernie. He also thought that Ernie was no longer screaming.

Helen straightened up. 'Come with me. Let's watch them,' she said, and drew John feebly, yet with determination, along the side of the barn towards the front doors.

Their slow walk seemed four times as long as it should have been. He gripped Helen's arm. 'Ernie *in* there?'

John asked, feeling as if he were dreaming, or perhaps about to faint.

'In there.' Helen smiled at him again, with her eyes half closed. 'I came down and opened the back door, you see – and I went up and woke Ernie. I said, "Ernie, something's wrong in the factory, you'd better come down." He came down and went in the back door – and I opened the coops with the lever. And then – I pulled the lever that opens the front door. He was – in the middle of the barn then, because I started a fire on the floor.'

'A fire?' Then John noticed a pale curl of smoke rising over the front door.

'Not much to burn in there – just the grain,' Helen said. 'And there's enough for them to eat outdoors, don't you think?' She gave a laugh.

John pulled her faster towards the front of the barn. There seemed to be not much smoke. Now the whole lawn was covered with chickens, and they were spreading through the white rail fence on to the road, pecking, cackling, screaming, a slow army without direction. It looked as if snow had fallen on the land.

'Head for the house!' John said, kicking at some chickens that were attacking Helen's ankles.

They went up to John's room. Helen knelt at the front window, watching. The sun was rising on their left, and now it touched the reddish roof of the metal barn. Grey smoke was curling upward from the horizontal lintel of the front doors. Chickens paused, stood stupidly in the doorway until they were bumped by others from behind. The chickens semed not so much dazzled by the rising sun – the light was brighter in the barn – as by the openness around them and above them. John had never before seen chickens stretch their necks just to look up at the sky. He knelt beside Helen, his arm around her waist.

'They're all going to – go away,' John said. He felt curiously paralysed.

'Let them.'

The fire would not spread to the house. There was no wind, and the barn was a good thirty yards away. John felt quite mad, like Helen, or the chickens, and was astonished by the reasonableness of his thought about the fire's not spreading.

'It's all over,' Helen said, as the last, not quite the last chickens wobbled out of the barn. She drew John closer by the front of his pyjama jacket.

John kissed her gently, then more firmly on the lips. It was strange, stronger than any kiss he had ever known with a girl, yet curiously without further desire. The kiss seemed only an affirmation that they were both alive. They knelt facing each other, tightly embracing. The cries of the hens ceased to sound ugly, and sounded only excited and puzzled. It was like an orchestra playing, some members stopping, others resuming instruments, making a continuous chord without a tempo. John did not know how long they knelt like that, but at last his knees hurt, and he stood up, pulling Helen up, too. He looked out of the window and said:

'They must be all out. And the fire isn't any bigger. Shouldn't we—' But the obligation to look for Ernie seemed far away, not at all pressing on him. It was as if he dreamed this night or this dawn, and Helen's kiss, the way he had dreamed about flying like Superman in the barn. Were they really Helen's hands in his now?

She slumped again, and plainly she wanted to sit on the carpet, so he left her and pulled on his blue jeans over his pyjama pants. He went down and entered the barn cautiously by the front door. The smoke made the interior hazy, but when he bent low, he could see fifty or more chickens pecking at what he knew must be Ernie on the floor. Bodies of chickens overcome by smoke lay on the floor, like little white puffs of smoke themselves, and some live chickens were pecking at these, going for the eyes. John moved towards Ernie. He thought he had braced himself, but he hadn't braced himself enough for what he saw: a

141

fallen column of blood and bone to which a few tatters of pyjama cloth still clung. John ran out again, very fast, because he had breathed once, and the smoke had nearly got him.

In his room, Helen was humming and drumming on the windowsill, gazing out at the chickens left on the lawn. The hens were trying to scratch in the grass, and were staggering, falling on their sides, but mostly falling backward, because they were used to shuffling to prevent themselves from falling forward.

'Look!' Helen said, laughing so, there were tears in her eyes. 'They don't know what grass is! But they like it!'

John cleared his throat and said, 'What're you going to say? – What'll we say?'

'Oh – say.' Helen seemed not at all disturbed by the question. 'Well – that Ernie heard something and went down and – he wasn't completely sober, you know. And – maybe he pulled a couple of wrong levers. – Don't you think so?'

Notes from a Respectable Cockroach

I HAVE moved.

I used to live at the Hotel Duke on a corner of Washington Square. My family has lived there for generations, and I mean at least two or three hundred generations. But no more for me. The place has degenerated. I've heard my great-great-great – go back as far as you like, she was still alive when I spoke to her – talk about the good old days when people arrived in horse-drawn carriages with suitcases that smelled of leather, people who had breakfast in bed and dropped a few crumbs for us on the carpet. Not purposely, of course, because we knew our place then, too, and our place was in the bathroom corners or down in the kitchen. Now we can walk all over the carpets with comparative impunity, because the clients of the Hotel Duke are too stoned blind to see us, or they haven't the energy to step on us if they did see us – or they just laugh.

The Hotel Duke has now a tattered green awning extending to the kerb, so full of holes it wouldn't protect anyone from the rain. You go up four cement steps into a dingy lobby that smells of pot smoke, stale whisky, and is insufficiently lighted. After all, the clientele now doesn't necessarily want to see who else is staying here. People reel into each other in the lobby, and might thereby strike up an acquaintance, but more often it's an unpleasant exchange of words that results. To the left in the lobby is an even darker hole called Dr Toomuch's Dance Floor. They charge two dollars admission, payable at the inside-the-lobby door. Juke box music. Puke box customers. Egad!

The hotel has six floors, and I usually take the elevator, or the lift as people say lately, imitating the English. Why climb those grimy cement air shafts, or creep up staircase after staircase, when I can leap the mere half-inch gap between floor and lift and whisk myself safely into the corner beside the operator at the controls? I can tell each floor by its smell. Fifth floor, that's a disinfectant smell since more than a year, because a shoot-up occurred and there was lots of blood-and-guts spilt smack in front of the lift. Second floor boasts a worn-out carpet, so the odour is dusty, faintly mingled with urine. Third floor stinks of sauerkraut (somebody must have dropped a glass jar of it, the floor is tile here) and so it goes. If I want out on the third, for instance, and the elevator doesn't stop there, I just wait for the next trip, and sooner or later I make it.

I was at the Hotel Duke when the U.S. Census forms came in in 1970. What a laugh. Everybody got a form, and everybody was laughing. Most of the people here probably haven't any homes to begin with, and the census was asking, 'How many rooms in your house?' and 'How many bathrooms have you?' and 'How many children?' and so forth. And what is your wife's age? People think that roaches can't understand English, or whatever is the going lingo in their vicinity. People think roaches understand only a suddenly turned-on light, which means 'Scram!' When you've been around as long as we have, which is long before the *Mayflower* got here, you dig the going yak. So I was able to appreciate many a comment on the U.S. Census, which none of the cruds at the Duke bothered filling out. It was amusing to think of myself filling it out – and why not? I was more of a resident by hereditary seat than any of the human beasts in the hotel. I am (though I am not Franz Kafka in disguise) a cockroach, and I do not know my wife's age or for that matter how many wives I have. Last week I had seven, in a manner of speaking, but how many of these have been stepped on? As for children, they're beyond count, a boast I've heard

146

my two-legged neighbours make also, but when it comes to the count, if the count is what they want (the more the merrier, I assume), I will bet on myself. Only last week I recall two egg capsules about to be delivered from two of my wives, both on the third (sauerkraut) floor. Good God, I was in a hurry myself, off in pursuit – I blush to mention it – of food which I had smelled and which I estimated to be at a distance of one hundred yards. Cheese-flavoured potato chips, I thought. I did not like to say 'Hello' and 'Good-bye' so quickly to my wives, but my need was perhaps as great as theirs, and where would they be, or rather our race be, if I could not keep my strength up? A moment later I saw a third wife crunched under a cowboy boot (the hippies here affect Western gear even if they are from Brooklyn), though at least she wasn't laying an egg at that time, only hurrying along like me, in an opposite direction. Hail and farewell! – though, alas, I am sure she did not even see me. I may never again see my parturient wives, those two, though perhaps I saw some of our offspring before I left the Duke. Who knows?

When I see some of the people here, I count myself lucky to be a cockroach. I'm at least healthier, and in a small way I clean up garbage. Which brings me to the point. There used to be garbage in the form of breadcrumbs, an occasional left-over canapé from a champagne party in a room. The present clientele of the Hotel Duke doesn't eat. They either take dope or drink booze. I've only heard about the good old days from my great-great-great-great-grandmothers and -fathers. But I believe them. They said you could jump into a shoe, for instance, outside the door, and be taken into a room along with the tray by a servant at eight in the morning, and thus breakfast on croissant crumbs. Even the shoe-polishing days are gone, because if anybody put shoes outside his room these days, they'd not only not be polished, they'd be stolen. Nowadays it's all you can hope for that these hairy, buckskin-fringed monsters and their see-through girls will take a bath once in a while and leave a few drops of water in the tub for me to drink. It's dangerous drinking out of a toilet, and at my age I won't do it.

However, I wish to speak of my new-found fortune. I'd just about had enough last week, what with another young wife squashed before my eyes by a lurching step (she had been keeping out of the *normal* path, I remember), and a moronic roomful of junkies licking up – I mean this – food from the floor as a kind of game. Young men and women, naked, pretending to be handless for some insane reason, trying to eat their sandwiches like dogs, strewing them all over the floor, then writhing about together amid salami, pickles and mayonnaise. Plenty of food this time, but unsafe to dart among those rolling bodies. Worse than feet. But to see sandwiches at all was exceptional. There's no restaurant any more, but half the rooms in the Hotel Duke are 'apartments', meaning that they have refrigerators and small stoves. But the main thing people have in the way of food is tinned tomato juice for vodka Bloody Marys. Nobody even fries an egg. For one thing, the hotel does not furnish skillets, pans, can-openers or even a single knife or fork: they'd be pinched. And none of these charmers is going to go out and buy so much as a pot to heat soup in. So the pickings is slim, as they say. And that isn't the worst of the 'service' department here. Most of the windows don't shut tightly, the beds look like lumpy hammocks, straight chairs are falling apart at the joints, and the so-called armchairs, maybe one to a room, can inflict injury by releasing a spring in a tender place. Basins are often clogged, and toilets either don't flush or keep flushing maniacally. And robberies! I've witnessed a few. A maid gives the pass key and someone's in, absconding with suitcase contents under an arm, in pockets, or in a pillowcase disguised as dirty laundry.

Anyway, about a week ago I was in a temporarily vacant room at the Duke, scrounging about for a crumb or a bit of water, when in walked a black bellhop with a suitcase that smelled of *leather*. He was followed by a gentleman who smelled of after-shave lotion, plus of course tobacco, that's normal. He unpacked, put some papers out on the writing table, tried the hot water and muttered something to himself, jiggled the running toilet, tested the shower which shot all over the bathroom floor, and then he rang up the desk. I could understand most of what he was saying. He was essentially saying that at the price he was paying per day, this and that might be improved, and could he change his room, perhaps?

I lurked in my corner, thirsty, hungry, but interested, knowing also that I would be stepped on by this same gentleman if I made an appearance on the carpet. I well knew that I would be on his list of complaints if he saw me. The old french window blew open (it was a gusty day) and his papers went in all the four corners. He had to close the window by propping the back of a straight chair against it, and then he gathered his papers, cursing.

'*Washington Square! – Henry James would turn in his grave!*'

I remember those words, uttered at the same time as he slapped his forehead as if to hit a mosquito.

A bellhop in the threadbare maroon livery of the establishment arrived stoned and fiddled with the window to no avail. The window leaked cold air, made a terrible rattle, and everything, even a cigarette pack, had to be anchored down or it would have blown off a table or whatever. The bellhop in looking at the shower managed to drench himself, and then he said he would send for 'the engineer'. The engineer at the Hotel Duke is a joke on his own, which I won't go into. He didn't turn up that day, I think because the bellhop made the final bad impression, and the gentleman picked up the telephone and said:

'Can you send someone sober, if possible, to carry my suitcases down? ... Oh, keep the money, I'm checking out. And get me a taxi, please.'

That was when I made up my mind. As the gentleman was packing, I mentally kissed good-bye to all my wives, brothers, sisters, cousins, children and grandchildren and great-grandchildren and then climbed aboard the beautiful suitcase that smelled of leather. I crawled into a pocket in the lid, and made myself snug in the folds of a plastic bag, fragrant of shaving soap and the after-shave lotion, where I would not be squashed even when the lid was closed.

Half an hour later, I found myself in a warmer room where the carpet was thick and not dusty-smelling. The gentleman has breakfast in bed in the mornings at 7.30. In the corridor, I can get all sorts of things from trays left on the floor outside the doors – even remnants of scrambled eggs, and certainly plenty of marmalade and butter on rolls. Had a narrow squeak yesterday when a white-jacketed waiter chased me thirty yards down the hall, stomping with both feet but missing me every time. I'm nimble yet, and life at the Hotel Duke taught me plenty!

I've already cased the kitchen, going and coming by lift, of course. Lots of pickings in the kitchen, but unfortunately they fumigate once a week. I met four possible wives, all a bit sickly from the fumes, but determined to stick it out in the kitchen. For me, it's upstairs. No competition, and plenty of breakfast trays and sometimes midnight snacks. Maybe I'm an old bachelor now, but there's life in me yet if a possible wife comes along. Meanwhile I consider myself a lot better than those bipeds in the Hotel Duke, whom I've seen eating stuff I wouldn't touch – or mention. They do it on bets. Bets! All life is a gamble, isn't it? So why bet?

Eddie and the Monkey Robberies

EDDIE's job was to open doors. Formerly, he had been cup-shaker for a recorder-player named Hank, a young man who hadn't been able to subsidize his poetry writing sufficiently by tootling, and it had been difficult to keep Eddie in the face of complaining landlords, so Hank had passed Eddie on to a girl friend called Rose, to whom he had just said good bye, and had taken a job. And Rose knew Jane, and Jane was an ex-convict, which was why Eddie was now opening doors of strange houses.

Being a young and clever Capuchin, Eddie had learned his new job quickly, and often approached doors gaily waltzing and swinging himself from any near-by object, such as a newel post or the back of a straight chair, towards his goal: the knob of a Yale lock, a button that undid a bolt, maybe a chain and bolt also. His nimble fingers flew, undoing everything, or experimenting until they could.

Thus he would admit the husky blonde woman called Jane, whose ring or knock he had usually already heard. Sometimes Eddie had the door open when Jane was still climbing the front steps or walking up the front path, her reticule in hand. Eddie would have got in through a window. Jane always paused for a moment on the threshold, and mumbled something, as if addressing someone standing in the house. Then she would come in and close the door.

Ka-*bloom*! This particular house was a solid one, and had a pleasant smell to Eddie, for there was a big cluster of yellow roses in a vase in the downstairs hall.

From the pocket of her loose coat, Jane produced a banana, its partly opened peel limp and blackening. Eddie gave a squeak of thanks, ripped the rest of the peel off and handed it back to Jane, who pocketed it. Jane was already walking towards the back of the house, towards the kitchen and dining-room.

She opened a drawer in the dining-room, then a second before she found what she wanted, and at once began loading her reticule with handfuls of silver spoons, forks and knives. She took a silver salt and pepper set from the dining-room table. Then she went into the living-room, went at once to the telephone table, where a silver-framed photograph stood. This she put into her bag, and also a handsome paper-knife which had what looked like a jade handle. By now barely three minutes had passed, Eddie had finished his banana, Jane whispered his name, opened her coat, and Eddie leapt. He clung to her big sweatered bosom with his twenty fingers and toes, aided also by his long tail, as he had clung to his mother when he was small.

They were out of the house. To Eddie, the hum of the car grew louder, then they were inside the car, Jane sat down with a thump, and the car moved off. The women talked.

'Easy, very easy, that one,' Jane said, getting her breath back. 'But I didn't bother with the bedrooms.'

'Silver?'

'You bet! Ha-ha! – Ah, a nice whisky'll taste good!'

Rose, younger than Jane, drove prudently. This was their seventh or eighth robbery this summer. Rose was twenty-one, divorced from a first marriage, and she'd fallen out with her boy friend two months ago. Someone like Jane, a little crazy excitement, had been just what she needed. But she had no intention of doing a stretch in prison, as Jane had done, if she could help it. 'So? The Ponsonby place now?'

'Yep,' said Jane, enjoying a cigarette. For two weeks, they had made telephone calls now and then to the Ponsonby house, and no one had ever answered. Two or three times in the last week, Jane and Rose had cruised past the big house, and had not seen any sign of life. Tommy, their fence, hadn't watched the house, hadn't had the time, he said. Jane thought the people were away on vacation. It was July. Lots of people were away, with only one neighbour or maybe a cleaning woman coming in to water the plants. But had the Ponsonbys a burglar alarm, for instance? It was a very swank section. 'Maybe we ought to phone one more time,' Jane said. 'Got the number handy?'

Rose had. She stopped the car in the parking area of a roadside bar-and-steakhouse.

'You stay here, Eddie,' Jane said, sticking Eddie under a disorder of plastic shopping bags and a raincoat on the back seat. She gave him a rap with her heavily ringed fingers to let him know she meant it.

The rap caught Eddie on the top of the head. He was only slightly annoyed. The two women were back before long, before it became unpleasantly hot in the car, and they drove on for a while, then stopped again. Eddie was still sitting on the back seat, hardly conspicuous in the débris except for the white cap of fur on the crown of his head. He watched as Rose got out. This was the way things always went when he had a job to do: Rose got out first, came back, then Jane put him under her coat and took him out of the car.

Jane hummed a tune to herself and smoked a cigarette.

Rose came back and said, 'No window open and the ones in back are locked. Nobody home, because I rang the bell and knocked front and back. – What a house!' Rose meant that it looked rich. 'Maybe breaking a back window is best. Let Eddie in that way.'

The neighbourhood was residential and expensive, the lawns generous, the trees tall. Rose and Jane were parked, as usual, around the corner from the house they were interested in.

'Any sign of life in the garage?' Jane asked. They had thought that there might be a servant sleeping there without a telephone, or with a different telephone from the Ponsonbys'.

'Of course not or I'd have told you,' said Rose. 'Have you emptied the tapestry bag yet?'

Jane and Rose did this, using the old grey raincoat to wrap the lot of silverware and the other objects up in, and this they put on the back seat, without themselves leaving the front seat.

'Why don't we try Eddie down a chimney?' Jane asked. 'It's so quiet here, I don't like the idea of breaking a window.'

'But he doesn't like chimneys,' Rose said. 'This house has three storeys. Pretty long chimneys.'

Jane thought for a moment, then shrugged. 'What the hell? If he doesn't like going all the way down, he can come up again.'

'And suppose he just stays up there – on the roof?'

'So – we've lost a good monkey,' said Jane.

A few weeks ago, they had practised with Eddie at a Long Island house which belonged to a friend of Jane's. The chimney top had been only twelve feet from the ground because it was a one-storey cottage. Eddie hadn't liked going down the chimney, but he had done it two or three times, with Rose on a ladder encouraging him, and Jane waiting to give him raisins and peanuts when he unlocked the front door for her. Eddie had coughed and rubbed his eyes, and made a lot of chattering noises. They'd tried him again the next day, tossing him on to the roof and pointing to the chimney and talking to him, and he'd done it well then, had come down and opened the door. But Rose remembered the worry wrinkles around his brows that had made him look like a little old man, remembered how pleased he was when she'd given him a bath and a brushing afterward. Eddie had given her a most endearing smile and clasped her hands. So Rose hesitated, wondering about Eddie, worried about herself and Jane.

'Well?' said Jane.

'Chi-chi,' said Eddie, knowing something was up. He scratched an ear, and looked attentively from one to the other of the women. He preferred to listen to Rose, her voice being gentler, though he lived with Jane.

Things got moving, but slowly.

Jane and Rose maintained an air of calm. Rose, in case of any possible interference at the door, someone asking what was her business, was prepared to say she was offering her services as a cleaning woman for four dollars an hour. If anyone accepted, Rose gave a false name and made a date which she never kept. This had happened only once. It was Rose who kept track of the houses they had robbed, and of the one house where someone had come to the door to answer her knock, even though no one had answered the telephone in that house just five minutes before. After they had robbed a certain neighbourhood, sometimes three houses in one hour, they never went back to it. In Rose's car, they had gone as far as a hundred and fifty miles from their base, which was Jane's apartment in Red Cliff, New Jersey. If they had to separate for any reason, they had a roadside café picked out or a drugstore somewhere, as a meeting place, the one who was carless (Jane) having to make her way there by taxi or bus or on foot. This had happened also only once so far in their two months of operations, one time when Rose had been perhaps unnecessarily anxious and had driven off. Today their rendezvous was the bar-and-steakhouse where they had just been to ring the Ponsonby house.

Now Jane, with Eddie under her lightweight woollen coat, walked up the rather imposing front path of the Ponsonby mansion. Such goodies in there Jane could scarcely imagine. They'd certainly be more than she could carry away in the reticule she called her tapestry bag. Jane rang, waited, then knocked with the brass knocker, not at all expecting anyone to answer, but she had to go through the motions in case a neighbour was watching. Finally Jane went round by the driveway to the back door, with

Eddie still clinging to her under her coat. She knocked again. Everything was as quiet as could be, including the garage with its one closed window over the closed doors.

'Eddie, it's the chimney again,' Jane whispered. 'Chimney, understand? Now you go right up! See it?' She pointed. Great elm trees sheltered her from view from any side. There seemed to be at least four chimneys projecting from the roof. 'Chimney and then the door! Right, Eddie? Good boy!' She released Eddie on to a drainpipe which went up one corner of the house.

Eddie managed well, slipping a few inches here and there, but he had no trouble in getting a hold on the somewhat rough exterior brick. Suddenly he was up, for a second silhouetted against the sky, leaping, and then he vanished.

Jane saw him jump to a chimney pot, peer down, hesitate, then run to another. She was afraid to call encouragement. Were the chimneys stopped up? Well, wait and see. No use worrying yet. Jane stepped back to see better, did not see Eddie, and made her way to the front door again. She expected to hear Eddie sliding bolts, but she heard nothing at all. She rang half-heartedly, for appearance's sake.

Silence. Had Eddie got stuck in a chimney?

A passerby on the sidewalk glanced at Jane and went on, a man of about thirty, carrying a package. A car went by. Rose, in the car, was out of sight around the corner. Eddie might be stuck, Jane supposed, might have been put out of commission by soot. And the minutes were passing. Should she play it safe and leave? On the other hand, Eddie was damned useful, and there were a good two more months of summer to operate in.

Jane went to the back of the house again. She looked up at the roof, but saw no sign of Eddie. Birds cheeped. A car shifted gears in the distance. Jane went to the kitchen window at the back, and at once the monkey leapt on to the long aluminium drainboard. He was black with soot, even the top of his head was dark grey, and he rubbed his eyes with his knuckles. He tapped on a pane and hopped from one foot to the other, wanting her to open a window.

Why hadn't they trained him for windows? Well, they'd have to get on to that. Just a matter of unscrewing – even from here, Jane could see the mechanism. 'Door!' said Jane, pointing towards the kitchen door, because any door would have done, but Eddie had the habit of going to front doors.

Eddie sprang down, and Jane heard him pulling bolts.

But the door did not open. Jane tried it.

Jane heard his 'Chi-chi-chi!' which meant he was annoyed or frustrated. The bolts were stiff, Jane supposed, or it was a mortice lock, requiring a key from inside to open. And some bolts took strength beyond Eddie's. Jane felt suddenly panicky. Ten or twelve minutes had passed, she thought. Rose would be worried. Maybe Rose had already gone off to the roadside steakhouse. Jane wanted to go back to Rose and the car. The alternative was breaking a window, and she was afraid to make that much noise and still get away with Eddie on foot.

Again making an effort to appear unhurried, Jane went down the driveway to the sidewalk. Around the corner, Jane saw with relief that Rose was still waiting in the car.

'Well,' said Jane, 'Eddie can't get a door open and I'm scared. Let's take off.'

'Oh? Where is he? He's still *in*?'

'In the kitchen in back.' Jane was whispering through the car's open window. She opened the door on her side.

'But we can't just leave him there,' Rose said. 'Did you see anybody – watching you?'

Jane got in and closed the door. 'No, but let's get going.'

Rose was thinking the police might connect a monkey with the robberies they'd done. How could anyone explain a monkey in a closed house? Of course, anyone who found Eddie might not at once telephone the police, might just give him to the S.P.C.A. or a zoo. Or mightn't Eddie break a window and escape – and then what? Rose realized she wasn't thinking logically, but it seemed to her that they ought to get Eddie out. 'Can't we break a back window?' Rose's hand was already on the door handle.

'No, don't!' Jane made a negative gesture, but Rose was already gone. Jane sat rigid. She'd get the blame if someone saw Rose breaking in. Rose would talk, Jane thought. And Jane had the police record.

Rose was forcing herself to walk slowly past a young man and a girl who were arm in arm, talking and laughing. The Ponsonby house. It was so grand, it had a name: Five Owls. Rose went into the driveway, still calm but not wanting to go through the motions of ringing the front doorbell, because she did not want to waste the time.

Eddie was in the kitchen, squatting on a table (she saw him through a side window), shaking something that looked like a sugar bowl upside down, and she had a brief impression of something broken, like a platter, on the yellow linoleum floor. Eddie must be desperate. By the time Rose came round the corner of the house, Eddie was on the drainboard just behind the back windows. Rose made an effort to raise a window and gave it up. She extricated a cuff of her white trousers from a rosebush. Almost at her feet, she found a rock the size of her fist, and tapped it once against a rectangular pane. She struck again at some jagged pieces of glass at the edges, but Eddie was already through, chattering with joy.

Rose gathered him quickly under her jacket, and walked into the driveway. She could feel Eddie trembling, maybe with relief. When Rose reached the corner, she saw that the car had gone. *Her* car. She'd have to find a taxi. Or walk to the roadhouse. No, that was too far. A taxi. And she'd left her handbag with her money in the car. Christ! She pressed Eddie's body reassuringly, and walked on, looking for some promising intersection where a taxi might be cruising. Where was Jane? Back at her own apartment? At the roadside place? What was the taxi driver going to say if she had no money to pay him? Rose couldn't tell the driver to go to the house of one of her friends, because she didn't want any of her friends to know about Eddie, about Jane, about what she'd been doing for the last weeks.

She had no luck spotting a taxi. But she did come to a shopping centre – supermarket, dry cleaning shop, drugstore, all that – and she had some coins in her jacket pocket so she went into the drugstore. With Eddie holding on under her jacket, Rose looked up a taxi company and dialled. The shopping centre was called Miracle Buy. She gave that name.

In about five minutes, a taxi arrived. Rose had been standing on a little cement island in the parking area, keeping a lookout for the taxi, because taxis weren't always painted in bright colours in neighbourhoods like this.

'Can you drive to Red Cliff, please? Corner of Jefferson Avenue and Mulhouse.'

They were off. Seventeen miles at least, Rose supposed. She didn't think Jane would have driven to the steakhouse, or have been able to find it. Jane wasn't a good driver. But she could have found her way home, and probably had. Rose had a key to Jane's apartment, but that was in her handbag too.

The taxi reached Jefferson and Mulhouse.

'Can you wait one minute? I want to speak to a friend, then I'll be back.'

'How soon?' asked the driver, looking around at Rose. His eyes moved over her, and Rose could see that he thought she had no pocket-book, therefore no money. 'What you got there, a *monkey*?'

Eddie had stuck an arm, then his head out of Rose's jacket before she could push him back. 'Friend's pet,' Rose said. 'I'm delivering him. Then I'll be down and pay you.' Rose got out.

Rose didn't see her own car. There were lots of cars parked at the kerbs. She rang Jane's bell, one of four bells in the small apartment building. She rang again, three short rings, one long, which was her ring by agreement with Jane, and to Rose's great relief, the release button sounded. Rose climbed the stairs, and knocked on a door on the third floor.

'It's Rose!' she said.

Jane opened the door, looking a bit frightened, and Rose went in.

'Here's Eddie. Take him. I need some money for the taxi. Give me twenty or thirty – or hand me my bag.'

'Anything happen? Anybody following you?'

'No. Where's some money? You brought my bag up?'

Eddie had scampered on to the sofa, and was sitting on his haunches, scratching his sooty head.

Rose went down with her handbag, and paid the driver. He said the fare was twenty-seven, though he had no meter, and Rose gave him three tens. 'Thanks very much!' Rose said with a smile.

'Right!' He drove off.

Rose didn't want to go back to Jane's, but she felt she had to say something. Make a speech and end it, she thought, and now was as good a time as any, and thank God, the taxi driver hadn't said anything more about Eddie. Rose gave her special ring again.

'What happened with the silverware?' Rose asked.

'Tommy just took it. I called him right away. – I'm sorry I got scared back there, Rosey dear, but I *did*. Breaking a window is nuts!'

Rose was relieved that Tommy had come and gone. He was a skinny, red-haired man with a stutter, inefficient looking, but so far he'd never made a mistake that Rose knew of. 'Don't forget to give Eddie a bath, will you?' Rose said.

'You always like to do that. Go ahead. – Don't you want a coffee? It's easy.'

'I'm leaving.' Rose hadn't sat down. 'I'm sorry, Jane, but I think I'd better pull out. You said yourself – I did the wrong thing today, breaking a window.'

Jane looked at Rose, braced her hands on her hips, and glanced at Eddie on the sofa.

Eddie was nervously examining the nails of his nearly hairless left hand.

'If something happened,' Jane said, 'it's better if you tell me. I'm the one who has to face it.'

'Nothing *happened*. I just want to quit and – I don't want any share of today's, thanks. I'll—You left the keys in my car? Where is the car?'

'What happened with the taxi driver?'

'Nothing! I paid him and that was that.'

'He saw Eddie?'

'Well, yes. I said he was a pet I was delivering. I'll be off, Jane. – Bye, Eddie.' Rose felt compelled to cross the room and to touch Eddie's head.

Eddie glanced up sadly, as if he had understood every word, and began nibbling his nails.

Rose moved towards the door. 'Don't forget to bathe him. He'll be happier.'

'To *hell* with him!' said Jane.

Rose went down the stairs, as scared and shaky as she'd ever felt ringing somebody's doorbell, or waiting in the car while Jane did her job. She'd ring up Hank. Hank White his name was, living somewhere in Greenwich Village. She hoped she could dig up the number somehow, because she didn't think it was listed under his name, and she might have to ring other people to get it. He'd come, if it concerned Eddie. She realized she was worried about Eddie. And Hank was the only person she could tell this to, because Jane kept Eddie hidden from her friends, kept him in a locked closet when anyone came (even Tommy), and spanked him later if he'd chattered. Rose found her car finally. The keys were in the dashboard. She drove towards her home, which was an apartment in a town about eight miles away.

Jane washed her face and combed her curly, blonde-rinsed hair by way of pulling herself together, but it didn't help. She picked up a paperback book and flung it at Eddie in a backhanded gesture. It caught Eddie in the side.

'*Ik-ik!*' Eddie cried, and leapt a couple of inches into the air. He turned a puzzled face towards Jane, and braced himself to jump to one side or the other, in case Jane tried to strike him again.

'You'll damn well stay in your closet *tonight*!' said Jane, advancing. 'Starting now!'

Eddie wriggled easily from her outstretched hands, and leapt to the frame of a picture over the sofa.

The picture fell, Eddie landed on the sofa again, and seized an icebag that had been lying there for some time. He hurled the icebag at Jane. It fell short. '*Chi-chi-chi-chi-chi!*' Eddie chattered without stopping, and his round eyes had gone wide and pink at the outer edges.

Jane was determined to catch him and stick him away. Suppose the cops for some reason suddenly knocked on the door? Or broke in? What kind of trail had that dumb Rose left behind? All Rose had to her credit was a nice face and a fast car. Jane picked up the end of the madras counterpane that covered the sofa, intending to throw it over Eddie and capture him, but Eddie leapt to the centre of the room. Jane pulled the counterpane all the way off and advanced with it.

Eddie threw an ashtray at close range and hit Jane in the cheek with it. The ashtray fell and broke on the floor.

Jane got angrier.

Now Eddie was on the drainboard in the kitchenette, brandishing a paring knife, chattering and squeaking. He picked up half a lemon and threw it.

'You little *insect*!' Jane muttered, coming towards him with the counterpane. She had him cornered now.

Eddie dove straight for Jane, landed with four feet on her left arm, and bit her thumb. He had dropped the knife.

Jane cried out. Her thumb began to bleed, the blood oozed and dripped. She picked up a straight chair. She'd kill the little devil!

Eddie dodged the chair and at once attacked Jane's legs from behind, nipped into one calf and sprang away.

'Ow!' Jane yelled, more with surprise than pain. She hadn't even seen him go behind her. She looked at her injury and saw that he'd drawn blood again. She'd fix *him!* She closed the one open window so he couldn't escape, and went for the paring knife on the floor. She felt inspired to sink it into his neck.

Eddie jumped on to her bent back, on to the back of her head, and Jane toppled over. She hurt her elbow slightly, and before she could get up, Eddie had bitten her nose. Jane touched her nose to see if it was still all there.

And Eddie dived for the door knob. He supported himself on one hind leg, and worked at the top bolt, turning the little knob. If he could turn the big knob at the same time, the door would open with a pull, but he had to abandon his effort when he heard Jane's steps close behind him. Eddie sprang down just as the knife point grated against the metal door.

'*Chi-chi!*'

Jane had dropped the knife. Eddie picked it up, ran up Jane's hip and shoulder and struck her in the cheek with the knife point. He used the knife as he had seen people do, sometimes with stabbing motions, sometimes sawing, and then suddenly he flung the knife away and leapt from Jane's shoulder to a bookcase, panting and chattering. Eddie smelled blood, and this frightened him. Nervously Eddie threw a book at Jane, which came nowhere near hitting her.

Jane was aware of blood running down her neck. Absurd that she couldn't catch the little beast! For an instant, she felt that she couldn't breathe, that she was going to faint, then she took a deep breath and gathered her strength.

Plock! A book hit Jane on the chest.

Well, well! One swat with a chair would do for Eddie!

Jane reached for the straight chair which had fallen on its side. When she had it in position to swing, Eddie was not

165

on the bookcase. Jane felt his fast little feet going up her back, started to turn, and had a glimpse of Eddie with the counterpane in his hands, climbing over her head with it. Jane lost her balance and fell, stumbling against the chair that she was lowering.

Eddie skipped from one side of the hump on the floor to the other, pulling the thin cloth over his enemy. He seized the nearest object – a conch shell from the floor near the hall door – and took a grip with both hands. He came down with this on the woman's slightly moving head under the counterpane. Eddie slipped and rolled over, but he kept his fingers in the crease of the shell, and struck again with it. The *crack* was a satisfying sound to Eddie. *Crack! Crack!* He heard a dreary moan from the heap.

Then for no reason, as he had dropped the knife for no reason, Eddie dropped the conch shell on the carpet and gave it a nervous kick with a hind foot. He allowed himself a few chatters, and peered about as if to see if someone else were in the room with him.

He heard only the *tick-tick-tick* of the clock in the bedroom beyond the hall. He was aware of the blood smell again, and withdrew some distance from the counterpane. Eddie sighed, exhausted. He loped to the window, fiddled with it for an instant, and gave it up. It had to be raised, and it was heavy.

It was growing darker.

The telephone rang. There flitted across Eddie's mind the familiar image of Jane or someone picking up the telephone, talking into it. Once Eddie had been told or allowed to do this, and he had dropped the telephone, and people had laughed. Now Eddie felt fearful and hostile towards the telephone, towards the hump on the floor. He kept looking to see if the hump stirred. It did not. He was thirsty. Eddie leapt to the drainboard, looked around and felt for a glass of water or anything with liquid in it, which he always smelled before drinking, but he saw no such thing. Using both hands, he turned a tap and cupped one hand and drank. He made a perfunctory effort to turn the tap off, didn't quite succeed, and left it trickling.

The telephone stopped ringing.

Then Eddie opened the refrigerator – a little uncomfortably because he had been scolded and slapped for this – and seeing no fruit in the lighted interior, scooped a handful of cooked stringbeans from a bowl and started to nibble them, kicked the door shut with a hind foot, and loped off on three legs. He felt at once tired, flung the beans down, and jumped into a rocking chair to sleep.

When the doorbell rang, Eddie was curled in the seat of the rocking chair. He lifted his head. The room was quite dark.

Suddenly Eddie wanted to flee. The smell of blood was uglier. He could open the front door and go, he realized, unless the woman had put on the special lock which required a set of jingling keys to open. She kept the keys hidden. Eddie had succeeded only once with a key, somewhere, for fun, with Jane and Rose. Keys were usually too stiff for him to turn.

Buzz-buzz.

It was the downstairs bell, different from the apartment door which gave a *ting*. Eddie was not interested in the bell, he simply wanted to escape now. He sprang to the doorknob again, and seized the smaller knob above with his left hand. It turned, but the door did not open. Eddie tried again, turning the doorknob also with his feet. Then he pushed the door jamb, and the door swung towards him. Eddie leapt down and loped silently down the stairs, swinging himself out at the turnings by one of the balusters. Downstairs the door was easier – he thought – and he could also slip out when the next person came in.

Eddie jumped up to the round white knob, slipped, and then tried turning it while standing on his hind feet. The door opened.

'Eddie! *Ed*-die! *What* the—'

Eddie knew the voice. '*Chi-chi!*' Eddie jumped on to

Hank's arm, flung himself against Hank's chest, chattering madly, and feeling that he had a long and desperate story to tell. '*Aieeee!*' Eddie was even inventing new words.

'What's goin' on, eh?' Hank said softly, coming in. 'Where's Jane?' He glanced up the stairs. He closed the door, settled Eddie more securely inside his leather jacket, and climbed the stairs two at a time.

Jane's door was ajar and there was no light on.

'Jane?' he called, and knocked once. Then he went in. 'Jane? – Where's the light here, Eddie boy?' Hank groped, and after a few seconds, found a lightswitch. He heard footsteps coming down from the next floor, and instinctively he closed the door. Something was wrong here. He looked around at Jane's living-room in astonishment. He'd been here before, but only once. 'What the hell happened?' he whispered to himself. The place was a shambles. A robbery, he thought. They'd dumped the stuff in the middle of the floor and intended to come back.

Hank moved towards the heap on the floor. He pulled the madras cover back slowly.

'Holy cow! – Holy *cow*!'

Eddie flattened himself against Hank's sweater and closed his eyes, terrified and wanting to hide.

'Jane?' Hank touched her shoulder, thinking maybe she'd fainted, or been knocked out. He tried to turn her over, and found that her body was a bit stiff and not at all warm. Her face, her neck were dark red with blood. Hank blinked and straightened up. 'Anybody else here?' he called towards the next room, more boldly than he felt.

He knew there was no one else here. Slowly it dawned on him that Eddie had killed Jane with his little teeth, maybe with – Hank was looking at a kitchen knife a few feet away on the floor. Then he saw the cream-and-pink coloured conch shell. 'Get down, Eddie,' he whispered. But Eddie wouldn't be dislodged from the sweater.

Hank picked up the knife, then the shell. He washed them both at the sink in the kitchenette, and saw a faint pinkness run off the shell. He turned the shell upside down, and shook the water out of it. He dried it thoroughly with a dishtowel. He did the same with the knife. Jane must have attacked Eddie. Hadn't Rose hinted as much? 'We're gettin' out, Eddie! Yes, sir, yes, sir!'

Then Eddie heard the comforting sound of the zipper that closed Hank's jacket all the way up. They were going down the stairs now.

Hank had not forgotten to wipe the doorknobs when he left Jane's apartment, and he had made sure the door locked behind him in a normal way. Hank had thought to telephone the police at once, when he'd been in Jane's apartment, then had thought to telephone them later once he got Eddie home safely. But he didn't. He wasn't even going to telephone Rose. Rose wouldn't want any part of it, and Hank knew she could be trusted to keep her mouth shut. The body would be found soon enough, was Hank's opinion, and he didn't want Eddie blamed for it. The police, if he'd rung, would have asked him what he knew about it, and they'd have found out somehow about Eddie, even if Hank had tried to hide him.

So Hank bided his time in Perry Street, Greenwich Village, where he shared an apartment with two young men, and two days later, he caught an item in a newspaper saying that Jane Garrity, aged forty-two, unemployed secretary, had been found dead in her apartment in Red Cliff, New Jersey, victim of an attack by an unknown assailant or assailants, maybe even children, because her wounds and blows had not been severe. The actual cause of death had been a heart attack.

The police would know Jane's record, Hank thought, and the company she kept. Let them worry about it. Hank reproached himself for having given Eddie to Rose, but she'd been fond of Eddie, and Hank had felt a bit guilty when he and Rose and broken up. But now that he had Eddie back, Hank was not going to part with him. Eddie showed no further interest in opening doors, because he was happy where he was. He had a small room to himself, with ropes to swing on, a basket bed, no door at all, and one of Hank's friends, a sculptor, constructed something like a tree for Eddie in the living-room. Hank began writing a rather long epic poem about Eddie, whose life story was to be veiled, metamorphosed, allegorized. *The Conqueror Monkey*. Only Hank and Eddie knew the truth.

Hamsters *vs* Websters

THE circumstances under which Julian and Betty Webster and their ten-year-old son Laurence acquired a country house, a dog, and hamsters, were most sudden and unexpected for the family, and yet it all hung together.

One afternoon in his air-conditioned Philadelphia office Julian suffered a heart attack. He had pain, he sank to the floor, and he was whisked to a hospital. When he had recovered some five days later, his doctor gave him a serious talk. Julian would have to stop smoking, reduce his working hours to six or less per day, and a country atmosphere would be better for him than living in an apartment in Philadelphia. Julian was shocked. He was only thirty-seven, he pointed out.

'You don't realize how you've been driving yourself,' the doctor replied calmly, smiling. 'I've spoken with your wife. She's willing to make the change. She cares about your health, even if you don't.'

Julian was of course won over. He loved Betty. He could see that the doctor's advice was reasonable. And Larry was hopping with joy. They were going to have a real country house with land, trees, space – a lot better than the silly paved playground of the big apartment building, which was all Larry could remember, since his family had moved there when he was five.

The Websters found a two-storey white house with four gable windows and an acre and a half of land, seventeen miles from Philadelphia. Julian would not even have to drive to his office. His firm had changed his job from that of sales manager to sales consultant, which Julian realized was another way of saying travelling salesman. But his salary remained the same. Olympian Pool built swimming pools of all sizes, shapes and colours, heated and unheated, and also provided vacuum and filter cleaning devices, purifiers, sprays and bubble-makers, and all kinds of diving boards. And Julian, he realized himself, made a good impression as salesman. His appointments were follow-ups of responses to mailed advertisements, so he was sure of being received. Julian was not high pressure. His manner was quiet and sincere, and he didn't mind disclosing difficulties and extra expenses from the start, if he saw that there were going to be any. Julian chewed his reddish brown moustache, pondered, and expressed his opinion with the air of a man who was thinking out loud about his own problems.

Now, Julian got up at eight, strolled around his garden-in-progress, breakfasted on tea and a soft-boiled egg instead of coffee and cigarettes, looked at the newspaper and worked the crossword – all according to doctor's orders – before departing in his car around ten. He was due home around four, and that was the end of his day. Meanwhile, Betty measured windows for curtains, bought extra rugs, and happily took care of all the details that were necessary to make a new, bigger house a home. Larry had changed schools and was getting along well. It was the month of March. Larry wanted a dog. And there were rabbit warrens in an outhouse on the property. Couldn't he have rabbits?

'Rabbits breed so,' said Julian. 'What'll we do with them unless we sell them, and we don't want to start that. Let's get a dog, Larry.'

The Websters went to a pet shop in their nearest town with the idea of inquiring about a kennel where they could buy a terrier or German shepherd puppy, but in the pet shop there were such splendid looking basset puppies, that Betty and Larry decided they had found what they wanted.

'Very healthy!' said the woman of the shop, fondling a floppy-eared, brown and white puppy in her arms.

That was obvious. The puppy grinned and slavered and wriggled in his loose hound's skin, which was so ready to fill out with the aid of Puppy-Spruce, Grow-Pup, dogbone-shaped biscuits and vitamins, all of which Julian bought in the shop.

'Look at these, Pop!' Larry said, pointing to some hamsters in a cage. 'They're smaller than rabbits. They could live in the little *rooms* we've got.'

Julian and Betty agreed to buy two hamsters. Only two, and they were so darling with their soft, clean fur, their innocent, inquisitive eyes, their twitching noses.

'All that space should be filled a little bit!' said Betty. She was as happy as Larry with the day's purchases.

Larry absorbed what the pet shop woman told him about hamsters. They should be kept warm at night, they ate cereals and grains of all kinds, and greenery such as carrots and turnips. They were nocturnal, and did not like direct sunlight. Larry installed his two in one of the cubicles in the rabbit warren. There were six such cubicles, three above, three below. He provided water and a pan of bread, plus a bowl of sweet corn from a tin he had found in the kitchen. He found an empty shoe box, which he filled with old rags, and this would be the hamsters' bedroom, he hoped. What to name them? Tom and Jerry? No, they were male and female. Jack and Jill? Too juvenile. Adam and Eve? Larry thought he would decide on names later. He could tell the male, because of a black patch between his ears.

Then there was the puppy. The puppy ate, peed, slept, and then awakened to play at two in the morning the first night. Everyone woke up, because the puppy had quit his box by the radiator and scratched at Larry's door.

'I *love* him!' said Larry, half asleep, rolling on the floor in pyjamas with the puppy in his arms.

'Oh, Julian,' said Betty, collapsing into her husband's

arms. 'What a wonderful day! Isn't this better than city life?'

Julian smiled, and kissed his wife on the forehead. It was better. Julian was happy. But he didn't want to make a speech about it. He'd had a tough time quitting cigarettes, and now he was putting on weight. If it wasn't one thing, it was another.

Larry, in his big room all his own, browsed in the Encyclopaedia Britannica on the subject of hamsters. He learned that they were of the order *Cricetus frumentarius*, belonging to the mouse-tribe *Muridae*. They made burrows some six feet deep which were vertical and sinuous. This burrow might have three or four chambers, in the deepest of which would be hidden the grain which the hamsters stored for the winter. Males and females and the young had separate rooms for sleeping. And when the young were only three weeks old, they were thrust from the parental burrow to fend for themselves. A female might have a dozen offspring at a time, and from twenty-five to fifty during her fertile eight months of the year. At six weeks, the female was ready for pregnancy. For four months of the year, or during winter, the hamsters hibernated, and fed upon the grain they had stored in their burrow. Among their enemies were owls and men who, at least in times past, had dug up their burrows in order to get at the grain the hamsters had stored.

'A dozen babies at a time!' said Larry to himself, astounded. A thought of selling them to his school chums crossed his mind, and just as quickly vanished. It was more pleasant to dream about a dozen tiny hamsters covering the floor of the three-foot by three-foot warren where his two now were. Probably they could fill all the six warrens before hibernation time.

Hardly six weeks had passed, when Larry looked into the barred front of the warren, and saw ten tiny hamsters suckling or trying to at the nether part of the female, whom Larry had named Gloria. Larry had just come home

176

from school on the yellow bus. He let his book satchel fall to the ground, and he pressed his face close to the bars.

'Golly! – Gosh! Ten – no, *eleven*!' Larry went running to tell the news. 'Hey, Mama!'

Betty was upstairs hemming a counterpane on the sewing machine. She came down to admire the hamster babies to please Larry. 'Aren't they adorable! Like little white mice!'

The following morning, there were only nine in the warren, which Larry had carefully barricaded with newspaper to a height of eight inches behind the bars, so the little ones could not fall out. Where had the other two gone? Then he remembered, with a twinge of horror, that the Encyclopaedia Britannica had said that the mother hamster often ate inferior or sickly babies. Larry supposed that that was what had happened.

Julian came home at 4.30, and Larry dragged him out to show him the little ones.

'That's awfully quick. Isn't it?' said Julian. He was not much surprised, as hamsters were related to rabbits after all, but he wanted to say the right thing to his son. Julian's mind just then was on a swimming pool, and he strolled out with his briefcase still under his arm to take another look at his lawn.

Larry followed him, thinking that the lawn would offer an ample burrowing area for his hamsters and their off-spring when winter rolled around – a long time away as yet. It would surely be better for the hamsters to hibernate in the ground than in straw in the brick warrens. They should have the right to store their grain supplies, as it said in the Encyclopaedia. The basset puppy had loped out to join Larry, and Larry scratched the top of the puppy's head, while trying to pay attention to his father.

'. . . or a nice pale blue pool, Larry my boy? What shape? Kidney shape? Boomerang? Clover?'

'Boomerang!' said Larry, pleased by the word at the moment.

Julian wanted to put in his order at once with his

company. Olympian Pool was terribly busy in the spring and summer months, and far from getting priority as an employee, Julian knew he might have to wait a bit. Olympian boasted of being able to create a swimming pool in a week. Julian hoped he could get one while there was still some summer left.

Larry had brought a few of his chums to his house for milk and cookies after school, and to show them his hamsters. The little ones were now a bigger attraction. A couple of the kids wanted to pick the little ones up, which Larry permitted, after separating the mother. Larry picked the mother up by the back of the neck, as his books advised.

'Your mother doesn't mind the babies?' asked Larry Carstairs, in a guarded way.

'Why should she?' Larry said. 'They're my pets. I take care of them.'

Eddie glanced over his shoulder, as if to see if Larry's mother might be coming. 'I'll give you more if you want. My parents want me to get rid of 'em. But my father doesn't feel like drowning 'em, you see? Well – if you want them—'

It was settled in a trice. The next afternoon, Eddie came on his bicycle around 4 p.m. with a cardboard carton on the handlebars. He had ten baby hamsters for Larry, of two different litters so they were not exactly the same age, plus three adult hamsters, two of which had orange spots, which Larry thought quite beautiful, since they introduced a new colour to his hamster warren. Eddie was furtive.

'You don't have to worry,' Larry said. 'My mother won't mind.'

'You never know. Wait and see,' said Eddie, and he declined politely to come in for milk and apple pie.

Larry released two of the adult hamsters in the garden, and watched with pleasure as they nosed their way about in their new freedom, sniffing irises, nibbling grass, moving on. Mr Johnson, the basset puppy, loped out just then, and started to chase one of the hamsters who at once disappeared into the lavender bushes, baffling Mr Johnson. Larry laughed.

A couple of days later, Betty noticed the new babies in two more warrens. 'Where'd they come from?'

Larry sensed a faint disapproval. 'Oh, one of the kids in school. I said I had room. And – well, you know I'm good at taking care of them.'

'That you are. – All right, Larry, this once. But we don't want too many, do we? All these are going to produce more, you know.'

Larry nodded politely. His thoughts swam. His status had risen at school because he could take on hamsters and knew a lot about them, and on his own property he had the warrens that hamsters needed, not some old crate or cardboard box. Another thought of Larry's was that he could release adults or even young hamsters from the age of three weeks onward whenever he wished in the garden. For the time being, he intended to be an outlet for hamsters among his friends. At least four of his schoolmates kept hamsters and had too many.

Three men arrived one afternoon with Larry's father to look over the lawn in regard to a swimming pool. Larry followed at a distance, keeping an eye on certain hamster burrow exits which he knew, and which he had concealed by discreet heaps of leaves and twigs. Some burrow outlets were obvious, however, and he had heard his father say, 'Damned *moles*!' once to his mother. His father was supposed to jog twice around the lawn every morning, but did not always do it.

Now a workman in blue overalls and with a tape measure sank into a burrow up to his ankle, and laughed. 'Moles'll help us out a little, don't you think, Julian? Looks like they've got it half dug already!'

'Ha-ha!' said Julian, to be friendly. He was talking to another workman about the boomerang shape, telling him at which point he wanted the outer arc of it. 'And don't forget with the excess soil, my wife and I want to create a kind of hill – a rock garden eventually, you know. Over there.' He pointed to a spot between him and a pear tree. 'I know it's on the blueprint, George, but it's so much clearer when you can see the land in front of your eyes.'

That was in late May. Larry now had a second litter from his original hamsters. The remaining single hamster was a female, and she soon had a litter by the original male, whom Larry had named Pirate, because of the black patch on his head. Larry thought if he held down his warren population to about twenty – three adults and a dozen or more little ones – his parents wouldn't complain. Since the hamsters were nocturnal, no one ever saw the garden hamsters in day-time, not even Larry. But he knew they were making burrows and doing all right, because he could see the burrow exits in various places in the lawn and garden, and could see that the grass seed, the corn kernels, also the peanuts that he put out in the afternoon were gone by the next day. Larry now had a bicycle, didn't have to take the school bus, and he spent much of his three dollars a week allowance on hamster food bought after school at the village grocery, which had a pet food section.

All that stored away! Or maybe eaten at once, Larry thought, because surely it was early to start saving for winter. He knew the garden was full of three-week-olds. Larry was tempted to demand twenty-five cents for every hamster he took on from his school chums and ten cents for a baby, to help pay for food, but he resisted. Larry in his fantasy imagined himself the protector of hamsters, the friend who gave them a happier life than the one they had known before, when they lived in cramped boxes.

'Hamster Heaven!' Larry said to himself as July rolled around. It was vacation time. Two litters had just been born in the warren. And maybe more were being born underground? Larry believed so. He imagined the burrows according to the Encyclopaedia's description: six feet deep and winding. How fascinating to know that the very ground he stood on was being used by families and their offspring as shelter and storage place, safe bedrooms – *home!* And no one could tell it from looking at the ground. What a good thing his father had stopped jogging, Larry thought, because even Larry sank in now and then if he stepped on a burrow entrance unawares. His father, being heavier, would sink in more, and might set about getting rid of the hamsters – even if his father still thought they were moles. Larry congratulated himself that his rather furtive feeding of the garden hamsters was paying off.

However, this same fact caused Larry to tell a lie, which weighed a bit on his conscience. It happened thus:

His mother remarked in the kitchen one afternoon, 'There aren't so many as I thought there'd be by this time. To tell you the truth, I'm glad, Larry. So much easier—'

'I've given a few away to kids at school,' Larry said, interrupting in his haste, and feeling awful at once.

'Oh, *I* see. I thought something was a little out of the ordinary about them.' Betty laughed. 'I was reading about them, and it seems they fight moles – destroy them. It might be a good idea if we put a couple in the garden. What do you think, Larry? Can you bear to part with a pair or two?'

Larry's slightly freckled face almost split with his smile. 'I think the hamsters would like that.'

After that, in a matter of ten days, things happened with lightning speed, or so it seemed to Larry. For a while, he was lying on his bed in his room, reading books propped on a pillow in lovely sunlight. His hamsters in the warren were plump and happy. Larry's father was looking forward to the last week in July and the first two weeks in August for his vacation, and Larry had learned that they were going to stay home this summer, because there was a river to fish in not far away, and a little gardening would be good exercise for Julian, his doctor had said. All was bliss, until the swimming pool men arrived in the last week in July.

They came early, around 7 a.m. Larry awakened at the noise of their two big trucks, and watched everything from his window. They were driving a bulldozer on to the lawn! Larry heard his father and mother talking in the hall, then Julian went downstairs and trotted on to the lawn. Larry saw it happen: his father's left foot sank suddenly, and he fell in a twisted way.

Then Julian gave a moan of pain.

One of the workmen took Julian gently by the shoulders. Julian was seated on the grass. Betty ran out. Julian was not getting up. Betty ran back to the house.

Then a doctor arrived. Julian was lying on the downstairs sofa, grimacing with pain, pale in the face.

'Do you think it's broken?' Betty asked the doctor.

'I don't think so, but we'd better take an X-ray. I've got some crutches in the car. I'll get them, and if your husband can just manage to get to my car . . .'

The bulldozer was already humming, groaning, stabbing at the lawn. Larry was more worried about his hamster burrows than about his father.

Julian was back in less than two hours, on crutches, his left foot thickly bandaged and with a metal bar underneath it to walk on when his ankle became better. And he was in a furious temper.

'That lawn is honeycombed!' Julian said to Betty and also Larry, who was in the kitchen having a second breakfast of milk and doughnuts. 'The workmen say they're hamsters, not moles!'

'Well, the digging, darling – the excavation will at least scare some of them off,' Betty said soothingly.

Julian focused his glare on his son. 'It's quite plain, Larry, you've been putting your hamsters right in the garden. You didn't tell us. Therefore you *lied*. You didn't—'

'But I didn't *lie*,' Larry interrupted in panic, because 'lie' was his father's most awful word. 'No one asked me about the – the—' Larry was on his feet, trembling.

'You led your mother to think, which is the same as

lying, that the two you released in the garden recently were the only two. This is patently untrue, since the lawn is full of holes and tunnels and God knows *what*!'

'Darling, don't get excited,' Betty said, fearing another heart attack. 'There are ways – even if there are a lot of holes and things. Exterminators.'

'You're damned right!' said Julian. 'And I'm going to call them up now!' He went off on his crutches in the direction of the telephone.

'Julian, *I'll* call them,' Betty said. 'Have a rest. You're probably still in pain.'

Julian wouldn't be dissuaded. Larry watched, breathing shallowly. He'd never seen his father quite so angry. *Exterminators.* That meant deadly poison, probably. Maybe men stood out there with clubs and hit the hamsters as they ran from their burrows. Larry wet his lips. Should he try to scare a few out now, and catch them, put them back in the warrens where it was safe? How many burrows with little ones were the pool men killing this very minute?

Larry looked out of the kitchen window. The bulldozer had already made a beginning on one wing of the boomerang shape, and was working now on the second wing, as if marking the land out. But not a hamster was in sight. Larry looked everywhere, even at the edges of the garden. He imagined his hamsters cringing far below in the earth, wondering what was causing all the reverberations. But they'd be only six feet below, and the pool would definitely be twelve feet deep in some places.

'*God damn the whole batch of 'em!*' Julian said in a voice like thunder, and crashed the telephone down.

Larry held his breath and listened.

'Darling, one said he could come possibly tomorrow. Call that one back,' said Betty.

Larry escaped out of the kitchen door, intending to watch the workmen, and to try to save some hamsters if he could. For this reason, he detoured and went to the toolhouse for an empty carton. When Larry reached the excavation, he was just in time to see the big toothed scoop rise with a load of earth, swing and dump it exactly on a spot where Larry knew there was a hamster exit. Larry seethed with helpless fury. He wanted to cry out and stop them. Fortunately the hamsters always had a second exit, Larry reminded himself.

His sense of reassurance was brief. When he looked into the hole the bulldozer was digging, he saw part of a burrow exposed as cleanly as if someone had taken a knife and cut downward, as in the Encyclopaedia diagram. And there at the bottom were three or four little ones – visible, barely four feet under, wriggling! Where were the hamster parents?

'Stop!' Larry yelled in a shrill voice, waving his arms at the man up in the orange bulldozer. 'There're animals *alive* there!'

The bulldozer man might not have heard him. The great jaw swung again and struck at a point lower than the baby hamsters' chamber.

'What's the matter, sonny?' asked a workman who had walked up beside Larry. 'There're plenty more of those, I can tell you!'

'But these are pets!' Larry said.

The man shook his head. 'Your father's plenty fed up with 'em, you know. Lawn's full of 'em! Just look. Now don't cry, kid! If we kill a few, you've got a hundred more around here!' He turned away before Larry could straighten up and assure the man he was not crying.

The rest of the day was a shambles. Julian was again on the telephone during the time the workmen stopped for lunch. Larry went out with his empty cardboard box to try to rescue a few hamsters, adults or babies, and didn't find a single one. Betty made a simple lunch, and Julian was still too upset to eat more than a bite. He was talking about getting at the hamsters himself, sticking burning brands down their holes, the way the farmers used to do with mole holes in Massachusetts where he'd been brought up.

'But Julian, the exterminators—' Betty glanced at her son. 'They'll probably be able to come in a few days. Friday, they said. You mustn't get excited over nothing. It's bad for you.'

'I'm damned well going to have a cigarette!' Julian said, and got up, dropped a crutch, picked it up, and made his way to the telephone table, where there were always cigarettes in a box.

Betty had cut her smoking down to five a day, which she smoked when Julian wasn't with her. Now she sighed, and glanced at Larry, who looked down at his plate.

His father, Larry thought, was mainly furious because he hadn't been able to smoke for the last several months, because the doctor had made him work shorter hours – little things like that. How could anyone get so angry just over hamsters? It was absurd. Larry said, 'Excuse me,' and left the table.

He went upstairs and wept on his bed. He knew it wouldn't last long, and it felt good to weep and get it over with. He was feeling a bit sleepy, when the sound of the bulldozer jolted him alert. They were at it again. His hamsters! Larry ran downstairs, with an idea of again trying, with his cardboard box, to save any refugee hamsters. He almost bumped into Julian who was coming in the kitchen door.

'Betty, you wouldn't believe it!' said Julian to his wife who was at the sink. 'There's not a square foot of that damned lawn that isn't undermined! Larry – Larry, you take the cake for destroying property! Your *own* property!'

'Julian, please!' Betty said.

'I can't understand why you hadn't noticed it!' Julian said to her. 'I can poke one of these crutches – *any* place and it sinks!'

'Well, I don't go around poking crutches!' Betty came back, but she was really wondering if she could get one of her tranquillizers (ancient pills, she hadn't taken one in at least two years) down Julian, or should she simply ring the doctor, their family doctor? Suppose he had another heart attack? 'Darling, would you take one of my Libriums?'

'No!' said Julian. 'I haven't time!' He turned on his crutches and went out again.

Larry went timidly out, drifted towards his hamster warrens, and felt a warm, happy relief at seeing Pirate and Gloria munching away at their bowl of wheat grain, and seven or eight young hamsters asleep in the hay.

'Hey there, Larry!' called his father. 'Gather some firewood, would you? Twigs! From anywhere!'

Larry took a deep breath, hating it, hating his father. His father was going to try to smoke the hamsters out. Larry obeyed with leaden feet, picking up twigs from under hedges and rose bushes, until after five minutes or so Julian yelled at him to move a little faster. Larry's mother had come out, and Larry heard her vaguely protesting, and then she too was recruited for his father's awful work. Betty took stakes from the toolhouse, stakes that had been destined for tomato plants, Larry knew.

As Larry advanced towards the barbecue grill on the terrace, he caught sight of something that made him freeze, then smile. A pair of hamsters stood on their hind legs in the laurel, chattering as if talking to each other, and in an anxious way.

'Larry, take that stuff to the grill!' Julian called, and Larry moved.

When Larry looked again, the hamsters were not there. Had he imagined them? No. He had *seen* them.

Kar-*rumph!* The bulldozer bit out another hunk.

Betty joined Larry at the grill, poured a bit of paraffin on the charcoal, and struck a match. Larry dutifully added his twigs.

'Hand me the stakes, dear,' Betty said.

Larry did so. 'He's not going to stab them with the stakes,

is he?' asked Larry, suddenly near tears. He wanted to fight his father with his fists. If he'd only been able to tackle his father man to man in a fight, he wouldn't be about to cry now, like a coward.

'Oh no, dear,' said his mother in her artificially soft voice, which always meant some crisis was at hand. 'He's just going to smoke them out. Then you can catch them and put them back in the warren.'

Larry didn't believe a word of it. 'And what about the little ones? All underneath? Without their parents?'

Betty only sighed.

Grimly, Larry watched his father poking with the tip of one of his crutches at the ground. He knew his father had found a hamster hole, and was trying to make it bigger, so a burning brand would go down there.

'Take these to your father, dear,' said Betty, handing Larry two burning sticks at least three feet long. 'Never mind if they go out. Hold them away from you.'

Larry trudged across the lawn with them.

'Ha!' laughed one of the workmen. 'You'll need more than that!'

Larry pretended not to hear. He handed Julian the stakes without looking into his face.

'Thanks, my boy,' Julian said, and stuck a smoking stick at once into a hole four inches in diameter. The stake all but disappeared and showed just a few inches above the ground. 'Ah, there we are!' Julian said in a tone of satisfaction. 'Take this. Follow me.'

Larry took back one stake, whose flame had gone out, but whose smoke made Larry close his eyes for an instant. His father had found two holes, the next just a yard or so away. The second stake went into this one.

'Splendid! More sticks, Larry!'

Larry walked back towards the terrace. The boomerang hole was now pretty deep, already looking like a boomerang shape, and Larry kept clear of it. He could not bring himself to glance at it, lest he see more destroyed hamster homes.

But the two hamsters he had seen above ground cheered him greatly: maybe they'd all have time to escape before they were overcome by asphyxiation. Larry carried more stakes to his father, six, eight, maybe twelve. The sun was sinking. The bulldozer pulled back and dropped its toothy scoop as if intending to rest for the night.

'Hamsters, come out!' Larry said aloud. 'It'll be dark soon! *Night!*' There must be some escape holes left, he thought.

The big rectangular lawn smoked from a dozen spots, but Larry was delighted to see that two or three stakes showed no smoke at ground level. He had relit several for his father. The puppy, Mr Johnson, had retreated to the house, not liking the smoke.

Julian was smiling broadly as he came on crutches towards the terrace fire, which Betty still tended. The workmen had departed. 'That'll give 'em something to think about!' he said, as he surveyed his land. 'Larry, go and collect the sticks that've gone out, would you, boy?'

'I'll do it, Julian,' Betty said. 'Go in and rest, dear. I'm sure you shouldn't be hobbling around with your ankle. The doctor would have a fit if he knew.'

'Ha-ha,' said Julian.

Larry avoided looking at his father. His father's grin seemed insane under the circumstances. Larry stood at a corner of the terrace, straining his eyes to see if any hamsters had come to ground level. But their babies! They were born blind, and some of the poor little things wouldn't even be able to see where to go to escape.

Betty came back with three stakes that had completely gone out, and stuck them on the charcoal.

'A little more paraffin!' Julian said. 'I think we're getting somewhere!'

'It's not good for the roses, all this heat and smoke, Julian,' Betty said.

Julian poured the paraffin himself, dropped the tin, and both he and Betty had to jump back as the flames leapt briefly. There hadn't been much in the tin. Julian laughed again. Betty became more nervous, and a little angry.

'These'll surely be enough, Julian,' she said. 'Let's let this be the end of it. Larry and I can take them out. It's almost too dark to see.'

'I'll put on the terrace light,' said Julian, and hobbled into the house and did so, but the lighted terrace only made the lawn seem darker. Julian found a flashlight. It was difficult for him to hold the flashlight and his crutches too, but it was his idea to hold the flashlight for Betty and Larry so they could find the hamster holes which still needed smoking stakes put into them.

The three of them went out to do this. Larry set his teeth trying to hold his anger and his tears back. He could hardly breathe. Partly it was because of the smoke, and partly because he was holding his breath. He saw a hamster, an adult that he didn't recognize, look at him with terrified eyes, then flee into some bushes. Larry, in a burst of rage, flung his burning sticks flat down on the lawn. The tips broke off, their flames went out.

'What're you doing there, Larry?' yelled his father. 'Pick those up!'

'*No!*' Larry said.

'It's because of *you* we're in this mess!' Julian shouted, moving towards Larry. 'You do as I say or you'll get the worst whipping of your life!'

'Julian, *please*, darling!' Betty said. 'We're finished now! Let's go in the house!'

'Will you pick up—' Julian toppled. One crutch had sunk deep.

Larry was quite near him, but stepped back in the darkness and dodged a smoking stick that stuck up from the grass.

'Oh, Lord!' Betty cried, and ran – in a curve because of the pool excavation – towards Julian whose white ankle bandage was the most visible part of him in the darkness.

She got a nasty whiff of smoke from somewhere, and coughed.

Larry heard the shriek of a fire engine siren, or maybe it was a police car. Under the cover of dark now, Larry removed every projecting stick he could see, and dropped them on the lawn. The rather dry grass was smouldering in some spots. Larry held his breath in smoky areas, and breathed only where it was a bit clearer. He saw that Julian was on his feet again. His father was yelling at him.

Larry didn't care. Now there were fire bells, rapid *clangs*. Good! A coal got into one of Larry's sneakers, and he had to remove his sneaker, knock it out, untie the lace and pull it on again.

Now the firemen were coming around the side of the house! With a hose! Larry could see them in the light of the terrace. Two or three firemen were getting the hose in position.

Hooray! Larry thought, but he didn't want the hamsters to be drowned either. He'd tell the firemen not to turn too much water on, he thought, and trotted towards the terrace.

Betty screamed from the lawn. 'The hamsters! They're *biting*!' Three or four were attacking her ankles.

Julian stabbed at a hamster with his crutch tip. '*Damn* them!' They were all around him and Betty. He lunged again, lost his balance and fell. One rushed at his face and nipped. Another sank its incisors into his forearm. Julian struggled up again, despite the fact that a hamster clung to his wrist. 'Betty! – *Tell the firemen*—'

At this point a spew of water like a battering ram caught Julian in the abdomen, and suddenly he was flat on his back with his breath knocked out. At once a half-dozen hamsters were attacking him.

'Julian, where are you?' Betty called. She debated trying to find Julian versus going to speak to the firemen – who must be thinking the whole lawn was on fire! She decided to run to the firemen. 'Careful!' she yelled at them. 'Be careful, my husband's on the lawn!'

190

'What?' came a man's voice from behind the horizontal torrent.

Betty got closer and shouted, nearly breathless. 'It's not a fire! We're trying to smoke out some hamsters!'

'Smoke out *what*?'

'*Hamsters!* Cut the hose off! It isn't necessary!'

Larry watched, standing in the dark near the terrace. The water from the hose had created more smoke.

The great canvas hose abated slowly, as if reluctant, and became limp.

'What's going on, ma'am? That's an awful lot of smoke!' said a huge fireman wearing a black rubber coat and a splendid red helmet.

In the few seconds of silence, they all heard Julian scream, a pained scream yet an exhausted one, as if it were not his first.

A dozen or more hamsters, crazed by smoke, shocked by the bursts of hose water, were attacking Julian as if he were the cause of their woes. Julian fended some off with his hands and fists and one crutch, which he wielded clumsily, holding it in the middle. He had wrenched his bad ankle again, the pain was awful, and he'd given up trying to stand up. His main task was to get the hamsters' teeth out of his own flesh, out of his calves, his forearm which braced him in a half-recumbent position on the smoking grass.

'Help!' Julian cried. 'Help *me*!'

And a fireman was coming, thank God! The fireman had a flashlight.

'Hey, what the hell is this?' the fireman said, kicking off a couple of hamsters with a thick boot.

Larry trotted towards the glow of the fireman's flashlight. Now Larry could see plenty of hamsters, scores of them, and his heart gave a jump as if he beheld a myriad fighters on his side. They were alive! They were lively and well! Larry stopped short. The fireman had dropped his father, having lifted him a little from the ground. What was happening?

The fireman had loosened his grip when a hamster bit him severely in the hand. The little beasts were running up his boots, falling, coming back. 'Hey, Pete! Give us a hand! Bring an *axe*!' the fireman yelled towards the terrace. Then he began to stomp about, trying to protect the man on the ground from the hamsters that were coming from all sides. The fireman uttered some round Irish curses. Nobody was going to believe this story when he told it!

'Get them off – off!' Julian murmured with one hand over his face. He had been bitten in the nose.

Larry observed it all from the darkness. And he realized he didn't care. He didn't care what happened to his father! It was a little like watching something on the TV screen. Yes, he *did* care. He wanted the hamsters to win. He wanted his father to get defeated, to lose, and he wouldn't have cared if his father fell into the pool pit – but he was a fair distance away from it. The hamsters had a right to their land, their homes, had a right to protect their offspring. Larry trotted in place and punched his fists in the air like a silent cheering squad. Then he found his voice. 'Come on, *hamsters*!' Larry yelled, and it crossed his mind to release Pirate and Gloria so they could join in – and yet they weren't even needed, there were so many hamsters!

Now a second fireman was trotting out with an axe. The two firemen got Julian up by putting one of Julian's arms around each of their necks. Julian's head sagged forward.

As the trio came into the terrace light, Larry saw hamsters at their feet flee back into the darkness of the lawn. His father's pale trousers, his shirt, were all splotched with blood.

And Larry's mother's face was absolutely white. An instant after Larry noticed this, his mother sank to the terrace tiles. She had fainted. One of the firemen picked her up and carried her into the living-room, which was brightly lit now, because the firemen had turned on all the lights.

'We've got to get this one to the hospital,' said the biggest fireman. 'He's losing blood.'

There was a pool of blood on the red tiles under Julian's half-supported feet.

Larry hovered and chewed a finger-nail.

'We'll take him in the wagon.'

'Think that's best?'

'Anything we can do for him now?'

'He's bleeding from too many places!'

'Put him on the wagon! The stretcher, Pete!'

'No time for that! Carry him and get going!'

Betty came to as Julian was being borne towards the driveway where the fire trucks were. A few neighbours stood there, and now they asked questions, questions about the fire. And what had happened to Julian?

'Hamsters!' said one of the firemen. 'Hamsters in the lawn!'

The neighbours were amazed.

Betty wanted to go with Julian to the hospital, but one of the firemen advised her not to. A couple of the women neighbours stayed with her.

Julian's jugular vein had been pierced in two places, and he had lost a lot of blood by the time he arrived at the hospital. The doctors applied tourniquets and stitched. Transfusions were given. The process was slow. In came the blood and out it flowed. Julian died within an hour.

Betty, under sedation that night, was not notified until the following morning. With the resources of an adult, Betty mentally gave herself two days to recover from the shock, knowing all the while that she would sell the house and move somewhere else. Larry, realizing factually what had happened, did not take it in at once emotionally, his father's demise. He knew his mother would never want to see another hamster, so he set about releasing those he could capture into territory where they might have a chance of survival. He made three or four expeditions on his bicycle, carrying his cardboard box loaded with adults and baby hamsters. There was a wood not far away with plenty of trees, underbrush, and not a house for half a mile.

So, his father was dead, Larry realized, finally. Dead because of hamsters which had simply bitten him. But in a way hadn't his father asked for it? Couldn't they have taken the time to save the hamsters in the boomerang area, and still gone on with the swimming pool construction? Much as Larry loved his father, and knew he should love his father – who had been a pretty good father as father's went, Larry realized – Larry was still somehow on the side of the hamsters. Because of his mother's feelings, Larry knew he had to part with Pirate and Gloria too. These with a few babies were the last to go one morning on Larry's bicycle in the cardboard box. Once more Larry fought against tears as he released this pair that he loved the best. But he did hold back the tears, and he felt he was at last becoming a man.

Harry: A Ferret

HARRY, a ferret of uncertain age, perhaps one or two, was the prize possession of Roland Lemoinnier, a boy of fifteen. There was no doubt Roland was fifteen. He was pleased to tell anyone, because he considered fifteen a great step forward over fourteen. To be fourteen was to be a child, but to be fifteen was to enter manhood. Roland took pleasure in his new deep voice, and looked into the mirror every morning before brushing his teeth to see if more hair had sprouted where a moustache might have been or under his sideburns. He shaved elaborately with his own razor, but only once a week, because seeing the hair on his face gave him more pleasure than shaving.

Roland's new adulthood had got him into trouble in Paris, at least in his mother's opinion. He had begun going out with boys and girls several years older than he, and the police had hauled him in among six other young people, all around eighteen, to caution them about possession of marijuana. Being tall, Roland could pass for eighteen and often did. His mother had been so shocked by the police episode, she had acted on the advice of her mother, with whom in this case she was in complete accord, and moved to her house in the country near Orléans. Roland's father and mother had been divorced since he was five. With Roland and his mother went the two servants Brigitte, maid and cook, and Antoine, the elderly chauffeur and factotum who had been with the family since before Roland was born. Brigitte and Antoine were not married to each other, and both were single. Antoine was so aged as to be a joke to Roland, something left over from another century and mysteriously still alive, frowning disapproval on Roland's blue jeans at the lunch table and his bare feet on the carpets and the waxed floors of La Source. It was summer, and Roland was free of the Lycée Lamartine, eight kilometres away, where he had gone for most of the preceding term after their move from Paris.

In fact Roland had been bored with country life in general until the day in late June when he had accompanied his mother to a nursery to buy plants for the garden. The nurseryman, a friendly old fellow with a sense of humour, had a ferret which he told Roland he had captured on the week-end while out hunting rabbits. Roland had been fascinated by the caged ferret which could hunch itself into a very short length as if its body were made like an accordion, then flash into its hole in the straw, looking three times that length. The ferret was black, light brown and cream, and to Roland looked part rat, part squirrel, and exceedingly mischievous.

'Careful! He bites!' the nurseryman said, when Roland put his finger against the wire of the cage.

The ferret had bitten Roland with a needle-like tooth, but Roland hid his bleeding finger in a handkerchief in his pocket. 'Would you sell him? With the cage too?'

'Why? Do you hunt rabbits?' the nurseryman asked, smiling.

'A hundred new francs. A hundred and fifty,' Roland said. He had that much in his pocket.

Roland's mother was bending over camellias yards away. 'Well—'

'You'll have to tell me what he eats.'

'A little grass, of course. And blood,' he added, bending close to Roland. 'Give him some raw meat now and then, because he's got the taste for it now. And mind you don't let him loose in the house, because you'll never catch him. Hay to keep him warm, like this. He made that tunnel himself.'

The ferret had darted into the little tunnel in the straw

and turned around so that only his lively face peered out with low-set, mouse-like ears and black eyes that slanted downward at the outer corners, making him look thoughtful and a bit melancholic. Roland had the feeling the ferret was listening to the conversation and hoping he would be able to go away with Roland.

Roland pulled out a hundred note and a fifty. 'How about it – with the cage?'

The nurseryman glanced over his shoulder, as if Roland's mother might interfere. 'If he bites, stick an onion at him. He won't bite you after he bites into an onion.'

Margaret Lemoinnier was surprised and annoyed that Roland had bought a ferret. 'You'll have to keep the cage in the garden. You mustn't take it in the house.'

Antoine said nothing, but his pink-white face took on a more sour expression than usual. He put lots of newspaper on the back seat of the Jaguar so that the cage would not touch the leather upholstery.

At home, Roland got an onion from the kitchen and went out on the lawn behind the house where he had set the cage. He opened the door of the cage slightly, onion at the ready, but the ferret, after hesitating an instant, darted through the door into freedom. He made for the woods at one side of the estate and disappeared. Roland warned himself to keep cool. He brought the cage, its door open, to the edge of the woods, then ran into the house via the back door. On a wooden board in the kitchen lay just what he wanted, a large raw steak. Roland cut off a piece and hurried back to the woods.

Slowly Roland entered the woods, intending to make a circle and drive the ferret back towards his cage. A ferret could probably climb a tree too. Roland had seen his sharp claws when the ferret had stood up in his cage at the nursery. The ferret had tiny pink-palmed hands that were rather like human hands, with miniature pads at the end of the fingers, and a freely moving thumb. Then Roland's heart gave a leap as he saw the ferret just a few yards away from him, sitting upright in the grasses, sniffing. The breeze blew towards the ferret, and Roland realized that he had smelled blood. Roland stooped and extended the raw meat.

Cautiously, rearing himself, then advancing a little, the ferret approached, eyes darting everywhere as if guarding against possible enemies. Roland was startled at the suddenness with which the ferret seized the meat in his teeth and jerked it away. The ferret chewed with bolting movements of head and neck, the brown and black hair on his back standing on end as he telescoped his lithe body. The steak was all gone, and the ferret looked at Roland, little pink tongue licking his face appreciatively.

Roland's impulse was to run back to the kitchen for more. But he thought it best to move slowly so the ferret would not become alarmed. 'Wait! Or come with me,' he said softly, because he wanted the ferret back in the cage. It would be dark soon, and Roland didn't want to lose him.

The ferret followed to the edge of the lawn and waited. Roland went to the kitchen and cut some more meat, then gently poured from the paper below the steak a tablespoon of blood into a saucer. He carried this out. The ferret was still in the same place, one paw raised, gazing expectantly. The ferret approached the saucer, where the meat was laso, but he chose the blood first, and lapped it up like a kitten lapping milk. Roland smiled. Then the ferret looked at Roland, licked his face again, seized the meat in his teeth and carried it in an uncertain route on to the grass, then seeing his cage, he made a straight line for it.

Roland was very pleased. The onion, still in Roland's pocket, might not be necessary. And the ferret was safely back in his cage on his own initiative. Roland closed the cage door. 'I think I'll call you Harry. How do you like that name? *Harry.*' Roland was studying English, and he knew that Harry was informal for Henry, and there was also an English word 'hairy' pronounced the same way, so the name seemed appropriate. 'Come up and see *my* room.' Roland picked up the cage.

In the house, Roland encountered Antoine who was coming down the stairway.

'M. Roland, your mother said she did not want the animal in the house,' said Antoine.

Roland drew himself up a little. He was no longer a child to be told what to do by a servant. 'Yes, Antoine. But I'll speak to my mother on the subject,' Roland said in his deepest voice.

Roland put the cage in the middle of the floor in his room, and went to the telephone in the hall. He dialled the number of his best friend Stefan in Paris, had to speak with Stefan's mother first, then Stefan came on.

'I have a new friend,' Roland said, putting on a voice with a foreign accent. 'He has claws and drinks blood. Guess what he is?'

'A – a vampire?' said Stefan.

'You are warm. – My mother's coming and I can't talk long,' Roland said quickly. 'He's a *ferret*. His name is Harry. Bloodthirsty! A killer! Maybe I can bring him to Paris! Bye-bye, Stefan!'

Mme Lemoinnier had come up the stairs and was walking towards Roland down the hall. 'Roland, Antoine says you have brought that animal into the house. I said you could keep it only if it stays in the garden.'

'But – the nurseryman told me to watch out that he doesn't get cold. It's cold at night, Mama.'

His mother went a few steps into Roland's room. Roland followed her.

'Look! He's gone to sleep in his burrow. He's perfectly clean, Mama. He'll stay in his cage. What's the matter with that?'

'You'll probably take him out. I know you, Roland.'

'But I promise, I won't.' Roland didn't mean that promise, and knew his mother knew it.

A minute later, Roland was reluctantly carrying Harry, now out of sight in the hay, down the stairway and into the garden. Harry was probably sleeping like a log, Roland thought, remembering what the nurseryman had said about ferrets falling asleep, often close to their victims for warmth, after they had drunk the blood of their prey. The primitiveness of it excited Roland. When his mother had gone back into the house (she had been watching him from the kitchen door), Roland opened the cage and lifted some of the hay, exposing Harry who raised his head drowsily. Roland smiled.

'Come on, you can sleep up in my room. Then we'll have some fun tonight,' Roland whispered.

Roland picked Harry up and put the hay back in place. Harry lay limp and innocent in Roland's hand. Roland opened a button of his shirt, stuck Harry in and fastened the button. He closed the cage door and latched it.

Up in his room, Roland got his empty suitcase from a wardrobe top, put a couple of his sweaters into it, and put Harry in, propping the suitcase lid open a little with the sleeve of one sweater. Then Roland got a clean ashtray from the hall table, filled it with water from the bathroom tap and put it in the suitcase.

Roland then flopped on his bed, lit one of the cigarettes which he kept hidden in a bookshelf, and opened a James Bond which he had already read two or three times. He was thinking of things he might teach Harry. Harry should learn to travel around in a jacket pocket, certainly, and come out on command. He should also have a collar and lead, and the collar, or maybe a harness, would have to be custom-made because Harry was so small. Roland imagined commissioning a leather craftsman in Paris and paying a good price for it. Fine! It would be amusing in Paris – even in Orléans – if Harry could emerge from his pocket on his lead and eat meat from Roland's plate in a restaurant, for instance.

At dinner, Roland and his mother and a man friend of hers, who was an antique dealer of the neighbourhood and very boring, were interrupted by Brigitte, who whispered to Mme Lemoinnier:

'Madame, I beg to excuse myself, but Antoine has just been bitten. He is quite upset.'

'Bitten?' said Mme Lemoinnier.

'He says it is the ferret – in M. Roland's room.'

Roland controlled his smile. Antoine had gone in to turn the bed down, and Harry had attacked.

'A *ferret*?' said the antique dealer.

Roland's mother looked at him. 'Will you excuse yourself, Roland, and put the animal back in the garden?' She was angry and would have said more if they had been alone.

'Excuse me, please,' Roland said. He went into the hall and saw Antoine's tall figure in the little lavatory by the front door. Antoine stooped to hold a wet towel against his ankle. Blood, Roland thought, fascinated to think that Harry had drawn blood from that old creature Antoine, who in fact looked as if he hadn't any blood in him.

Roland ran up the stairs two at a time, and found his room in disorder. Antoine had obviously abandoned the bed-turning-down midway, an armchair was askew where Antoine must have dragged it looking for Harry, or maybe trying to protect himself. But the bed in disorder meant more to Roland than an explosion: Antoine would not have left a bed in that state unless he was ready for extreme unction. Roland looked around for Harry.

'Harry? – Where are you?' He looked up at the long curtains, which Harry would certainly be able to climb, in the wardrobe, under the bed.

The door of his room had been closed. Evidently Antoine had wanted to guard against Harry escaping. Then Roland looked at the folds in the bedcovers where nothing, however, twitched.

'Harry?'

Roland lifted the top sheet. Then he saw the counterpane move. Harry was between counterpane and blanket, and he sat up and regarded Roland with a desperate anxiety. Roland noticed another beautiful thing about Harry: his whole torso was beige and soft looking, from his little black chin down to the counterpane on which he stood, and a fine line of brown fur perhaps caused by the fur pressing together down the centre of his body, gave the effect of a stripe, turned Harry into a bifurcated piece of beige fluff, quite concealing where his hind legs began and ended. Harry's dainty hands sought either side of the counterpane's folds, not to keep his balance which he had perfectly, but nervously, as the hands of a highly strung person might do. And perhaps Harry was asking, 'Who was that giant who tried to shoo me, scare me, catch me?' But as Roland looked at Harry, Harry's face seemed to lose some of its terror. Harry lowered himself and advanced a little. Now he might be saying, 'I'm delighted to see you! What's happening?'

Roland extended a hand without thinking, and Harry went up his arm and down his shirtfront – the collar of his shirt was open – and nestled with scratchy little claws against Roland's waist. Roland found his eyes full of tears which he could not explain. Was it pride because Harry had come to him? Or anger because Harry had to stay in the garden tonight? Tears, explained or not, had a poetic value, Roland thought. They signified importance of some kind.

Roland took Harry out of his shirt and put him on a curtain. Harry ran up the yellow curtain to the ceiling, Roland took the bottom of the curtain in his hands, and Harry ran down the slope. Roland laughed, lowered the curtain, and Harry ran up again. Harry seemed to enjoy it. Roland caught Harry at the bottom of the curtain and stuck him into the suitcase. 'I'll be back in a minute!' This time Roland fixed the lid down with a straight chair turned sideways.

Roland intended to go back to the dining-room until the meal was over, then ask Brigitte for some meat before he took Harry to the garden. But it seemed the meal was over. The dining-room was empty. The antique dealer sat in the drawing-room where the coffee tray already stood on the table, and Roland heard his mother's voice and Antoine's voice from the room opposite the drawing-room. Its door was not quite closed.

'. . . disobeyed me,' Antoine was saying in his shaky old man's voice. 'And *you*, madame!'

'Now you must not take it so seriously, my dear Antoine,' Roland's mother said. 'I am sure Roland will keep the animal in the garden . . .'

Roland made himself move away. Gentlemen did not eavesdrop. But it irked him that Antoine had said, 'M. Roland disobeyed me.' Since when did Antoine think he controlled him? Roland hesitated at the doorway of the drawing-room, where the antique dealer sat smoking and gazing into space, his white trousered legs crossed. Roland wanted coffee, but it was not worth walking into that boredom for, he thought. Roland went through the dining-room into the kitchen.

'Brigitte, may I have some meat for the ferret? Preferably raw,' Roland said.

'M. Roland, Antoine is very upset, you know? A ferret is a *bête sauvage*. You must realize that.'

Roland said courteously, 'I know, Brigitte. I am sorry Antoine was bitten. I am going to take the ferret to the garden. In his cage. Now.'

Brigitte shook her head and produced some veal from the refrigerator and cut a morsel grudgingly.

It wasn't bloody but it was raw. Roland flew up the stairs to his room, gently lifted the suitcase lid, whereupon Harry stood upright like a jack-in-the-box. Harry took Roland's offering with both front paws and his teeth, chewing it and turning it so he could get at the edges.

Roland extended his hand fearlessly, saying, 'You've got to sleep in the garden tonight, sorry.'

Harry flitted through the gap above Roland's shirt cuff, went up to his shoulder and down to his waist. Roland cradled him in his shirt, and went down the stairs like a soldier, the cage in his other hand.

It was dark, but Roland could see by the light from the kitchen window. He stuck Harry into the cage and closed the door with its pin latch which dropped through a loop. Harry had a tin mug of water which still held enough. 'See you tomorrow, Harry my friend!'

Harry stood up on his hind legs, resting a pink palm lightly against the wire, black nose sniffing the last of Roland, who looked back at Harry as he walked across the lawn.

The next morning, a Sunday, Roland was brought tea by Brigitte at 8 o'clock, a ritual that Roland had started a few weeks earlier. It made Roland feel more grown-up to fancy that he couldn't awaken properly without someone handing him a cup of something hot in bed.

Then Roland pulled on blue jeans, tennis shoes and an old shirt, and went down to see Harry.

The cage was gone. Or at least it was not in the same place. Roland looked in the corners of the garden, behind the poplar trees on the right, then next to the house. He went into the kitchen, where Brigitte was preparing his mother's breakfast tray.

'Someone's moved the ferret's cage, Brigitte. Do you know where it is?'

Brigitte bent over the tray. 'Antoine took it, M. Roland. I don't know where.'

'But – did he take the car?'

'I don't know, M. Roland.'

Roland went out and looked in the garage. The car was there. Roland stood and turned in a circle, looking. Could Antoine have put the cage in the toolhouse? Roland opened the toolhouse door. There was nothing there but the lawnmower and garden tools. The woods. Antoine had probably been told, by his mother, to take Harry to the woods and turn him loose. Frowning, Roland started off at a trot.

He pulled up when some brambles caught at his shirt and tore it. Old Antoine wouldn't have gone too far in these woods, Roland thought. There weren't any real paths.

Roland heard a groan. Or had he imagined it? He was not sure where the sound had come from, but he plunged on the way he had been going. Now he heard a crackling of branches and another groan. It was unmistakably a groan from Antoine. Roland advanced.

He saw a splotch of dark through the trees. Antoine wore dark trousers, often a dark green cotton jacket. Roland stood still. The darkish splotch was pulling itself up only thirty feet away. But there were so many leaves in between! Roland saw a golden light streak from the left towards the vague form which was Antoine, heard Antoine's rather shrill cry – feeble, almost like the cry of a baby.

Roland went closer, a little frightened. Now he could see Antoine's head and face, and blood flowed from one of Antoine's eyes. Then Roland saw Harry make a flying leap at Antoine's thigh, saw Antoine's hand slap uselessly against his leg, because Harry was already at Antoine's throat. Or face. Antoine staggered back and fell.

He ought to go and help, Roland thought, grab a stick and fend Harry off. But Roland was spellbound and couldn't move. He saw Antoine try a swingeing backhand blow at Harry, but the branch Antoine held struck a tree and shattered. Antoine stumbled again.

In a way it serves Antoine right, Roland was thinking.

Antoine got up clumsily and flung something – probably a rock – at Harry. Roland could see blood down the front of Antoine's white shirt. And Harry was fighting like a mysterious little bullet that came again and again at Antoine from different directions. It looked as if Antoine was trying to flee now. He was stumbling through the underbrush to the left. Roland saw Harry leap for Antoine's left hand and apparently cling there with his teeth. Or had it been a streak of sunlight? Roland lost sight of Antoine, because he fell again.

Roland gasped. He had not been breathing for several

seconds, and his heart was pounding as if he had been fighting too. Now Roland forced himself to walk towards the place where he thought Antoine lay. Everything was silent except for Roland's footfalls on the leaves and twigs. Roland saw the black, white and green of Antoine's clothes, then Antoine's face streaked with blood. Antoine was lying on his back. Both his eyes were bleeding.

And Harry was at Antoine's throat!

Harry's head was out of sight under Antoine's chin, but his body and tail trailed down Antoine's chest – as a furpiece might do from someone's neck.

'*Harry!*' Roland's voice cracked.

Harry might not have heard.

Roland picked up a stick. 'Harry, get away!' he said through his teeth.

Harry leapt to the other side of Antoine's throat and bit again.

'Antoine?' Roland went forward, raising the stick.

Harry lifted his head and backed on to Antoine's green lapel. His stomach was visibly larger. He was full of blood, Roland realized. Antoine didn't move. Seeing Roland, Harry advanced a little, nearly stood up on his hind legs, came down again and, staggering with the weight of his stomach, stepped down on to the leaves beside Antoine's outflung arm, lay down and lowered his head as if to sleep. Harry was in a patch of sun.

Roland felt considerably less afraid, now that Harry was still, but he feared now that Antoine might be dead, and the possible fact of death frightened him. He called to Antoine again. The blood was drying and darkening in the eye sockets. His eyes seemed to be gone, just as Roland had thought, or at least nearly entirely eaten out. The blood everywhere, on Antoine's clothing, down his face, was dark red and crusty now, and no more seemed to be coming, which was a sign that the heart had stopped beating, Roland thought. Before Roland realized what he was doing, he had stooped very close to the sleeping Harry and was holding Antoine's wrist to feel for a pulse. Roland tried for several seconds. Then he snatched his hand from the wrist in horror, and stood up.

Antoine must have died from a heart attack, Roland thought, not just from Harry. But he realized that Harry was going to be taken away, even hunted down and killed, if anybody found out about Antoine. Roland looked behind him, in the direction of La Source, then back at Antoine. The thing to do was hide Antoine. Roland felt a revulsion against Antoine, mainly because he was dead, he realized. But for Harry he felt love and a desire to protect. Harry after all had been defending himself, and Antoine had been a giant kidnapper, and possibly a killer too.

It was still only a little past 9.30, Roland saw by his watch.

Roland began to trot back through the woods, leaping the bad patches of underbrush. At the edge of La Source's lawn he stopped, because Brigitte was just then tossing a pan of water on to some flowers by the back steps. When she had gone inside the house again, Roland went to the toolhouse, took the fork and spade, and carried these into the woods.

He dug close beside where Antoine lay, which seemed as good a place as any to try to dig a grave. His exertions sobered him, and took away some of his panic. Harry continued to sleep on the other side of Antoine from where Roland was digging. Roland worked like one possessed, and his energy seemed to increase as he laboured. He realized he was in terror of Antoine's body: what had been the living fossil, so familiar in the household in Paris and here, was now a corpse. Roland also half expected Antoine to rise up and reproach him, threaten him in some way, as ghosts or corpses did in stories that Roland had read.

Roland began to tire and worked more slowly, but with the same determination. The job had to be done by mid-day, he told himself, or his mother and Brigitte would be searching for Antoine by the lunch hour. Roland tried to think of what he would say.

The grave was deep enough. Roland set his teeth and pulled at Antoine's green jacket and the side of his trousers, and rolled him in. Antoine fell face downward. Harry, ruffled by Antoine's arm, stood on four legs looking sleepy still. Roland shovelled the earth in, panting. He trod on the soil to make it sink, and there was still extra soil which he had to scatter, so it would not catch the eye of anyone looking in the woods. Then with the fork he pulled branches and leaves over the grave so it looked like the rest of the forest floor.

Then numb with fatigue, he picked Harry up. Harry was very heavy – as heavy as a pistol, Roland thought. Harry's eyes were closed again, but he was not quite limp in sleep. His neck supported his head, and as Roland lifted him to his own eye level, Harry opened his eyes and looked at Roland. Harry would never bite him, Roland felt sure, because he had always brought meat to him. In a way, he had brought Antoine to Harry. Roland trudged back with Harry towards the house, saw the cage in the woods and started to pick it up, then decided to leave it for the moment. Roland put Harry down beside a sun-warm rock not far from the lawn.

Roland put the fork and spade back in the toolhouse. He washed his hands as best he could at the cold water tap by the toolhouse, then thinking Brigitte might be in the kitchen, he entered the house by the front door. He went upstairs and washed more thoroughly and changed his shirt. He put on his transistor radio for company. He felt odd, not exactly frightened any longer, but as if he would do everything clumsily – drop or bump into things, trip on the stairs – though he had done none of these things.

His mother knocked on the door. He knew her knock.

'Come in, Mama.'

'Where have you been, Roland?'

Roland was lying on his bed, the radio beside him. He turned the radio down. 'In the woods. I took a walk.'

'Did you see Antoine? He's supposed to fetch Marie and Paul for lunch.'

Roland remembered. People were coming for lunch. 'I saw Antoine in the woods. He said he was taking the day off, going to Orléans or something like that.'

'Really? – He was letting the ferret loose, wasn't he?'

'Yes, Mama. He'd already let the ferret loose. I saw the cage in the woods.'

His mother looked troubled. 'I'm sorry, Roland, but it was not an appropriate pet, you know. And poor old Antoine – we've got to think of him. He's terrified of ferrets, and I think he's right to be.'

'I know, Mama. It doesn't matter.'

'That's a good boy. But Antoine, just to go off like that— He'll go to a film in Orléans and come back this evening probably. He didn't take the car, did he?'

'He said he was taking the Orléans bus. – He was very annoyed with me. Said he might be gone a couple of days.'

'That's nonsense. But I'd better hop off now for Marie and Paul. You see what trouble you caused with that animal, Roland!' His mother gave him a quick smile and went out.

Roland managed to save some meat from dinner, and took it out around 10.30 p.m., when Brigitte had gone to bed and his mother was in her room for the night. Roland sat on the rock where he had left Harry earlier that day, and after seven or eight minutes, Harry arrived. Roland smiled, almost laughed.

'Meat, Harry!' Roland said in a whisper, though he was a good distance from the house.

Harry, slender once more, accepted the underdone lamb, though not with his usual eagerness, having eaten so much that day. Roland stroked Harry's head for the first time. Roland imagined coming to the woods in the day-time, training Harry to stay in his pocket, teaching him certain commands. Harry didn't need a cage.

After two days, Mme Lemoinnier sent a telegram to Antoine's sister who lived in Paris, asking her please to telephone. The sister telephoned, and said she hadn't heard a word from Antoine.

It was curious, Mme Lemoinnier thought, that Antoine had just walked off like that, leaving all his clothes, even his coat and raincoat. She thought she should notify the police.

The police came and asked questions. Roland said he had last seen Antoine walking towards the Orléans road where he intended to catch the bus that passed at 11 a.m. Antoine was old, Mme Lemoinnier said, a little eccentric, stubborn. He had left his savings bank passbook behind, and the police were going to ask the bank to communicate if Antoine came to make a withdrawal or to get another passbook. The police went over the ground that Roland showed them. They found the empty cage, its door open, which Antoine had carried into the woods. The Orléans road was to the right, the opposite direction from where Antoine was buried. The police walked all the way to the Orléans road. They seemed to believe Roland's story.

Every night that Roland could go out unobserved, he fed Harry, and usually once during the day too. The few nights Harry did not turn up, Roland supposed he was hunting rabbits or moles. Harry was wild, yet not wild, tame, yet not reliably tame, Roland knew. Roland also realized that he didn't dare think too much about what Harry had done. Roland preferred to think that Antoine had died from a heart attack. Or – if Roland ever thought of Harry as a murderer, he put it in the same realm of fantasy as the murders in the books he read, real yet not real. It was not true that he was guilty, or Harry either.

Roland liked best to imagine Harry as his secret weapon, better than a gun. Secret because no one knew about him, though Roland intended to tell Stefan. Roland had fantasies of using Harry to kill a certain mathematics professor whom he detested in his lycée. Roland was in the habit of writing letters to Stefan, and he wrote Stefan the story of Harry killing Antoine, in fiction form. 'You may not believe this story, Stefan,' Roland wrote at the end, 'but I swear it is true. If you care to check with the police, you will find that *Antoine has disappeared!*'

Stefan wrote back: 'I don't believe a word of your ferret story, obviously inspired by Antoine walking out, and who wouldn't if they had to wait on *you*? However it is mildly amusing. Got any more stories?'

Goat Ride

BILLY the goat was the main attraction at Playland Amusement Park, and Billy himself was the most amused – not the children or their parents who fished out endless quarters and dimes, after having paid the one-dollar-fifty admission for themselves and seventy-five cents per child. Hank Hudson's Playland wasn't cheap, but it was the only place of amusement for kids in or around the town.

Screams and cheers went up when Billy, pulling his gold-and-white cart, made his entry every evening around 7. Any President of the United States would have been heartened by such a roar from his adherents, and it put fire into Billy too. All sinew and coarse white hair, brushed to perfection by Mickie, Billy started on the gallop, dashed past a white rail fence against which children and adults pressed themselves out of his way and at the same time urged him on with 'Hurrahs!' and 'Ooooohs!' of admiration. The run was to take a little froth off Billy's energy, as well as to alert the crowd that Billy was ready for business. Back at the start of the Goat Ride, Billy skidded to a halt on polished hooves, hardly breathing faster but snorting for effect. The ride cost twenty-five cents for adult or child, and Billy's cart could take four kids, or two adults, plus Mickie who drove. Mickie, a red-headed boy whom Billy quite liked, rode in front on a bench.

'Gee up!' Mickie would say, slapping the reins on Billy's back, and off Billy would go, head down at first till he got the cart going, then head up and trotting, looking from side to side for mischief or handouts of ice cream and caramel popcorn which he was ever ready to pause for.

Mickie wielded a little whip, more for show than service, and the whip didn't hurt Billy at all. Billy understood when Hank yelled at Mickie that Hank wanted them to get on with the ride in order to take on the next batch of customers. The Goat Ride had a course round the shooting gallery, through the crowd between the merry-go-round and the ice cream and popcorn stands, round the stand where people threw balls at prizes, making a big figure-eight which Billy covered twice. If Mickie's whip didn't work, Hank would come over and give Billy a kick in the rump to tear him away from a popcorn or peanut bag. Billy would kick back, but his hooves hit the cart rather than Hank. Still it was seldom that Billy could call himself tired, even at the end of a hard week-end. And if the next day was a day when the park was closed, and he was tied to his stake with nothing to butt, no crowds to cheer him, Billy would dig his horns into the grass he had already cropped. He had a crooked left horn which could tear into the ground, giving Billy satisfaction.

One Sunday, Hank Hudson and another man approached the post at the start of the Goat Ride, and Hank held his hands out palms down, a signal to Mickie to stop everything. The man had a little girl with him who was hopping up and down with excitement. Hank was talking, and slapped Billy's shoulder, but the little girl didn't dare touch Billy until her father took one of his horns in his hand. Ordinarily Billy would have jerked his head, because people loved to laugh and turn loose before they were thrown off their balance. But Billy was curious now, and continued chewing the remains of a crunchy ice cream cone, while his grey-blue eyes with their horizontal pupils gazed blandly at the little girl who was now stroking his forelock. The four kids in Billy's cart clamoured to get started.

Hank was taking lots of paper money from the man. Hank kept his back to the main part of the crowd, and he counted the money carefully. Hank Hudson was a tall man with a big stomach and a broad but flat behind which once or twice Billy had butted. He wore a Western hat, cowboy boots, and buff-coloured trousers whose belt sloped down in front under his paunch. He had a wet pink mouth with two rabbit-like front teeth, and small blue eyes. Now his wife Blanche joined the group and watched. She was plump with reddish-brown hair. Billy never paid much attention to her. When Hank had pocketed the money, he told Mickie to get on with the ride, and Billy started off. Billy did his usual twelve or fifteen rides that evening, but at closing time he was not led back to his stable.

Mickie unhitched Billy near the entrance gate, and Billy was tugged towards a pick-up whose back hatch was open.

'Go on, git in theah, Billy!' Hank shouted, giving Billy a kick to show he meant business.

Mickie was pulling from the front. 'Come on, Billy! Bye-bye, Billy boy!'

Billy clattered up the board they had put as a ramp, and the hatch was banged shut. The car started off, and there was a long bumpy ride, but Billy kept his balance easily. He looked around in the darkness at whizzing trees, a few houses that he could see whenever there was a street-light. Finally the car stopped in a driveway beside a big house, and Billy was untied and pulled – he had to jump – down to the ground. A young woman came out of the house and patted Billy, smiling. Then Billy was led – he let himself be led mainly because he was curious – towards a lean-to against the garage. Here was a pan of water, and the women brought another pan of a vegetable and lettuce mish-mash that tasted quite good.

Billy would have liked a gallop, just to see how big the place was and to sample some of the greenery, but the man had tied him up. The man spoke kindly, patted his neck, and went into the house, where the lights soon went out.

The next morning, the man drove off in his car, and then the woman and the little girl came out. Billy was taken for a sedate walk on a rope. Billy pranced and leapt, full of energy but content to stay on the rope until he realized that the woman was taking him back to the lean-to. Billy dashed forward, head down, felt the rope leave the woman's hands, and then he galloped and rammed his horns, not too hard, against the trunk of a small tree.

The little girl shrieked with pleasure.

Billy's rope caught under a white iron bench, and he made circles around the bench until there was no more rope left, then butted the bench, knocked it over, and tossed his head. He liked making his bells ring, and he looked gaily at the woman and the little girl who were running towards him.

The woman picked up his rope. She seemed to be a little afraid of him. Then much to Billy's annoyance, she tied the end of the rope to a near-by stone statue. The statue, which looked like a small fat boy eating something, stood by a little rock pond. Billy was alone. He looked all around him, ate some grass which was delicious but already cut rather short. He was bored. There was no one in sight now, nothing moving except an occasional bird, and one squirrel which stared at him for a moment, then disappeared. Billy tugged at his rope, but the rope held. He knew he could chew through the rope, but the task struck him as distasteful, so he made a good run from the statue and was jerked back and thrown to the ground. Billy was on his legs at once, prancing higher than ever as he assessed the problem.

Billy took another run and this time put his back into it, chin whiskers brushing the ground. A solid weight struck his chest – he was wearing his harness – and behind him he heard a *crack!* then a *plop!* as the statue fell into the water. Billy galloped on, delayed hardly at all as his plunging legs hauled the statue over the brim of the pond. Billy went on through hedges, over stone paths where the statue gave out more *cracks!* and became ever lighter behind him. He found some flowers and paused to refresh himself. At this point, he heard running feet, and turned his head to see the woman of the house plus a boy of about Mickie's age coming towards him.

The woman seemed very upset. The boy untied the rope from the remnant of statue, and Billy was tugged firmly back towards the lean-to. Then the woman handed the boy a big iron spike which the boy banged into the ground with a hammer. Billy's rope was then tied to the spike.

The boy smiled and said, 'There you go, Billy!'

They went away.

A day or so passed, and Billy became more bored. He chewed through part of his rope, then abandoned the project, knowing he would only be tied up again if he were walking around free. Billy was well fed, but he would have preferred Playland Amusement Park with its noise and people, pulling his cart with four passengers plus Mickie, to being tied to a stick doing nothing. Once the man put the little girl astride Billy's back, but the man held the rope so short, it was no fun for Billy. Billy shied at something, the little girl slid off – and that seemed to be the end of his giving her rides.

One afternoon a rather large black dog came loping on to the lawn, saw Billy and started barking and nipping at him. This infuriated Billy, because the dog seemed to be laughing at him. Billy lowered his head and bounded forward, determined to pull up the iron stake, but the rope broke, which was even better. Now the dog was on the run, and Billy bore down at full speed. The dog went round the corner of the greenhouse. Billy cut the corner close, and there was a shattering of glass as one of his horns hit a pane. Blind with rage, Billy attacked the greenhouse for no reason – except that it made a satisfying sound.

Crash! – *Bang!* – Clatter-tinkle! And again *Crash!*

The dog nipped at Billy's heels, yapping, and Billy kicked and missed. Billy charged the dog, his hooves thundering on the lawn. The dog, a streak of black, disappeared off the property and headed down a street. Billy went after him, but stopped after a few yards, feeling that he had routed his enemy. Billy upturned the nearest hedge for the hell of it, gave a snort and shook himself so his bells jingled like a full orchestra. Then he trotted up the street with his head high, in the general direction of his own lawn. But some flowers by a gate attracted him. There was a scream from one of the houses. Billy moved off at once.

More shouts and yells.

Then a policeman's whistle. Billy was rudely taken in hand by the policeman who jerked him by horn and harness, and then whacked him on the haunch with his nightstick. In retaliation, Billy rammed the policeman in the belly and had the pleasure of seeing the man roll on the ground in agony. Then four or five boys jumped on Billy and threw him to the ground. Much noise, yelling and dragging – and Billy was back on the lawn where the iron stick was, and the broken greenhouse. Billy stood foursquare, breathing hard, glaring at everyone.

That evening, the man of the house loaded Billy on to the pick-up, and tied him so securely he could not lie down. Billy recognized from afar the cheerful cymbal clashes and the booms of the merry-go-round's music. They were back at Playland!

Mickie ran up smiling. 'Hey, Billy! Back again!'

Hank wasn't smiling. He stood talking solemnly with the man, pulling his underlip and shaking his head. The man looked sad too, as he went away back to his car. That very evening Billy was harnessed to his cart and made nearly a dozen rounds before closing time. There was much laughter from Mickie and Hank as they put Billy into his stable that night and fed him. Billy was already quite full of hotdogs and popcorn.

'*Billy!* . . . There's *Billy* back!' The yells from the crowd echoed in Billy's ears as he fell asleep in his old straw bed. *Some* people in the world liked him.

Billy slipped into his old routine, which wasn't at all bad, he thought. At least it wasn't boring. In the day-time, five days a week, he could wander over the deserted grounds where there wasn't much grass but a good many remnants of hotdog buns and discarded peanut bags with a few peanuts generally in them. All was as usual. So Billy was surprised one busy evening to be unhitched from his cart by Mickie and dragged by Hank towards an automobile with a box at the back of it big enough for a horse.

Billy knew what was happening. Hank was pushing him off somewhere else. Billy braced his legs and had to be lifted on to the ramp by Hank and another man in a Western hat similar to Hank's, while a third man pulled his horns from inside the box. Billy gave a twist of his body, landed on his feet, and at once bounded into freedom.

Freedom! But where was he to go? The place was fenced in except for the car entrance, and this Billy made for. Two men tried to block him, but jumped aside like scared rabbits as Billy hurtled towards them. Billy rammed the side of a car, not having seen it in the semi-darkness, and knocked himself nearly out. A cry went up from the car occupants. Two huge men fell on Billy and held him down. Then three men carried him back towards the car with the horse box. This time his feet were tied together, and Hank himself jerked Billy's legs from under him, and Billy fell on his side. Billy kicked to no avail. He hated Hank at that moment. He had never liked Hank, and now Billy's hostility was like an explosion in him. Once more Billy witnessed from his horizontal position Hank receiving lots of paper money from the man who owned the horse box. Hank shoved the money deep in a pocket of his baggy trousers. Then they closed the box door.

This time it was a longer ride, far out into the country, Billy could tell from the smell of fresh-cut hay and damp earth. There was also the smell of horses. The men untied Billy's feet and put him in a stable where there was straw and a bucket of water. Billy gave a mighty kick – *tat-tat!* – against the side of his stable, just to show everyone, and himself, that there was plenty of fight in him yet. Then Billy blew his breath out and shook himself, jingling all his bells, and leapt in place from hind feet to front feet again and again.

The men laughed and departed.

The next day, Billy was tied to a wooden stake in the centre of a broad field of grass. Now he had a chain, not a rope. Billy was indifferent to the horses, though he attempted to charge one which had whinnied and looked scared. The horse broke away from the man's hold on his rein, but stopped in a docile fashion, and the man caught him again. Billy thought the morning quite boring, but the grass was thick, and Billy ate. A saddle fit for a child was put on Billy, but there wasn't a child in sight. There were three men on the place, it seemed. One man mounted a horse and led Billy, trotting, around a circular area that was fenced in. When the horse trotted, Billy galloped. The man seemed pleased.

This went on for a few days, along with more complicated routines for the horses. They walked and strutted, knelt, and galloped sideways to music from a record player which one of the men operated outside the fence. They tried to get Billy to do something with a ribbon to which a piece of metal was attached. Billy didn't understand what they wanted, and started eating the ribbon, whereupon they snatched it out of his mouth. The man kicked him in the haunch to make him pay attention, and tried again. Billy wasn't trying very hard.

A couple of days later they all went off with the horses to a place with the biggest crowd Billy had ever seen. These people were mostly sitting down in a great circle with a clear space in the middle. Billy wore his saddle. One of the men got on a horse and led Billy – amid a lot of other men and women on horses – twice round the arena in a big parade. Music and cheers. Then Billy was led to the sidelines, and the man stood beside him on foot. They were near a gap in the wall, which was a good thing, because they had to use it when a wild horse, bucking and kicking, came very near them and threw his rider off. Now Billy and the man were in a kind of pen with no top, people leaned over the edge above them, and someone dropped what looked like a sizzling hotdog on Billy's back. The man brushed it off Billy and was trying to stamp on it when it exploded with a terrible *Bang!*

Billy bolted forward and was in the middle of the arena suddenly. A roar of delight went up from the crowd. A man in a clown's costume spread his arms to stop Billy, or deflect him. Billy aimed himself straight at the clown who jumped nimbly into an ashcan, and Billy's horns hit the ashcan with a *Clang!* and sent it rolling yards away with the clown in it. The people yelled with glee, and Billy's blood tingled. Then a big man who looked purposeful came running for Billy, grabbed his horns as Billy attacked, and Billy and the man both fell to the ground. But Billy's hind feet were free, and he kicked with all his might. The man gave a scream and released him, and Billy trotted away triumphant.

Bang!

Someone had fired a gun. Billy hardly noticed. It was all part of the fun. Billy looked around for more targets, started for a man on horseback, but was distracted by two men on foot who were running towards him from different directions. Billy didn't know which to aim at, decided on the closer, and picked up speed. He whammed the man at hip height, but an instant later a rope hissed around Billy's neck.

Billy charged the rope-thrower, but still a third man threw himself at Billy and caught him round the body. Billy twisted, fighting with his crooked left horn, and got the man in the arm, but the man held on. Someone else banged Billy in the head, stunning him. Billy was dimly aware of being carried off, amid the continuing cheers of the spectators.

Ka-plop!

Billy was dumped into one of the horse boxes. The man who mainly took care of him was tying up his legs now. His arm was bleeding, and he was muttering in an unpleasant way.

When they all got home to the ranch that night, the man took a whip to Billy. Billy was tied in one of the stables. The man kept shouting at him. It was a long strong whip and it hurt – a little. Another man watched. Billy butted the side of the stable in wrath, and on the rebound aimed himself at the man with the whip. The man jumped back, and was closing the stable door when Billy's horns banged into it. Then the man went away. It was a long time before Billy calmed down, before he began to feel the stings of the whip on his haunches and his back. He hated everybody that night.

In the morning, all three men escorted Billy to one of the horse boxes, though when Billy saw the horse box, he went along readily. Billy was willing to go anywhere that was somewhere else.

Once more, it was a longish ride. Then Billy heard the peculiar rattle under the wheels that cars made going over the metal roller bridge in front of Playland Amusement Park. They stopped, and Billy heard Hank's voice. Billy was let out. Billy was rather pleased. But Hank didn't seem pleased. Hank was frowning and looking at the ground, and at Billy. Then the men went away in their car, and when they were gone, Hank said something to Billy and laughed. He grabbed Billy's harness with one hand and steered him on to the grassier part of the park where cars and people never went. But Billy was too disturbed to eat. His back hurt worse, and his head throbbed, maybe from the blow he'd got in the arena.

Where was Mickie? Billy looked around. Maybe it was one of the days when Mickie didn't come.

As dusk fell, Billy was sure it was one of the evenings when no one came to Playland Amusement Park, not even Mickie. Then Hank put the usual lights on, or most of them, and hitched Billy to his cart. This was strange, Billy thought. Hank never took a ride all by himself.

'Come along, Billy, ni-ice Billy,' Hank was saying in a soothing tone.

But Billy sensed fear in him. Hank's weight made the cart creak as if he were several people.

'Gee up, Billy. Easy does it,' Hank said, and slapped the reins as Mickie always did.

Billy started off. It felt good to put some of his anger into pulling the cart. Billy's trot became a gallop.

'*Ho theah, Billy!*'

Hank's command made Billy run all the faster. He hit a tree, and knocked a wheel off the cart. Hank yelled for him to stop. Then Hank bounced out of the cart, and Billy made a curve and stopped, looking back. Hank was sitting on the ground, and Billy charged. Hank had just about got to his feet when Billy struck, and knocked him down.

'Ho theah, Billy,' Hank was saying, more softly now, as if he were still guiding Billy by the reins. Hank wobbled towards Billy, pressing a hand to one of his knees, the other hand to his head.

Then Billy saw Hank evidently change his mind, and veer towards the popcorn stand for protection, and Billy charged again. Hank trotted away as best he could, but Billy whammed into Hank's broad, highly buttable backside. *Whoof!* Hank fairly doubled backward, and fell in a heap on the ground.

Billy trotted in a circle, oblivious of the half-a-cart behind him. Hank lifted a blood-stained face. Billy lowered his head and attacked the mass which was now about his own height. One curved horn, one crooked horn hit God knew where, and Hank rolled over backward. Billy gave an uppercut, pulled his horns out, backed a little, and came at Hank again.

Thuck! Hank's body seemed to be growing softer.

Billy struck again, backed a little, then footed it daintily over Hank's body, cart-wreck and all. Dark blood ran into the grassless, much-trodden earth. The next thing Billy knew, he was yards away, trotting with his head up. The cart behind him seemed to weigh nothing at all. Was it even there? But Billy heard a bush – which he had leapt – crackle behind him, and felt the cart bump against the corner of a booth.

Then Hank's wife appeared. '*Billy!* . . .' She was yelling excitedly.

Billy trembled with left-over fury, and was on the brink of butting her, but he only snorted and shook himself.

'Hank! Where are you?' She hurried away.

The sound of 'Hank!' made Billy jump, and he started off at a run, made a swipe at the gatepost by the car entrance, and knocked off the other wheel of the cart.

Hank's wife was still screaming somewhere.

Billy dashed down the road, took the first dirt road that he came to, and kept on into the darkness, into the country. A car slowed, and a man said something to Billy, but Billy ran on.

Finally Billy trotted, then walked. Here were fields and a patch of woods. In the woods, Billy lay down and slept. When he woke up, it was dawn, and he was thirsty, more thirsty than hungry. He came to a farmhouse, where there was a water trough behind a fence. Billy couldn't easily get to it, so he trotted on, sensing that there was water somewhere near. He found a brook in a sloping place. Then he ate some of the rich grass there. One shaft of his cart remained attached to his harness, which was annoying, but more important was that he was free. He could go in any direction he chose, and from what he could see there was grass and water everywhere.

Adventure beckoned.

So Billy took another dirt road and pushed on. Only two cars went by all morning, and each time Billy trotted faster, and nobody got out to bother him.

Then Billy caught a scent and slowed down, lifted his nose and sniffed again. Then he went in the direction of the scent. Very soon he saw another goat in a field, a black and white goat. For the moment, Billy felt more curious than friendly. He walked towards the goat, came to an opening in the rail fence, and entered the field, dragging the one gold-and-white shaft behind him. Billy saw that the other goat was tethered. She lifted her head – the goat was a female, Billy now realized – looked at him with mild surprise and went on chewing what she had in her mouth. Behind her was a long low white house, and near it clothes fluttered on a line. There was a barn, and Billy heard the 'Moo' of a cow from somewhere.

A woman came out of the house and threw a pan of something on the ground, saw Billy, and dropped the pan in astonishment. Then she approached Billy cautiously. Billy stood his ground, chewing some excellent clover which he had just wrenched up. The woman made a shooing motion with her apron, but as if she didn't really mean it. She drew nearer, looking very hard at Billy. Then she laughed – a nice laugh. Billy was an expert on laughs, and he liked this woman's laugh at once, because it was easy and happy.

'Tommy!' the woman called to the house. 'Georgette! Come out and see what's here!'

In a minute, two small children came out of the house and screamed with surprise, a little like the children at Playland.

They offered Billy water. The woman finally got up courage and unbuckled the shaft from Billy's harness. Billy was still chewing clover. He knew the thing to do was not to look aggressive, and in fact he felt not in the least like butting any of them. When the woman and the children called him towards the barn, he followed. But nobody tried to tie him up. The woman seemed to be inviting Billy to do what *he* wanted to do, which was a nice relief. She would have let him walk away, Billy thought, back down the road again. Billy liked it here. Later, a man arrived, and looked at Billy. The man took off his hat and scratched his head, then he laughed too. When the sun went down, the woman untied the other goat, and led her towards the barn outside which Billy was walking about, looking things over. There were pigs, a water trough, and chickens and ducks behind a fence.

'Billy!' said the man, and laughed again when Billy recognized his name and looked at him. He gave Billy's harness a shake, as if he admired it. But he took it off and put it away somewhere.

The barn was clean and had straw in it. The man put a leather collar on Billy, patted him and talked to him. The other goat, which they called Lucy, was tied up near Billy, and the woman milked her into a small pail.

Billy opened his mouth and said 'A-a-a-a!'

It made everybody laugh. Billy jumped back and forth from front feet to hind feet. The memory of Hank, of the smell of his blood, was fast fading, like a bad spell of temper that had happened longer ago than yesterday, although he knew he had given Hank more butts than he had ever given anyone or anything.

In the morning when the woman came into the barn, she looked surprised and really happy to see that Billy was still there. She said something friendly to him. Evidently he wasn't going to be tied up ever, Billy thought as he trotted into the meadow with Lucy. Now that was fair play!